To Alison— Hope you enjoy

Death of a Flapper

A Max Hurlock Roaring 20s Mystery

By John Reisinger

Glyphworks Publishing
2012

This book is a work of fiction. Except for specific historic references, names, characters, places and incidents are products of the author's imagination and are not to be construed as real, and any resemblance to any actual place, event, organization or person living or dead, is unintentional and purely coincidental.

ISBN 978-0-9838818-0-3

Acknowledgments

Although Death of a Flapper is a work of fiction, a lot of research was necessary to get the details right. Here are some of the people who contributed their time and knowledge to make the job easier.

My wife and unofficial research assistant, Barbara, who finds out things I never could, and who never runs out of ideas, encouragement, or patience

Dr. John Santaspirt- who provided his files of the Wilson-Roberts case and his contacts in Moorestown.

The present owners of the Moorestown house where the murder/suicide that inspired the story took place.

The Historical Society of Moorestown, especially William Archer for his generous assistance and wealth of hard to find information.

Dr. Charles Tumosa, former head of the Criminalistics section of the Philadelphia Crime Lab- who expertly answered my questions about the forensic and medical aspects of the story.

Joseph Fishera- expert in aviation history and classic aircraft restoration, who provided insights into early flying history and lore.

H.P. Ketterman, formerly of the Maryland State Police- Who provided technical information about firearms and ammunition.

Henry Leonard, CPA- Who provided information on accounting fraud.

Barbara Reisert, owner of Claiborne Cottage by the Bay in Claiborne, Maryland

Alexandra Zullo, manager of the Tidewater Inn, Easton, Maryland

Kristin P. Ketterman

Carl Gardella

Judge Robert North– Who provided information on log canoe racing, history, and lore.

The Scene of the Crimes

Death of a Flapper takes place in 1922 and is based on a real life case. The details are in the notes at the back of the book.

The Great War, later to be called World War I, was over and America was in the throes of the Roaring 20s. The return to "Normalcy" after the war brought widespread social change with Model Ts, flappers, movies, radio, jazz music, the Florida land boom, the resurgence of the KKK, and the Great Red Scare. Prohibition brought speakeasies, bathtub gin, bootleggers, and Chicago gangsters. Mary Pickford, Clara Bow, Douglas Fairbanks and Charlie Chaplin ruled Hollywood, while Babe Ruth, Red Grange, and Jack Dempsey were the stars of the sports world. Other famous figures were Amelia Earhart, Will Rogers, Duke Ellington, Annie Oakley, and Al Capone.

In spite of all these changes and the widespread hope for a better world, however, human nature hadn't changed, so crime flourished, especially organized crime involved in bootlegging. The huge profits from the illegal liquor trade caused corruption and drew mobsters who murdered each other over territories. In addition to the Roaring 20s and the Jazz Age, the era was sometimes called the Lawless Decade.

Cast of Characters

Max Hurlock
Allison Hurlock

Charlie Bradwell
Martha Bradwell
Peter Bradwell- Robert's younger brother
Robert Bradwell-Bradwell's oldest son
Doris Gentry, secretary
Fred Madison, accountant

William Taylor
Ruth Taylor
Miriam Taylor

Otto Pfeiffer, Chief of Police
Detective Anderson
Pedigree Pettigrew. reporter

Danny Greene
Mrs. Greene
Tim Walsh

Horace Caldwell
Joe Bryant

Ben Daniels
Emma Manelli

Chapter 1

The light in the window

"That's odd. There's a light on in Miriam's room."

In the darkness on a warm July night in Moorestown, New Jersey, Ruth Taylor squinted through the leaves of a low hanging tree branch, and saw the faint square of yellow light in the distance, the window of her daughter's upstairs bedroom.

"Really, William," she remarked to her husband beside her. "It's after midnight. Miriam is usually asleep long before this. I wonder what's wrong?"

The Taylors were making their way home after a late Mah Jongg game with neighbors. Although William Taylor sometimes grumbled that Mah Jongg was a game that was more fit for opium dens than polite society, the Taylors had found the new game both enjoyable and engrossing, and before they realized, it was almost midnight. So they had set off for a pleasant walk home along the darkened street, hearing only the soft hum of the crickets and the hollow echoing of their own footsteps. The sudden sight of the light in daughter Miriam's window, however, reminded them of their trouble at home.

"She's worried about that Robert Bradwell, I suppose," said Mrs. Taylor in a soft voice as if she was afraid of being overheard, "Ever since Miriam broke off their engagement two months ago, he's been making a pest of himself. He comes calling all the time. I really don't see how she'll ever get rid of him."

William Taylor squinted towards the light from beneath the brim of his straw hat. "A lot of damned foolishness if you ask me. That Bradwell boy should give it up as a bad job and find someone else. Miriam is being too nice to him; give him the bum's rush, I say. If something isn't resolved soon, I may have to intervene."

Ruth looked at him. "Intervene? What do you mean?"

But William Taylor didn't reply.

They mounted their front steps. The rambling Victorian mansion loomed as a dark and faintly ominous shadow in front on them, towering into the night sky and showing only a single light from Miriam's second floor window. William Taylor took out his key and was annoyed to find the front door was ajar.

"I realize Miriam is upset," he scolded, "but this carelessness is inexcusable. Why, who knows what could have happened?"

He opened the front door and looked toward the kitchen, thinking Miriam may have come down for some chamomile tea to help her sleep, but the kitchen was dark. He switched on the hall light. A wide central hallway framed in dark woodwork and decorated with gold framed oil landscape paintings passed darkened rooms on each side and a curved stairway on the left.

"William, look," Ruth whispered hoarsely, "there's a man's straw hat on the hall chair."

"Good God!" William sputtered, "So he was here tonight, and while we were out as well. This has got to stop! Miriam!"

William Taylor started up the polished oak stairway, still calling out his daughter's name until he came to the door of her room. The door was locked and there was no sound from inside the room. A thin streak of light glowed along the gap beneath the door.

"Miriam! Open the door this minute!" William Taylor pounded on the heavy wooden door, but it didn't budge. The room on the other side was still silent.

Ruth put her hand to her mouth. "William, this isn't like Miriam. I think something is wrong! Could Robert be in there with her now?"

William Taylor frowned. The same thought had occurred to him, and he didn't like it one bit.

"If he is, he'll rue the day he ever crossed her threshold. I'm going to get out on the porch roof. I can reach the window of Miriam's room from there. We'll soon get to the bottom of this!"

The moon had risen, casting shifting dappled shadows from an overhanging tree on the porch roof and throwing a pale, bluish gray light over the yard below. William Taylor lifted the window in his room and climbed out on the porch roof. A few yards away, he could see a square of light cast on the porch roof from Miriam's room, but couldn't yet see inside. His shoes crunched and scraped on the shingles as he made his way closer. Finally, he came to Miriam's open window. The light from inside the room turned the highlights on his face yellow as he slowly peeked around the edge of the window frame.

"Oh, my God!" he gasped.

A few minutes later and several miles away, in a house that was comfortable but somewhat more modest than that of the Taylors, a telephone rang distantly in the darkness. The repeated ringing slowly penetrated the sleep of the two figures in the upstairs bedroom.

"Charles, would you get that?" said a sleepy voice. Charles Bradwell grunted, then rolled over, sat up on the edge of the bed, and felt around for his slippers.

"Who could be calling at this time of night? It's almost one in the morning," he complained. He fumbled to put on a plaid flannel robe and shuffled downstairs towards the insistent telephone.

"Robert's probably run out of gas somewhere again. I keep telling him not to wait until it's running on fumes, but..."

The phone sat on a small table in the entrance hallway, lit only by the gray moonlight filtering through the glass transom over the front door. Bradwell reached the jangling phone and picked it up.

"Hello?.....Yes, this is Charles Bradwell....What? Oh, my God...When? Are they all right? ....Oh, I see. Yes...yes...We'll be right over."

He placed the phone back in the stand. His mouth was dry and filled with a metallic taste, and his hand was shaking.

"Charles," said a voice from upstairs. "Who was that?"

"Martha, get dressed. Something terrible has happened!"

Chapter 2

A Race on the Chesapeake

The biplane was a speck in a cloudless blue sky that seemed to go on forever. In the padded twin cockpits, Max and Allison Hurlock slowly banked the wings of Gypsy, their war-surplus Curtiss Jenny and flew a lazy arc high above the sparkling waters of the Chesapeake Bay. A long white streak far below them marked the progress of the bay steamer Cambridge as it steered between clusters of workboats harvesting crabs and oysters. Ahead, just short of where the blue-green water met the hazy dark green shoreline to the east, a group of sleek and graceful log canoe sailboats heeled over precariously as their large sails filled tightly with wind and strained their tall pine masts.

Max looked up again. In the front cockpit he could see the back of his wife Allison's leather flying hat, her white silk scarf flapping in the wind. As if by telepathy, she became aware of his gaze, turned around and grinned. Max gestured downward and Allison nodded. They dropped down and circled closer to shore to have a better look at the scene below.

The small waterfront town of Claiborne, on the Eastern Shore of Maryland had seen its population swell by hundreds in just the past few hours. Men in straw hats and women in bright summer dresses with parasols occupied every square foot of available space along the shoreline, in the trees, and all over the long wooden steamship pier, even the part with the railroad tracks that led eastward to Ocean City on the Atlantic coast. Most of the crowd had come down for the day on the steamship from Baltimore. Some carried picnic baskets while others bought fried chicken and crab cakes from the circulating local vendors as they watched a race between some of the fastest and most beautiful sailboats ever built. The crowd was festive and reacted to every change in the racing boats' positions. Many of the spectators were city dwellers from Baltimore and Annapolis, and stared wide-eyed at the spectacle.

But Allison Hurlock, viewing the scene from the cockpit, was less enthusiastic. She picked up the speaking tube and shouted to be heard above the roar of the engine. "What's going on down there, Max?"

"Take a good look," he shouted back. "That's a genuine log canoe sailboat race."

"You call that a race?" Allison shifted her goggles up for a better look. "Those things are barely moving. It's like a race between turtles. Oh, they're graceful, and I suppose it takes a great deal of skill to keep them upright, but wouldn't a Chris Craft runabout be much faster?"

Max cut back the engine speed back so they could talk without the speaking tube. "Sure it would, and an airplane would be faster still. But there's more to it than just speed. There's skill and strategy. See that boat in the lead? That's the Island Blossom. I can tell by her sail markings. Did you notice how she's cutting back and forth in front of the Billy Hall and the Island Lark? That's a maneuver to keep the others from passing."

"Well, that hardly seems fair."

"Allison, I love you, but you're not on the Western Shore any more. This is a serious sport around here."

She smiled back at him. "You're so handsome when you're defending local traditions."

"And you're beautiful when you're attacking them," Max replied, laughing. "Let's get a closer look."

Allison slid her goggles back down.

"Tally ho!"

They descended to 200 feet and roared over the boats and over Claiborne, wagging the wings to greet the crowd. As they dipped the wing they could see the steam trail from the engine of the Ocean City Flyer on the horizon as it chugged its way toward the railhead at Claiborne.

They made a slow turn to the northeast, passing over miles of wide flat tidal lands of farm fields shimmering in the summer haze and planted with tomatoes that would soon be harvested and taken to the cannery in nearby St Michaels. As they steadily descended, the ground below seemed to rush past faster until they felt the slight bump as Max brought the Jenny down gently in a grassy field, bounced along the uneven ground and rolled to a stop by a barn with a hand painted wooden sign that read "Hurlock's Flying Service".

Max cut the engine, jumped out of the airplane and gave his hand to Allison. She was wearing a leather flying jacket over a green print dress.

"Nice flight. Gypsy's running pretty frisky today."

"Yes," Allison agreed. "It's nice to make a flight without an emergency landing."

A few minutes later, Gypsy was back in the barn and they were strolling down the driveway of a two-story white clapboard house set by a creek amid marshy wetlands. They mounted the steps to the wide front porch and soon were seated at the kitchen table eating leftover stew warmed up from the night before. Allison removed her flying hat revealing a wide white scarf around her head, flapper fashion. She had already removed a similar scarf around her neck.

"So Max, what does the winner of the log canoe race win?" she asked.

"I think it's $25 with maybe $15 for second place and $5 for third. Then of course the last place finisher gets a cured ham."

"What? Look, I understand the prizes awarded the winners, but why would they give a ham to the crew that came in last?"

Max chuckled. "An old tradition around here. The idea is that the crew will use it to grease the bottom of their boat so it will do better in the future."

Allison shook her head. "Well, it appears my education was lacking such essentials. Maybe I should ask Goucher for a refund."

"Forget the refund. You learned plenty. Say, how is the article coming?"

Allison sighed. "The life of a freelance magazine writer is not an easy one, I'm afraid. I sent off the article on the crossword puzzle craze to Modern Girls Magazine and I'm looking for my next topic. I'm thinking of something about flappers."

"Flappers? Now you're cooking with gas. I'd read that article myself."

The black phone in the living room rang and Allison went to answer it. A few seconds later she returned.

"Max, when you were in the navy did you know someone named Bradwell?"

Max looked up. "Charlie Bradwell? Sure. He was a Lieutenant Commander and Executive Officer of my ship, the USS Carson. We called him Mr. Social Register because he came from one of those upper crust Philadelphia families, although I think he lived across the river in New Jersey. He ran some kind of real estate company that bought and sold commercial properties. Pretty decent guy all in all. What about him?"

"Thelma at the switchboard in town said he called you today. He'll call back tonight."

"Charlie Bradwell? I haven't talked to him since the war. I wonder what he wants? We were cordial, but not best pals or anything. He's the one who started calling me Sherlock Hurlock after we had that murder on the ship."

"Maybe he wants to enter the USS Carson in the next log canoe sailboat race. That should liven things up."

"I guess we'll find out," said Max. "It's funny he'd wait all this time. It must be something unusual. I thought I'd never see him again when I left the Carson. Well, we'll just have to wait. Do you have any ideas how we can pass the time waiting for Charlie to call back?"

She untied the scarf around her head and let her hair tumble down.

"Maybe."

An hour later, darkness had fallen and they lay in bed half asleep. The long green curtains rustled gently at the open windows, and above the hum of the electric fan, the phone was ringing downstairs. It rang several times before there was any sign of life from the rumpled bed.

"You really ought to get that," Allison said finally. "It's probably what's-his-name from the navy. He probably couldn't find the signal flags."

Max reluctantly swung his feet over the edge of the bed and slowly stood up. "It'd be just like Charlie Bradwell to call when I'm busy. Sailors have no sense of timing."

The phone was still ringing when he finally got to it.

"Max. Is that you? This is Charlie Bradwell.... from the Carson." The voice on the phone was surprisingly clear.

"Sure Charlie. How are you doing?" Max stifled a yawn.

"Listen, Max. I'm here in Easton, just up the road from you and I need to see you as soon as possible. I've got a big problem and I really need your help."

"You say you're up in Easton? I thought you lived in New Jersey. What are you doing in Easton?"

"I came down to see you, Max. I'm at the Avon Hotel, along with my son Peter. Max, I have to see you. I rented a car from a local garage and I can come to your house."

"Sure, Charlie. How about tomorrow?"

"How about tonight?"

Max looked at the clock and saw it was almost 8:30. Whatever Charlie Bradwell wanted must be urgent.

"Tonight? Well, all right, Charlie. Let me give you directions."

As Max hung up the phone, he heard Allison's voice behind him.

"It's not a real estate problem, is it?"

Max turned to see his wife standing in the doorway in a long blue robe. Several strands of brown hair hung down over her face in a way Max had always found erotic, but her expression was serious.

"No, I don't think it is. It's something a bit more important. I could tell it from his voice alone. He'll be here in about an hour."

"At this time of night? Max this has to be something big. Well, let's get dressed and I'll squeeze a pitcher of lemonade."

Max nodded absently. "Of course. Say, Allison, when they get here, how about sticking around to hear what they have to say? I'd be interested in your opinion."

Allison nodded as she rinsed out the lemonade pitcher in the kitchen sink. "Sure. I'll be discrete, though. I wouldn't want to scare them off."

Max looked out the window into the darkness. "I wouldn't worry about that. From the urgency in his voice, I have a feeling that nothing would scare them off."

Chapter 3

The icy mitt

Almost an hour later, they heard the first faint sounds of tires crunching on the road. As the sounds grew louder, the pale wash of headlights appeared, making drifting shadows among the trees.

Max looked out the window. "I think he's here, and in record time."

As Max watched, a model T materialized from the darkness and stopped at the end of the drive. Two figures emerged and walked towards the house.

"Hello, Max," said Charlie Bradwell, appearing in the glow from the porch light. He looked older than Max remembered, and wearier, but he still had thick wiry hair the color of a brick. Max noticed he was carrying a small valise.

Charlie Bradwell stepped into the living room and introduced his son Peter, a somewhat shorter and younger version of himself. Although the night was warm, they were wearing hats and vested suits.

"Thanks for seeing us, Max. I didn't know where else to turn."

"Always willing to help an old shipmate, Charlie. Come on into the parlor here and have a seat. Welcome to Hurlock's Hideaway."

"The man at the hotel said you were running some sort of flying service."

"That's right," said Max. "After we got married, Allison and I bought a surplus Jenny from the army. They were practically giving them away, and you know how I always liked to tinker with engines. So now we do occasional barnstorming, ferry businessmen around and even haul mail once in a while. Of course I still do engineering work to pay the bills."

Charles Bradwell nodded absently, but did not comment further. He obviously had other things on his mind.

The Bradwells sat on the old mohair sofa in front of the fireplace as Allison appeared from the kitchen with a pitcher of lemonade and some glasses. She had changed in to a blue print dress and the Bradwells momentarily seemed to forget their mission. Max smiled to himself. Allison had that effect on men. It probably had something to do with her resemblance to movie star Mary Miles Minter. Charlie and Peter Bradwell rose awkwardly from their seats and Max told them to sit down again as he introduced them.

"Allison, this is my old navy shipmate Charlie Bradwell and son Peter."

Allison smiled and discretely slipped into a chair near Max.

For about a minute, the Bradwells sat silently, with Charles fidgeting with the valise and Peter just looking uncomfortable. Outside a chorus of frogs was tuning up for the night and in the distance a duck protested. Finally Charlie cleared his throat and spoke.

"I'm sorry for barging in on you and your wife this time of night, Max, but I'm sure you will understand when I explain. We've come about an urgent matter. I came all the way down here from New Jersey because I had to see you in person. This is too important to discuss over the phone."

Max, seated in the armchair by the side of the fireplace, leaned forward slightly. "Of course, Charlie. Go ahead."

Charlie Bradwell took a deep breath, as if bracing himself for an ordeal. "You remember me speaking of my son Robert; Peter's older brother?"

Max nodded. "Yes, of course. When we were on the Carson he was starting at Rutgers if I remember correctly. Is he in some sort of trouble?"

"Robert is dead."

The only sound was Allison's faint gasp.

"I'm really sorry to hear that, Charlie," Max said finally. "What happened?"

Charles Bradwell suddenly looked determined.

"That is what I want you to find out."

Bradwell opened his valise and took out a stack of newspaper clippings. "The whole story, or at least the newspaper version of it is in these articles, but they give only a hint of what a nightmare the last few days have been."

"I can look at them later," said Max. "Why don't you tell me about it?"

Charles Bradwell looked at Peter, and then took another deep breath. "Robert was shot to death a week ago, along with his former fiancée, Miriam Taylor. They were found dead in her locked bedroom, each shot in the head at close range."

"Did you say she was his former fiancée?"

"That's right. She broke it off about three months ago with no warning and no apparent reason."

"She gave him the icy mitt." Peter, somewhat unnecessarily, provided the vernacular term.

Max sat back in his chair and studied Bradwell.

"And now," said Max, "everyone is saying Robert killed her then shot himself."

Bradwell nodded. "So you've read about the case."

Max shook his head. "No, I haven't. The Easton Star-Democrat barely covers local crime, let alone one that took place in New Jersey."

"Then how did you know?"

Max waved his hand in a dismissive gesture. "It was a logical inference, and it would account for why you came to see me. You don't believe Robert is to blame and you want his name cleared."

"Geez, Dad," said Peter. "No wonder you call him Sherlock Hurlock."

Max looked at Allison and smiled faintly.

"You're right, Max. I don't believe Robert would have done anything like that. I believe they were both killed by someone else."

"I see. Any idea who?"

"None. They were both popular and didn't have an enemy in the world. Still, it had to be someone else. It just had to be."

Max looked uncomfortable. "Charlie, I'm willing to do anything I can to help, but I'm not with the police and I'm not even a private detective. I'm just a guy who helps assemble facts in a logical way. Most of my work is engineering, not criminal investigation. You're talking about a capital crime; and in another state to boot."

"Max, I'm not asking you to gather the suspects in the drawing room at midnight and reveal the murderer,

I just need you to help us make sense of this whole thing. I'm too close to it and I don't want a reporter finding out I'm asking questions and use it to write more sensational articles to cheapen Robert's good name. They're already referring to Robert and Miriam as 'socialites'. One headline said 'Society Suitor kills Rich Girl, Then Self.' It's like Robert isn't even a person anymore."

"I can't do anything about what they write, Charlie," Max reminded him.

"You can if you find out the truth. That's all I'm asking. Look, Max; you're a damned good man for finding the pieces and putting them together the right way. You proved that on the Carson. I'll pay whatever you charge and any expenses, but I'm begging you to come up to Moorestown and look into it. You can stay with us or I'll put you up in the hotel for as long as you need; Allison, too. Will you do it?"

Max's face gave no hint of what he might be thinking. "Tell me the rest."

"Robert had a bright future," Bradwell began. "He graduated a year ago and was working at my firm, Bradwell Properties. We do a lot of commercial development and property management. Robert was learning the business; just as a way of getting started you understand. Everything changed when he met Miriam Taylor. She was the daughter of William and Ruth Taylor, also of Moorestown. William Taylor is a prominent attorney in Philadelphia."

Max nodded. "What can you tell me about Miriam Taylor?"

"Miriam was a nice girl, but something of a flapper. Oh, I don't mean she carried around a flask of bathtub gin or anything like that, but she liked parties and nightclubs, and referred to Charles's car as a "jalopy", even though it's a Packard. I'm not saying she did anything sordid, but the point is, she was a little sophisticated; worldly, perhaps. I mean she was still a nice girl, but, well, maybe her manner dazzled Robert and made his rejection all the harder to take. Most of the other girls Robert knew before Miriam were conventional. Miriam was more of a free spirit."

"She wore her dresses pretty short, too," Peter added. "And cut her hair into one of those short bobs. Oh, and she wore silk stockings...rolled below her knees!" Peter made it sound scandalous.

"Yes," Charlie continued. "She had all the trappings of a flapper, but for the most part she seemed like a level headed girl as far as we could tell. Well, a lot of this flapper business is really youthful rebellion I suppose, like the way we used to leave our knickers unbuckled when I was a youngster. Anyway, Robert was crazy about her. They became engaged and everything seemed fine, but then suddenly.."

"She just up and gave him the heave-ho ," said Peter. "No warning; no nothing."

"What was the problem?" Max asked.

"That's the strange part," said Charlie. "We never knew. She just decided to break it off one day and that was that. Even Robert was in the dark."

"So how did he react?"

Charlie shook his head sadly. "He was devastated and confused. Robert went to see her a few more times after that, trying to understand and maybe get her to change her mind. The strange thing is they were still on cordial terms and even went out together sometimes. This went on for about three months."

"Old man Taylor was sticking his nose into it," Peter added. "He said if Robert didn't stop bothering Miriam he would put a stop to it himself."

Max raised his eyebrows slightly. "What did he mean by that?"

"Who knows?" Charlie answered. "We only heard it second hand. It was probably said in a fit of anger. William Taylor does have a bad temper. He once threw a paperweight through the front window of his office."

"So tell me about the night of the...incident." said Max.

"Robert and Miriam went to Atlantic City for the day with two friends. As I said, they were still on cordial terms in spite of the breakup. That night the Taylors went to a neighbor's house to play Mah Jongg. It's a new game from China, or some such place."

"I've heard of it," said Max. "Go on."

"Robert and the others dropped Miriam off at her house around 10 or so then they took Robert home, but he must have gone back to see her. The Taylors got home a little before midnight and found the front door to the house ajar. They also noticed Robert's hat on a chair in the hall and the door to Miriam's room locked, so naturally they were quite alarmed. When no one answered repeated knocks on the locked door, William Taylor climbed out on a roof and looked in her window. He saw Miriam and Robert lying on her bed. Miriam was wearing only her stockings and a light robe, while Robert was dressed, except for his jacket. He was lying partly off the edge of the bed, as if he had slipped off of her. She was shot twice in the head and he was shot three times. There was a .22 pistol lying on the floor near Robert's hand. The door key was on the floor next to him as well."

Charlie looked thoughtful. "It's amazing how quickly you can wake up when you hear bad news. We got a phone call around midnight. The next thing we knew we were standing in the Taylor house looking at

Robert's body. God, but it was horrible. A patrolman had helped William Taylor move Miriam's body to her parents' room by this time, so our Robert simply lay there alone. It's funny what you think of at a time like that. They say your whole life flashes before your eyes when you're about to die. Well, I saw Robert's whole life. His mother was crushed. Martha's been inconsolable ever since. I insisted on her remaining at home to recuperate somewhat."

"One question," Max interrupted. "Was there a carpet in the room?"

Charles Bradwell and Peter looked at each other in confusion. "A carpet? Well, let's see. Uh, no. I think it was just a wooden plank floor. Why?"

Max nodded. "Just a detail I wanted to clear up. Please go on."

"Anyway, the police were there when we arrived at the Taylors', as was the coroner, Dr. Carstairs. Otto Pfeiffer, the chief detective investigated and asked us some questions, but you could tell he had made his mind up already. As far as he was concerned, Robert shot Miriam and then killed himself. It was a simple case of a rejected lover's revenge. The coroner said there would be an inquest, but a day later he called and said the county prosecutor, a fellow named Hillsborough, had decided that no inquest was needed. Hillsborough's an elected official and I suppose he didn't want an inquest to turn up any facts that might conflict with Pfeiffer's tidy conclusion of murder-suicide. So now my son has been officially branded a killer without a trial or even an autopsy. Pfeiffer said the gun was such a small caliber that Robert had to shoot himself several times...in the head!"

Bradwell's voice was getting hoarse with fatigue and emotion. Allison poured him a glass of lemonade, which he drank gratefully before resuming his story.

"I was outraged that they had closed the case so quickly, so I gave an interview to the Moorestown paper just before we left to come here. I told them the case was insufficiently investigated and I called on County Prosecutor Hillsborough to open a formal inquest, complete with autopsies. I even threatened to write to President Harding. I was desperate. Max, they're wrong. I know they are. Robert is not a killer. He would never do anything like this. He really loved that girl, and would never hurt her. Even if he wanted to, how could anyone shoot himself three times in the head? Someone murdered them both. Isn't it obvious?"

Max chose to ignore this question. "What about the gun they found? What kind of a gun was it?"

"A .22 caliber revolver."

"A .22? Seems like kind of a puny gun to use for a double murder. Do they have any idea where it came from?"

Charlie looked embarrassed. "They did trace the gun the next day."

"..and?"

"It was mine," said Peter.

"Yours?" said Max. In the background, Allison gasped again.

"I got it in a pawnshop two years ago," said Peter, wringing his hands. "I bought some cheap black powder ammunition and used it for target shooting in the woods for a while, then put it away in the back of a closet. I hadn't touched it for months."

"Did you give it to Robert?" Max asked.

"No, of course not. I didn't know Robert even knew about it. He never mentioned it. I had forgotten I even had the gun, so I didn't miss it when it was taken."

In the silence that followed, Max sighed and cleared his throat. "Charlie, when you were XO on the Carson you always insisted on a full and honest report, no matter how bad it was, so here's what I get so far: We have two people dead. One of them has a strong motive to feel rejection and resentment of the other one. No one else seems to have any reason to wish ill to either one of them, let alone both. We know this occurred in a locked room in a private home, a place no one else is likely to either know about or have access to. We know the murderer used Peter's gun, and that no one outside the family had access to the closet in which it was kept or even knew it was there. We know the local authorities on the scene investigated, not thoroughly perhaps but they did investigate, and determined it was a murder-suicide. As for Robert shooting himself three times in the head, that does seem unlikely, but with small caliber bullets and old black powder loads, it's at least possible that the first shots didn't penetrate the skull. Charlie, I'd love to help in any way I can, but do you really want me to investigate further? It sounds hopeless. I'll probably wind up agreeing with the local officials."

Charlie Bradwell took another drink from the lemonade glass Allison had just refilled, then resumed in a quiet voice. This time, however, he addressed Allison.

"Mrs. Hurlock...Allison... Did Max ever tell you about that time on the Carson, when we found that bosun's mate stabbed to death in the engine room? I know I'll never forget it. We were three days out to sea in a convoy. The ship was in a panic. Everyone thought there was a German spy aboard and he was going to kill us one by one. The captain called the officers together in the wardroom and told us to question everyone on the ship and conduct background checks for anyone with German ties until we found out who the spy was. Then Ensign Maxwell Hurlock, the most junior officer on the ship spoke up, and told the captain he was going about it all wrong. Max said the key was to find out what a bosun's mate was doing in the engine room. For some reason the captain listened and told him to follow that angle on his own. Two days later, Max had the killer and it wasn't a German spy. That's when we started calling Max Sherlock Hurlock. Max was.."

"I've told her the story, Charlie," Max interrupted. "What does it have to do with Robert's death?"

"Just this, Max. On the Carson, everyone *knew* there was a German spy aboard, and everyone *knew* that extensive questioning and background checks were the way to catch him. It was obvious. You alone looked beyond the obvious and found the truth. Well now everyone *knows* Robert killed Miriam Taylor then killed himself. I believe you're still the only one who can find the truth whatever it is. That's why I came here to appeal to you in person. I owe it to Peter, I owe it to Robert's mother, I owe it to myself, and most of all, I owe it to Robert. Yes, I still want you to investigate. If you find Robert really was the killer, at least we'll know the truth came out, painful as it might be. I'm not even worried about that possibility, though. I have faith in Robert."

Max looked at Charlie and Peter and saw they were leaning forward expectantly. Then he glanced at Allison and saw the sympathy in her eyes.

"All right, Charlie. I'll need a couple of days to finish up a few things here and make arrangements, and then

I'll come up to Moorestown. Meanwhile, I'll need for you to make a list of names and addresses of the people involved. Oh, and leave me the clippings so I can bone up on some of the details in the meantime."

"Thank you, Max. I knew I could count on you."

"I'd like to fly up if possible," said Max. "Are there any airfields nearby?"

"I don't think so, except over towards Philadelphia maybe. But there is a farm nearby. I can arrange for you to land there if you'd like."

"Perfect. We'll be there."

Later that night, long after Charlie and Peter Bradwell had gone, Max and Allison lay in bed listening to the frogs croaking outside and the electric hum of the fan inside. In the warm darkness, they lay silently for a long while. Finally Allison spoke.

"Well, Max. You always like a challenge. Looks like you've got a corker."

Max sighed. "That's putting it mildly. I really hate to let Charlie Bradwell down, but it looks like he's clinging to a very fragile hope and all I'll be able to do is step on his fingers."

"It does look that way at the moment, but he seems to have a strong faith in Robert's innocence. Doesn't that count for anything?"

"Strong faith is all well and good," said Max, shaking his head in the darkness, "but I prefer strong facts. As far as I can see, though, the facts are all pointing the other way."

Chapter 4

Inquest

"Max, should I pack a coat? It can get cold in New Jersey."

Three days had passed since the nighttime visit of the Bradwells, and Max and Allison were finishing packing.

"The only thing cold up there is the reception we're likely to get from the local police," said Max.

Allison frowned. "I'd better take it anyway. Just to be on the safe side. Even if New Jersey isn't cold, the trip up there in Gypsy will be. By the way, did you pack your straw hat?"

Max groaned. "I hate that hat. It makes me look like I'm a vaudeville performer. All I need is a cane and a soft shoe routine."

"Straw hats are all the rage," Allison insisted. "If you're going to hobnob with the Philadelphia upper crust, you don't want to look like you're there to check their plumbing. They'll already be inclined to regard you as a bumpkin; you don't want to dress like one. If you forget to pack it, I'll get you a good straw boater when we arrive."

"I can hardly wait."

"Good. So do you have any theories on the case yet, Max?"

Max looked out the window and sighed. "Several of them; unfortunately, they all involve Robert being the killer."

Allison looked at him. "So much for having a satisfied client. I think I hear the phone, Max. Could you get it?"

"I'm halfway there," Max said, walking towards the stairs.

"Max, this is Charlie Bradwell," came the tinny voice on the other end. "There have been some developments you should know about before you get here."

"Sure, Charlie. What happened?"

"The Prosecutor's office decided to hold an inquest after all, complete with autopsies. They just finished up this morning."

"That's good news, but why the change?" Max asked.

"They said it was to deal with 'unanswered questions', but I think the real reason is the public pressure. Everybody's been talking about the case and how it was handled. I think the governor got hold of the prosecutor and told him to hold the inquest to quiet everyone down once and for all. It was quite a change of heart. Prosecutor Hillsborough had gone on record saying autopsies were a waste of time in this case and would be against his principles."

Max smiled. "You know what they say, Charlie. In politics, you sometimes have to rise above principles. So how did it go?"

"It was a circus," Bradwell said. "I've never seen anything like it. Sensation-seeking crowds gathered around the cemetery, carloads of the curious arrived in town from miles around, and a parade of witnesses testified all day long."

"Anything new turn up?"

"The testimony was pretty much the same as what had been in the papers, but the autopsy revealed that two shots had failed to penetrate the skull due to the small caliber of the bullets and the deterioration of the black powder loads in the shell casings."

"I'm not really surprised," Max said.

"The trouble is I listened to all the testimony and I didn't hear anything about someone else at the house that night or about anyone who might have had a reason to commit murder. From what I heard, I'm afraid Robert was the only one with a credible motive. He's certainly the only one who was definitely at the house. The inquest didn't turn up anyone who had a reason to even dislike them, let alone murder them. I don't know; maybe it was a random act of some sort. Maybe they were killed by a maniac, or a passing tramp of some kind."

"The problem with that theory is figuring out how a maniac could get Peter's gun," said Max, "not to mention the problem of how a stranger could have found his way to Miriam Taylor's room in a house he was unfamiliar with. And the fact that the room was locked."

"I know, I know," Bradwell sighed. "I'm afraid there's no obvious alternative. I believe in Robert's innocence, but the facts don't seem to agree. Maybe you can make sense out of all of this when you arrive tomorrow, Max, but I'm afraid your job just got even harder."

"So the case is now officially closed?" Max asked.

"That's right. That's what we're up against, Max. If you've got any miracles in your bag of tricks, we're going to need them."

The next morning dawned warm and muggy. As Max oiled the rockers on the engine preparing for takeoff, Allison made final adjustments to the stowed baggage in the compartment behind the rear cockpit.

"I hope Gypsy can get airborne with all the luggage," said Max.

"Have a little faith, Max."

"Faith? There's that word again," said Max, grasping the propeller.

"Contact!" shouted Allison. Max pulled on the propeller and the engine sprang to life. Then after a slightly longer takeoff run than usual, the biplane lifted into the sky with room to spare. As they headed north over the bay at 75 miles an hour, Max saw a line of clouds far to the south and hoped he could outrun them. They found the Delaware River at Wilmington and followed it until they saw the skyline of Philadelphia rising on the left and Camden on the right. Allison looked down and signaled to Max.

"That must be Petty's Island below," she shouted into the speaking tube.

Max nodded. "I see it. We turn due east when we're over the northern tip."

They made the turn and crossed over the New Jersey countryside. On the horizon was a faint gray smudge of smoke.

"There it is," said Max. "Do you see it?"

"Yes," said Allison. "Just a little to the left."

Charlie Bradwell had arranged for a nearby farmer to have a smoky fire burning in an old oil drum by one of his empty fields, so that both Moorestown and the landing area were easy to find from the air. The smoke also made it easy to judge the wind.

Max circled the field once, then brought Gypsy in for a smooth landing. Charlie Bradwell and the farmer were waiting by some hay bales. Max noted with satisfaction, that Bradwell was wearing a fedora, not a straw hat.

"Welcome to New Jersey," said Charlie. "So that's your Jenny, is it? It looks like it's in pretty good shape."

"We have to work at it, but Gypsy is holding together nicely. She'll do almost 90 with a good tailwind, too. It saved us a long day on the train getting here."

The farmer, meanwhile, just walked around inspecting Gypsy, marveling at the flimsy looking fabric-covered wings, the wooden struts and the bracing wires that seemed to hold it all together.

"This looks like a big kite. You flew all the way up from Maryland in this thing?"

"All the way," Max assured him. "Half way might have been a problem."

Allison, wearing the green print dress she preferred for flying, stifled a laugh.

The farmer traced the maze of wires between the wings in amazement.

"How do you know you've still got all the wires you need?"

"That's easy," said Max, winking at Charlie. "You just put a pigeon between the wings. If he can get out, you know one of the wires is missing!"

After transferring their luggage and getting Gypsy safely put away in a barn, they set off towards Moorestown in Bradwell's red Packard.

"I really appreciate you both coming here like this," Bradwell said as they chugged along. "What can I do to help?"

"If I can get a copy of the autopsy and the inquest testimony it will save a lot of spade work," Max said. "Allison will help too, but she's really here to research a magazine article on flappers".

Bradwell nodded. "Flappers, eh? Well, we've got a lot of those. You should have plenty of material, Mrs. Hurlock."

"Please, call me Allison. After all, you've been a guest in our house."

Bradwell smiled. "Now that I've met Allison, I know why you were always anxious to get home, Max."

"I still am," Max assured him.

Moorestown was a small Quaker farming town that was starting to become home to businessmen who worked in Camden and Philadelphia. With quiet, tree lined streets, it was not the sort of place people would associate with sordid murders. Charlie Bradwell took Max and Allison to Cole's Hotel, which like pretty much everything of consequence in Moorestown, was located on Main Street. Cole's was not too fancy, but it was clean and had its own restaurant. Once they checked in and dropped off their bags, they were taken to the Bradwells' for dinner.

The Bradwells lived in a white painted Victorian house just off of Main Street. A hedge of roses along the side was obviously the work of Martha Bradwell, a no-nonsense sort of a woman who took an instant shine to Allison once she learned that Allison wrote one of the articles she had just read in Eastern Living magazine. Charlie, however, soon brought the conversation around to the terrible subject that had brought them all there.

"Max," said Charlie Bradwell, "When you solved that stabbing on the Carson, and we asked you how you did it, you said something about logical connections. Just what was that all about?"

Max shrugged. "Oh, it's simple, really; cause and effect. Everything is connected to something else. It's just engineering applied to human activity. That was pretty much what I did with the stabbing on the Carson. When a bosun's mate is found in a place a bosun's mate almost never goes something very out of the ordinary had to be involved. It was just a matter of working backwards to figure out how and why he got there. It's like seeing only the upper part of a house in the fog. Even if you can't see it, you know a foundation exists underneath and how big it is."

"Well," said Charlie. "I'm still not sure how you did it, but I hope you can do the same for us."

"I promise," Max answered, "I'm going to do everything I can to find out what happened to Robert, including chasing down any logical connections I can find. I thought I'd start by visiting the scene of the..uh..incident. Maybe you could drive me past there tonight, just to get a feel for the layout. Later I'd like to speak with the Taylors as well."

Charlie shook his head. "I doubt that William Taylor is willing to talk about it, especially with someone who is working on my behalf. As far as he is concerned, our son murdered his daughter. He made that pretty clear on the night it happened and I don't think anything has changed his mind since then. Obviously it's a pretty sore subject with him."

"I understand," said Max. "Sometimes I use a cover story to get people to open up, but I don't think that's playing fair with people who have lost a daughter. Take me past the place and I'll think about it."

"Well, that sounds like a good place to start. You can have Robert's Packard to use while you're here, but I can take you past the Taylors' place tonight so you'll know where it is. If you've finished your dessert, let's take a ride."

Chapter 5

The red Packard

The Taylor house on Montgomery Street stood on a large lot in the midst of a grove of stately oak and elm trees. The house had two half-timbered gables over a wide winding front porch. A driveway on the left side of the house led to a separate garage in the back that looked like a converted carriage house. The house exuded wealth and comfort.

"Be it ever so humble," said Max. "Where's Miriam's room?"

"It's that second floor window on the left hand side."

Max saw a window above a porch roof. He could picture William Taylor making his way across that roof inch by inch and finally looking in that window to see his daughter lying dead. Max knew he would have to treat William Taylor with delicacy.

"All right. I've seen enough for now. Tomorrow I'll contact Mr. Taylor. Now tell me some more about this chief detective that's so convinced it was a murder-suicide."

"Well, Otto Pfeiffer is an old hand at police work, and a damned good detective in his own right. He's rough around the edges and can be either charming or obnoxious, depending in his mood, but he knows his job. He gets confessions by getting the goods on the suspect, not with the third degree. Around here everybody puts a lot of stock in anything he says because they know he does things the smart way and never tries to beat up a suspect. Pfeiffer has a lot of credibility, so if he says a case is suicide, that's pretty much that."

"I'll need to find out what he's uncovered so far," said Max. "How do you think he'll view an out-of-state investigator?"

"Like ants at a picnic would be my guess."

"Very encouraging," said Max. "What about the coroner?"

"Carstairs. I don't know that much about him. He's a doctor and was made coroner about five years ago. He's a political appointee, but mostly keeps out of politics and out of the newspapers as far as I can tell."

"How about the prosecutor who suddenly decided to hold the inquest?"

"He's elected and is a political operator; very beholding to the governor. Most of the time he does all right in his job, but when a case gets a lot of public attention, he's been known to change course abruptly the way he just did."

"An interesting cast of characters," Max remarked. "Do any of them have any reason for wanting a murder to be considered a suicide?"

Charlie shook his head slowly. "None whatsoever, I'm afraid. As far as I can tell, they all genuinely believe it because of the evidence."

Max nodded. "Can't say as I blame them at this point, but we'll see what we can turn up."

Once back at Cole's, Max and Allison read through most of the additional newspaper articles Charlie Bradwell had provided before they went to bed.

"This is disgusting," said Allison. "All they talk about is how Robert and Miriam were supposedly 'rich' or 'socialites', or 'upper crust', as if that's the most important part of the story. The fact that two people with their whole lives ahead of them are now dead seems to be a minor footnote."

Max shrugged. "They're selling papers. They have to make it as sensational as possible."

"A double shooting in a locked room isn't sensational enough?"

"Apparently not."

"Anyway, the inquest jury seems pretty sure it was a murder-suicide," Allison said, placing the last page in the stack.

"Yes, but there are a few questions I'd have liked to have asked."

"It's never too late, Max. I can think of a few questions as well."

"I'll start with Miriam's father and maybe her mother, although from what Charlie says, they're not likely to be very talkative."

"Especially if you come zipping up to the curb in Robert Bradwell's car. I'd advise parking down the street."

"Good point."

The next morning as the sun was rising through the trees, Max left the hotel with his coat over his shoulder and headed back to the Taylor house. Everything was quiet except for the shrill chirping of the Cicadas. Parking Robert's red Packard around the corner, Max waited outside for a while, and then spotted William Taylor as he was departing for his office in Philadelphia. As the chauffeur held the car door open, Max approached.

"Good morning Mr. Taylor. My name is Max Hurlock and I'd like to have just a moment of your time."

Taylor, a stocky man who looked perpetually irritated, fumed at the interruption of his routine and looked as if the only reason he wasn't beating Max with a club was there was a law against it.

"I'm an independent consultant and I've been asked by Mr. Bradwell to try to organize and perhaps clarify some of the contradictory aspects of the recent tragedy to ease the minds of all concerned. If you could answer a few quick questions, I would sure appreciate it."

Taylor was becoming red faced. "So Bradwell's hired a private eye, has he?"

"No, Mr. Taylor. I am not a private eye; I am simply an independent investigator. I am looking for the truth, whatever it is, so everyone can be satisfied all the leads have been covered."

"Damned nonsense. I can't speak for the parents of my daughter's killer, but I for one am completely satisfied with the investigation and the inquest. I see nothing to be gained by continuing to drag this out."

"I certainly understand, Mr. Taylor, but I can assure you that my conclusions will be based solely on the facts, not on any preconceived notion."

Taylor eyes narrowed shrewdly. "I know what this is about. It's the insurance, isn't it? Bradwell's after the insurance money. Well, I'll have no part of it. None! Now if you'll excuse me, I have to get to my office."

Sensing he was losing the encounter, Max played his last card. "Suit yourself, Mr. Taylor, but I'm staying at Cole's Hotel here in Moorestown if you decide to talk."

"To you? Why in the devil would I do that?"

"Well, it would be a shame if I had to reach my conclusions without taking your side of the story into account. It's your chance to get your side out. Otherwise I'll just have to rely on what Mr. Bradwell tells me."

"My 'side' as you call it is already out," Taylor growled. "It's called the truth, and you'll find it contained in the pages of the official inquest, especially in the verdict. If you wish to try to single-handedly overturn that verdict, you are certainly free to waste your time doing so, but I have no intention of allowing you to waste mine. Good day."

Taylor got in the car and sped off.

Attracted by the commotion, Mrs. Taylor had drifted out on to the porch and was watching with almost equal disapproval. Max turned to her and lifted his fedora respectfully. "I'm sorry to disturb you, Mrs. Taylor. I know how terrible this ordeal has been for all of you."

"No, Mr...."

"Hurlock. Max Hurlock."

"No, Mr. Hurlock, I don't believe you know at all."

"Of course not, Mrs. Taylor. It must have been awful when you approached your house and saw that the Bradwell boy was here."

"Actually, we had no idea he was here until we saw his hat on the chair."

Max shook his head in sympathy. "I'm sorry, I just assumed that when you saw Robert's car out front, you realized...."

"I'm afraid you assumed incorrectly. We never saw his car."

"Oh, well; I suppose you missed it in the dark," ventured Max.

"It was a red Packard and there was a full moon. We did not miss it. The car was not here. Now, Mr. Hurlock. I suggest that you follow the car's example and not be here as well."

"Of course. Good day, Mrs. Taylor."

After he left the Taylors, Max went to the county detective's office in the town hall on Main Street and asked for Chief Detective Otto Pfeiffer. The sun was higher in the sky now and heating up Moorestown rapidly. In contrast to William Taylor, Pfeiffer was an easy man to see. Pfeiffer saw just about anyone because he picked up a lot of leads from casual information people gave him. Accordingly, the secretary ushered Max into a small cluttered office where a stocky, bald headed man with a bushy mustache waited behind a desk with what appeared to be a human skull on one corner. Pfeiffer noticed Max looking at it.

"So you're admiring old Oscar, are you? Well, go ahead and look. He won't mind." Pfeiffer laughed heartily at a joke he had no doubt made many times before. He seemed unusually affable and outgoing for a detective.

"Oscar is from a skeleton we found over by Clink Creek about two years ago. We investigated for a month and never found out who it was. I keep it as a reminder not to get too cocky because some cases you just can't solve."

"Well, that's exactly what I'm here about, Mr. Pfeiffer. I'm Max Hurlock and I'm looking into the Taylor-Bradwell killings at the request of Mr. Bradwell.

I'm just trying to help him clarify everything and how it fits together."

Pfeiffer cocked his head and looked at Max suspiciously. "You a reporter?"

"No, I'm simply investigating..."

"Well ain't that the limit?" The chief's smile had become a sneer. "So Bradwell went and hired a private dick. I suppose my investigation wasn't good enough for him."

"I'm not a private 'dick' as you put it. I'm an investigator. I'm only trying to find out what happened."

"Well, Mr. 'Investigator', let me save you some trouble. Here's what happened; Robert Bradwell killed Miriam Taylor then shot himself, period."

Max tried to keep his patience. "That may well be what happened. It's just that there are some details that I'm a little confused about. It may be grasping at straws, but the Bradwell's desperately want all the pieces to fit. They've had a great loss and they're trying to live with it as best they can. I'm sure you can understand."

Pfeiffer looked suddenly suspicious. "What do you mean by details?"

Max smiled to himself. He felt he had Pfeiffer nibbling at the hook and just had to reel him in. "Oh, you know; little things that probably don't really mean anything but might be confusing to someone who isn't a professional as you are."

"Nix on the flattery. Like what?"

"Well, like the car for instance."

"Car? What car?"

"Robert Bradwell's red Packard. The Taylors said it wasn't there at the house when they got home. So then how did Bradwell get back to the Taylors' house after being dropped off at his home that night if he didn't have a car? He lives several miles away."

Pfeiffer smiled a superior smile. He had the advantage now. "Well you're wrong, wise guy. Bradwell did drive back there that night; he just didn't park in the driveway. We found his car parked around the block."

Max pretended to be surprised, although it was exactly what he had expected. "Around the block? But why would Bradwell park around the block? Why not just park in front of he house, or in the driveway. There was plenty of room."

Pfeiffer shook his head. "Some investigator," he snorted. "Obviously because he didn't want it to be seen."

"...didn't want it to be seen," Max repeated slowly. "I understand. Just one more question if you don't mind. If Robert Bradwell was going in to commit murder then suicide, he knew he was going to be dead in a few minutes, and he knew he would be found there fairly soon. So why would he care if anybody saw his car outside?"

Pfeiffer looked surprised, but recovered quickly and went on the offensive. "You tell me, Mr. Investigator."

"Maybe because he <u>wasn't</u> going in to commit murder and suicide. Good day, Chief Pfeiffer. You've been a big help."

The late afternoon sun cast lengthening shadows by the time Max returned to the hotel. Allison had gone out along Main Street to observe and collect information for her article and the room was empty and quiet. He turned on the ceiling fan, opened the windows to let the cooler evening air in, then made some notes on the case and sat back in the chair. A few minutes later, the sound of a key in the door told him Allison had returned. She stuck her head in the room, still wearing her hat, and flashed Max a dazzling smile.

"Hey, Max. I've been pounding the pavements of Moorestown and got a lot a great stuff about local jazz babies. Really darb as the young bearcats would say. I feel like dancing the Charleston." She flopped down on the edge of the bed and pulled out her notebook from her bag. "And you'll be pleased to know it doesn't mention short skirts and rolled down stockings; well, not yet at least. But what about your investigation? How did it go?"

Max didn't reply.

"Max?"

"Oh, sorry. I was thinking about short skirts and rolled down stockings. What was the question again?"

She crossed her arms and tapped her foot. "Your investigation?"

"Oh, that. Well, William Taylor wouldn't talk to me, but Mrs. Taylor let slip that they didn't see Robert Bradwell's car the night they came home. When I mentioned it to Pfeiffer, he said the car was there, but parked around the block so nobody would see it."

Allison looked startled. "So nobody would see it? But why would......"

Max held up a hand. "If he was going to kill himself, why would he care if someone saw the car? I asked the same thing. Pfeiffer didn't have an answer."

"Max, you know what I think? I think maybe Charlie Bradwell might be right after all. Maybe Robert didn't do it."

Max thought a moment, then walked over and looked out the window.

"I'm thinking the same thing. Of course if Robert didn't do it, that brings up an even stickier problem; who did?"

"And of course, if it wasn't a murder/suicide, how did the killer get out of a room locked from the inside?" Allison reminded him.

Max waved his hand in a dismissive gesture. "Getting out of the locked room? Oh, that's not a problem. I knew how that was done as soon as I heard there was no rug on the floor. No, the real problem is finding someone with a motive to kill two popular and harmless people and figuring out how everyone happened to come together in a room with Peter Bradwell's gun."

Chapter 6

The Volstead Tavern

While Max and Allison were discussing the events of the day at their hotel, Peter Bradwell set out to find a place to enjoy with his friends, if only for an hour or two, and take his mind off the tragedy that had engulfed his family. Just being away from his gloomy house was a relief, and Peter was grimly determined to enjoy himself.

Just outside of Philadelphia, on the Trenton Road, they found an old barn with a sign out front that read The Broken Axle. A smaller sign read simply Food. The Broken Axle was a roadhouse, one of a number that were springing up along the roads to provide food, entertainment, and sometimes illegal drink to travelers in the motor cars that were becoming more numerous every day. The place was newly painted and looked respectable, even dull from the outside, but the Model T Fords, Chevrolet coupes, and a few other cars parked along both sides of the road hinted that the place offered more than just a good meal.

Peter and his friends entered a low ceiling room with tables and booths scattered about. A handful of late diners were eating and a few appeared to be almost asleep. Lively music could be heard, but it was muffled and distant. Since the windows were open against the heat, the smoke wasn't too thick. Peter was familiar with roadhouses and realized this one was even less respectable than normal.

"Nice place," said Peter, sarcastically.

"Just wait," said his friend Frank, gesturing to a narrow hallway with three doors. "Over here."

A small panel slid back in a scuffed looking door at the end of the corridor past the rest rooms, and an eye appeared and looked them over. The door opened and they entered a back room that was almost as big as the front, but with a difference. A bar stretched along the back wall and people crowded around tables and a dance floor. In one corner, a small band played the latest ragtime and jazz tunes on a saxophone, piano, trumpet and banjo, while couples danced with abandon.

The far reaches of the room were barely visible in the pall of hazy smoke, and above the din was the constant clink of bottles and glasses. On one wall hung a sign that announced the name of the place as the Volstead Tavern, a sarcastic reference to the Volstead Act recently passed by Congress, that outlawed the manufacture, sale, and consumption of alcohol, thus creating nationwide Prohibition.

"Come on, let's grab a table."

The tabletop was covered with wet rings left by the cold glasses of the pervious occupants. No one bothered to wipe them off. People didn't go to the Volstead Tavern for the service. Finally, a somewhat greasy-looking waiter drifted over to the table.

"What'll it be, gents?"

"Got any Canadian gin?" one of them asked. Alcohol smuggled in from Canada was of much higher quality and less likely to be watered down, or even poisonous than the various cheap homemade concoctions now being sold under the table.

"Sure, boys. Why, everything we have is Canadian," the waiter lied smoothly. "Except for the applejack; that's strictly local. Made from genuine Jersey apples."

"Then give us your best Canadian gin."

The waiter smiled, went back behind the bar, and began to fill four glasses from a gallon jug with a paper label that said "Gin" in crayon.

Four glasses appeared and the group tried the contents warily.

"Say, is this gin or paint thinner?" said Peter, looking at his glass sourly. "I have a feeling this stuff hasn't been any closer to Canada than the north side of Trenton."

As Peter and his friends were laughing about the peculiar gin, Peter suddenly heard the word Bradwell from the table behind him. He strained to listen a little more closely in case someone was calling him. Above the din, he could just make out what was being said.

"....all wrong, that's what it was. They all got it wrong; the police, the detectives, the newspapers, everybody. It wasn't a suicide; not even close. It was murder, plain and simple."

Peter felt a lump in his stomach, and not just from the gin. He couldn't get away from his brother's murder, no matter where he went. Even here people were speculating about the case. The gin must be more potent than he thought. In spite of his distaste, he listened further.

"That's horse feathers, Danny," someone else said. "You think you know more than all those people?"

"A lot more," came the reply. "Because they didn't know where to look and I did. That's how I know it was murder."

"So why didn't you tell the police when you had the chance?"

"I didn't have all the information when I testified, but I do now. Pretty soon I'm telling all, but not until I'm ready. You'll see. I know it was murder and I know who did it and why. But I'm not saying any more about it until I'm ready."

Peter felt a chill at the reference to testifying. Maybe this wasn't some babbling drunk after all. Peter turned to see who was talking. With a shock, Peter realized the speaker was Danny Greene, one of Robert's friends. Robert had recently spoken of Greene, but didn't see him often. What could he know? Was it just the gin talking?

"I'm not wasting my breath on you mugs anymore," said Greene, rising from his chair. "I'm going to the can, and then I'm going home. See ya in the funny papers."

Seeing his chance, Peter waited until Greene was in the men's room before rising to place himself in a position to intercept him when he left. He had to know what Greene meant.

"Hang on," he said to his friends, "I'll be back in a few minutes."

He made his way through the crowd and stood near the front door where he could talk to Greene when he left the men's room. Peter's mind was racing. Could Greene really prove that his brother was murdered? Peter stared at the scarred brown restroom door, willing it to open.

"Raid! Everybody out!" someone shouted.

Chaos erupted. Suddenly everyone seemed to be running at once. Panicky customers overturned tables and chairs and stumbled over each other to get out or at least get to the restaurant section before the police caught them. Bartenders slid panels over the liquor shelves behind the bar while waiters frantically gathered up glasses from the tables and emptied them into a sink. Someone turned over the Volstead Tavern sign to reveal lettering on the other side that said simply "special event room". Peter was almost knocked over in the crush of escaping people. He didn't see Danny Greene.

Outside, people piled into cars and sped off into the night as three police cars and a paddy wagon arrived. Obviously, someone had tipped off the owners that a raid was imminent. Police tried to stop the escaping patrons, but it was like trying to push back the tide with a broom. About a dozen loudly protesting people were herded into the paddy wagon while the rest scattered in all directions. Peter stood by the only door waiting to latch on to Danny Greene, but Greene didn't appear.

The police were in the Volstead Tavern now, confronting a handful of innocent looking patrons and a lot of recently emptied bottles. Peter had moved to the restaurant section and wasn't trying to flee, so he wasn't arrested. A red-faced policeman stopped near him to confer with another one.

"I checked the bathroom and it looks like the ones in there got out through the window."

"Well, kiss 'em goodbye, I guess. My shift'll be over in an hour anyway. Just another night enforcin' Prohibition."

Chapter 7

Witnesses

When Max stopped by the Bradwells' the next morning, Charlie eagerly told him about Peter's experience at the Volstead Tavern the night before.

"Wait a minute," said Max. "Who is Danny Greene, exactly?"

"He was a pal of Robert's, but a couple of years older. He lived right across the street from the Taylors; that is, he used to. He got married last year and bought a house over in Palmyra."

"Okay," said Max. "Anything else?"

"Well, there is one more thing," said Charlie. "Danny used to see Miriam Taylor a while before Robert did. In fact, they were engaged as well."

"Interesting," said Max. "Was there any jealousy between Robert and Danny Greene?"

"I don't think there was. Robert certainly never said so. Anyway, by the time Robert started seeing Miriam, Danny was engaged to his current wife."

Max turned to Peter. "Did Robert see Danny Greene often?"

"Not really," said Peter. "Danny was busy with his new wife and getting his business going and Robert was going to school up in New Brunswick except during the summer. Robert did mention him a few times in the weeks before he died, though."

"Oh? What did Robert say about him?"

Peter looked slightly uncomfortable. "Oh, nothing special. He just wondered how he was doing in his business. That sort of thing."

"So what do you think, Max? Could Danny Greene have any useful information?" Charlie broke in.

"It's hard to say, Charlie. If he does, why didn't he tell it at the inquest? Besides, an overheard conversation in a speakeasy is not the most reliable source of information in the best of circumstances. Still, it's worth investigating. Even if it's all talk, he did testify at the inquest and might have some small piece of the picture that could help. I'll go over and see him."

Martha, who had been listening quietly, spoke up. "Danny Greene? You know, I think I just read something about him in the society pages. His family's very well off."

She picked up a newspaper and started rustling through the pages. "Now where did I see that? Here it is; 'Mr. And Mrs. Daniel Greene of 212 Highfields Road, Palmyra will be visiting relatives in Florida for a week. They leave on August 2.'"

"August 2?" said Charles. "That's today. If they're heading for Florida, they probably left first thing this morning."

"Danny Greene seems to have remarkably bad timing," said Max. "Well, all right. I'll just have to catch up to him when he returns."

"So what do you think so far, Max?"

"Charlie, I've only been here a little over 24 hours, so there's still a lot to do, but..."

"What?"

"There are a few inconsistencies in the testimony that seem to raise at least the possibility that Robert did not intend to kill Miriam and himself when he went there that night."

"You mean it might have been accidental?" Charlie looked both hopeful and confused. "But how could.."

Max held up a hand, palm outward. "Maybe not accidental exactly, but unplanned at least. Anyway, it's too soon to even speculate. All I'm saying is that what I've found so far has certain aspects that are inconsistent with the official story. That doesn't necessarily mean that Robert didn't do it, just that he might have done it in a different way and for a different reason than everyone thinks."

"All right, Max. It isn't much, but it's a hope. That's about all we've got at this point."

Sitting in the shade of an Oak tree on Main Street, Max started to go through the list of Robert's friends Charlie had provided, as well as the list of people who testified at the inquest. Max took off his jacket. It looked like another warm day. A familiar blue sign told him a pay telephone was nearby and he used it to start calling people. After a few calls, Max was able to find Horace Caldwell, the friend Robert and Miriam had gone to Atlantic City with the day of the killings. He seemed surprised, but agreed to meet Max at the hotel in 20 minutes.

Caldwell proved to be a thin, awkward young man who wore a loud blazer in spite of the heat. He sat squirming slightly and adjusting his already-adjusted tie.

"Well, Mr. Hurlock, it's like I told them at the inquest. We all went to Atlantic City in the morning and got back to Miriam's around maybe ten that night. Then we dropped Robert off at his house around 10:15. That's all I know."

"Wasn't it unusual for a couple to split up but still go out together?"

"I guess it was, but they weren't really romantic or anything. They were just friends. It was like taking your sister somewhere."

"Did Robert say or do anything unusual on the trip to Atlantic City?"

"Well, I thought he was sort of quiet and withdrawn; like he had something on his mind, but he didn't really say anything unusual."

"Do you have any idea why Miriam broke off the engagement?"

Caldwell frowned in a way that indicated he would rather be talking about something else. "Well, I never asked Miriam, and she never talked about it to me, but I heard from some of her girlfriends that she thought Robert was too..."

"...too what?"

"Dull. I don't mean he was a drip or anything, but Miriam, well, she got bored easily. She was always on the lookout for something new. It was as simple as that."

"So you don't think she would have changed her mind?"

"Not a chance. I even told Robert that once. I said 'Robert, she wants someone different. The only way she'd want you now would be if you were reincarnated.'"

"Reincarnated, huh? Interesting choice of words in view of what happened."

Caldwell jumped as if struck by an electric shock. "Well, jeez Louise, Mr. Hurlock. How was I to know?"

That afternoon, while the sun burned down on the nearly empty streets, Max went to the offices of the Moorestown News-Chronicle and looked through archived copies of past editions to see if there was any additional information about either Charlie Bradwell or William Taylor. You never knew if someone might be hiding some scandal or other. After an hour, he stifled a yawn. There didn't seem to be anything out of the ordinary about the principals in the case, nothing public at any rate.

As his final stop for the day, Max drove over to Danny Greene's house about two miles away. He knew Greene would be in Florida for another week, but he didn't want to miss him when he returned, so he decided to leave him a note on his front door. He approached the neat cottage and knocked, just in case. As he expected, there was no one home, so he wrote out a note. The note said simply.

I understand you have some information about the Taylor Bradwell case. Please contact me at Cole's Hotel as soon as possible. *Max Hurlock*

The next morning, Max and Allison were up and dressed, but were taking their time getting ready for their day. A leisurely room service breakfast of bacon and scrambled eggs soon had them feeling contented and optimistic.

"I think I'm making some progress," said Max. "Pfeiffer is suspicious of me and not very cooperative at this point, but he seems like he's competent, so he might be a help since he's the only detective who was on the scene the night of the killings."

"My flapper article is taking shape, too," Allison said. "I've made a list of local places where flappers might shop or congregate. Of course the article won't be exactly in depth, but I think I can gin up some new insights, if you'll pardon the expression. By the time I'm finished with it, the article will be the cockatoo's shoes."

"Maybe you could gin up some insights into Charlie Bradwell's case in your spare time," said Max, "especially regarding Danny Greene. The more I think about it the more possible it seems that Greene saw or heard something that affects this case."

Allison nodded. "Yes, but it was quite inconsiderate of him to biff off to Florida just when he's needed here. Let's hope he doesn't buy property and stay there like everyone else seems to be doing these days. I saw an advertisement just yesterday for Florida land; only $150 for ten acres. Of course nine of them are probably underwater."

"No, I think he'll resist that temptation. He'll be back next week and by then I'll have all the other pieces in place. I can't wait to talk to him."

"Of course, he could be just a blowhard," Allison observed. "The hot air that gets expelled from braggarts in the average speakeasy could fill a Zeppelin."

Max nodded. "Of course he could be. That's why I need to talk to him to find out."

As they spoke, they heard the sound of several sets of heavy footsteps clumping in the hallway.

"I think someone's out in the corridor," said Allison. "Someone with size 14 boots from the sound of it. The management of Cole's really ought to invest in thicker carpeting."

The door shook with the sound of a pounding fist. “Max Hurlock? Open up. This is the police!”

Max and Allison looked at each other. “The police?” said Max. “That sounds like Pfeiffer’s voice. What could he want?”

Max opened the door to find Otto Pfeiffer standing in the hall with two other policemen. They were not smiling.

“Good morning, Otto,” said Max. “Nice to see you again so soon. To what do I owe..."

“Mr. Max Hurlock,” said Pfeiffer with obvious satisfaction. “You are under arrest for the murder of Danny Greene.”

Chapter 8

Danny Greene

Max and Allison stood at the doorway in stunned silence for a few seconds. Finally, Max spoke.

"But Danny Greene's in Florida. You mean he..."

"Danny Greene," Pfeiffer corrected him, "is on the floor of his parlor lying dead with a bullet in his chest."

"Dead? But what makes you think I had anything to do with it?"

"A neighbor saw someone matching your description leaving the house yesterday afternoon, and we found this in Greene's pocket."

He handed Max a folded piece of paper. Max opened it.

I understand you have some information about the Taylor Bradwell case. Please contact me at Cole's Hotel as soon as possible. *Max Hurlock*

Max was recovering his wits. "Come on, Pfeiffer. If he had his grocery list in his pocket would you arrest the guy who runs the A&P? What kind of murderer would leave a note making an appointment with someone he intends to kill?"

Pfeiffer stood with his hands on his hips. "Dunno, but I mean to find out. Come along down to the station and we'll have a nice little chat."

Max turned to Allison. "Get hold of Charlie Bradwell. Tell him I need his bail money and maybe his lawyer right away. Take the car and see what else you can find out."

"But Max,.."

"Go ahead. I'll get it straightened out on this end if I can."

One of the police grabbed Max's arm in a clamp-like grip and ushered him out. Allison followed them down the hall and past the disapproving stares of several people in the lobby. A minute later they were in a police car and gone, leaving her standing by the curb with the key to Charlie Bradwell's Packard in her hand.

"Yes, we're making real progress," she remarked, shaking her head.

A few minutes later, Max found himself on a hard wooden chair in a dark and stale-smelling room at police headquarters. A row of file cabinets lined one institutional green-painted wall, and wanted posters crowded a bulletin board on the opposite side, but otherwise the room contained only a table and several battered wooden chairs. The room looked as if the only reason it wasn't being used to store boxes of old files was that the atmosphere might turn the paper brown. A place this unpleasant could only be the interrogation room. Otto Pfeiffer stood in a corner smoking a cigarette and eyeing Max. Without a word, he flicked on a bright overhead light in the center of the room. Max squinted as his eyes adjusted.

"Now why don't you save yourself a lot of trouble and tell me all about it?" Pfeiffer asked. "Did Danny Greene have some information that reflected badly on Robert Bradwell? Is that why he had to be shut up?"

Max looked at Pfeiffer, who looked more sinister than ever with the back lighting. "I'll tell you anything you want to know if you'll tell me something first; why did Danny Greene come back early from Florida?"

"He never went," said Pfeiffer. "His wife went by herself. She's already been notified and is on her way home."

"But the newspapers said they went together."

Pfeiffer let out a long stream of smoke. "You can't always believe what they say in the papers, can you, Hurlock? She went and he stayed home. Now are you ready to talk to me, or do I have to use other methods?"

Max squinted in the harsh light. "Other methods? I doubt it. I checked up on you, Pfeiffer. You're a little rough around the edges, but you're a real detective. You're not a thug with a badge. You outsmart the criminal, but you don't use the third degree. It's not your style."

Pfeiffer ground out the cigarette and moved closer. His features looked grotesque in the light. "I'm flattered, but how do you know I won't make an exception for an out of town smart guy who murders a leading citizen?"

"Like I said, you don't do that sort of thing because you don't have to. Besides, I'll be glad to tell you what I know. You didn't even have to arrest me."

"So start telling. What did you want to see Danny Greene about?"

"I understood he was talking in a speakeasy about knowing the real story behind the Taylor Bradwell killings."

"Do tell. And what, according to Mr. Greene was the real story?"

Max shrugged. "He said Robert Bradwell was murdered and he knew who did it and why. That's all I know. I never got to talk to him."

"Or maybe you did talk to him and decided he knew too much to keep breathing. The fact is that you were the last person seen at his house, and nobody else had a motive."

"Nobody else had a motive that you know about yet, Pfeiffer, and I didn't have a motive at all. He died before I ever found out what, if anything, he knew."

Pfeiffer was silent a few moments, then started pacing back and forth. "That may be, but I've got a dead man on my hands and only one person so far has motive, means, and opportunity."

"Come on, Pfeiffer, you're too good a detective for this. I don't have a motive because I have no idea what he knew. I don't have means because my gun is a Mauser .32, and I'll bet Greene was killed with something bigger if it was only one shot. I don't have opportunity because he wasn't home when I arrived. I thought he was still in Florida."

"Says you, but all I know is that you show up at my office second guessing my investigation, and less than 24 hours later a prime witness turns up dead. Now I don't believe in coincidences, so I have to wonder."

Max stared back at him. "Look; do you seriously believe that I went to Greene's house and left a note with my name on it, then came back a few hours later and shot him, but never bothered to retrieve the note? You don't believe that and neither would a jury."

After glaring at his suspect briefly, Pfeiffer abruptly walked out of the room without saying another word, leaving Max to wonder whether he had convinced him or not. A few minutes later another detective came in and asked Max routine questions about date of birth, residence, and the like. Then he left as well. Max slumped back in his chair.

"Well," he said ruefully, "this investigation is certainly off to a great start. Charlie Bradwell wanted me to produce a murder suspect and it seems that's just what I've done."

A few minutes later, Charles Bradwell appeared at Pfeiffer's office along with Allison. Pfeiffer informed them that bail had not yet been set since he had not yet taken Max before the magistrate.

"Pfeiffer, you can't keep a man without a warrant and without a magistrate deciding on bail," Bradwell reminded him.

"We are still investigating," said Pfeiffer smoothly. "I can hold a nonresident for 48 hours while we get things sorted out. That way we don't have to worry about him skipping town."

"But this is preposterous," Bradwell protested. "Max is investigating for me. He's not a hit man. He should be released at once."

"My boys are beating the bushes for more information at the moment. This will give us a little breathing space in case Mr. Hurlock knows more than he's sayin'."

"Oh, for heaven's sakes," sputtered Allison. "You could throw a dart at the telephone directory and find a more likely suspect than Max. He never even met the man."

Pfeiffer just looked at his watch. "Only about 47 hours to go."

"Pfeiffer can't really believe all that," grumbled Allison as they left the office.

"Whether he does or doesn't, Max is stuck there for the moment," said Charlie Bradwell. "I'll go see the prosecutor, but he's been ducking me."

"We've got to get Max out of jail and cleared of the murder charge," said Allison. "Where is Danny Greene's house, anyway?"

"I'll take you over there, if you'd like."

"Just give me the address and I'll take care of it. But first I need to stop at the railroad ticket office."

"Sure. It's about three blocks from here. I'll take you."

The ticket office was a small white clapboard building at the Haddon Avenue station in Palmyra. Allison and Bradwell went to the stationmaster seated behind an old-fashioned ticket window. Allison smiled sweetly and said, in what Max sometimes called her "damsel in distress" voice, "Hi. I hope you can help me. I have to meet an old friend coming up from Florida and I lost the paper with the train information on it. I took everything out of my purse, but it's not there."

The stationmaster looked gallantly concerned. Middle aged men get few opportunities to assist attractive young women and tend to tackle such jobs eagerly.

"That's too bad, miss. Maybe I can help. When is she getting in? It is a she isn't it?"

Allison shook her head. "I don't know when. That's what I lost."

"I see."

"But I know she was in Miami, and I know she was leaving sometime today."

The stationmaster smiled. "Well, maybe we can figure it out. Let me look at the schedule here....Miami to Moorestown via Baltimore, Philadelphia, and Camden..... Well, there are two trains she could take. One is at 10:15 this morning..."

Allison did some quick calculating. "No, that's a little too early. I think she'd take the later train."

"All right." The ticket agent flipped through more pages of timetables. "The other train leaves Miami at 2:45 this afternoon. It goes to Baltimore and she'd have to change trains there. She'll arrive in Philadelphia tomorrow at 8:15 am. Then, allowing for time to get to the ferry, she should get into Camden around nine or so tomorrow morning. Then she would take the Camden and Amboy line right up to this station in Palmyra. She'd probably get in around ten tomorrow morning."

Allison smiled and looked relieved. "Then that's it. I'm sure it is. Thank you so much."

The stationmaster beamed. "Not at all, miss. Glad to help. These train schedules can be confusing."

Thanks again," Allison said, turning to leave. "Oh, by the way...."

"Yes, miss?"

"Could I buy a ferry ticket for tomorrow?"

"Certainly, miss. Here you are. That'll be 15 cents."

"You're a dear. Good bye."

The stationmaster grinned and flushed slightly.

As they got back in the car, Bradwell shook his head. "Gee, I never get service like that."

After Bradwell dropped her off back at the hotel, Allison took the Packard and drove to Danny Greene's house on Highfield Road. Two police cars were parked in front and two more were slowly searching the grounds for whatever they could find. Allison parked up the street and walked to the house next door. She rang the bell and a pale woman with black hair and a two-year-old hanging on the hem of her skirt answered. Although not yet fluent in English, the two-year-old contributed to the conversation by emitting occasional ear-splitting screams, which the mother apparently failed to notice.

"You from the police?" the woman asked. "I already told the officer everything I know about it."

"No," said Allison, "I'm investigating privately; to sort of help out the police."

The woman nodded. "If you ask me they could use the help."

"Can you tell me what you saw yesterday?"

"It was around maybe 4:00 or 4:30. I looked outside and saw someone coming out of the house. He was a tall guy, good-looking, with brown hair and a brown suit; maybe in his twenties. At first I thought it was Danny, but when I looked again, I could see it wasn't. Anyway, the guy walked out and got into a red Packard and drove away."

Allison tried to hide her disappointment. The woman had described Max.

"You said he was leaving the house," said Allison. "Did you actually see him open the front door?"

"Well, no. He was coming down the steps when I first saw him, but I didn't actually see him come through the door."

"And you didn't see or hear anything..."

The baby screamed for a few seconds, forcing Allison to wait.

"You didn't see or hear anything after that?"

"No, not a thing. I got little Dudley here in bed around seven and I was so tired, I went to bed myself. My husband's away for a few days you see."

"Thank you. You've been a big help."

Little Dudley screamed goodbye as she left.

The people in the next house had seen and heard nothing, so Allison trudged to the house across the street without much hope.

A short elderly lady wearing a black dress with a cameo brooch at the neck answered the door.

"Mercy, dear. I thought you were one of those encyclopedia salesmen, or maybe one of those Fuller brush men."

"Well, no, I...."

"You're not selling vacuum cleaners are you?"

"No, I'm..."

"Good! That Hoover salesman that came by last week dumped ashes on my new rug to show me how good the vacuum cleaner was. A lot of nerve if you ask me."

"Well, actually...."

"Of course, he was able to vacuum them up, but what if the power had been off?"

"Yes, but...."

"Oh, lord! And that man who came by last week selling magazines. I thought I'd never get rid of him. I told him I already get Colliers and Look and the Ladies Home Journal, and that's quite enough for me. I thought that man yesterday was headed my way, but he wasn't. When you knocked I thought he was back again."

"Well, I'm investigating...Wait a minute, what man are you talking about?"

"The one that came by last night around 7:30 or so. I knew he was selling something. I figured he was working the other side of the street first, but I guess he ran out of time."

"You saw a man on the other side of the street around 7:30 last night? Did you tell the police?" asked Allison excitedly.

"Humph! I never got the chance. Some young man from the police asked me if I saw a tall man in a brown suit around 4:30 or so. I said no and he just said thank you and good bye before I could tell him about the man I did see. Can you imagine? Nobody wanted to hear about it."

Allison smiled. "Well I want to hear about it; every little detail, and I promise not to dump ashes on your rug or try to sell you a magazine subscription. Now what did this man look like and where did he go?"

The lady lit up, glad to have an attentive audience. "He was about average height and wore a dark suit. He had on a hat with a broad brim, so I really didn't see his face. I'm sorry, but that's all I can tell you."

"Don't worry," Allison reassured her. "You've already told me plenty."

Chapter 9

The Man in the Model T

Max Hurlock sat in the small interrogation room in the detectives' office. He was on one of the chairs at the table, while on the opposite side sat Otto Pfeiffer casually smoking another cigarette. The room was quiet except for the hum of a flickering fluorescent light in the ceiling. The air was thick with stale tobacco smoke.

"All right," said Pfeiffer, grinding out his cigarette and almost simultaneously lighting another one, "let's go over it again. How do you know Charles Bradwell?"

"We were in the navy together; on the USS Carson."

"And why did he ask you to come here?"

"He asked me to investigate the circumstances surrounding the death of his son, Robert. He doesn't think it was suicide."

Pfeiffer eyed him sharply. "Do you work for the insurance company?"

Max frowned. This was the second time Pfeiffer had mentioned insurance. "No. I told you. I'm an independent investigator. I find the facts, whatever they are. Why do you keep mentioning insurance?"

Pfeiffer took a deep drag on his cigarette and raised one eyebrow. "You mean he didn't tell you? Some navy buddy he is. Robert Bradwell had a $25,000 life insurance policy, payable to his parents in the event of his death. All the Bradwells have similar policies. I think Charles got to be a real cautious man during the Great War- saw too many cases of sudden death, I guess. Anyway, only problem is a life insurance policy doesn't pay if the death is a suicide, but it does if the death..."

"...is a murder." Max finished the sentence for him.

"Right," said Pfeiffer. "You see, Bradwell's real estate company was doing pretty well until he went in the navy, but by the time he came back things had turned around, and he started having trouble making ends meet. My guess is he could really use the money right about now. Funny he never told you. He expects you to dig out the facts and he doesn't give you the ones he has. Maybe you can ask him about it at your trial."

Max was silent a moment, lost in thought until Pfeiffer spoke again, more slyly this time. "Well, now that you know your buddy isn't playing straight with you, there's no reason to protect him, is there? Why don't you tell me what happened, and you'll get off a lot easier. Did he ask you to kill Danny Greene to keep him from talking?"

"Pfeiffer, Danny Greene would be the last person Bradwell would want dead. If Danny Greene had lived to talk, he might have proved Robert was murdered. That's what he said in the speakeasy."

"Correction," sneered Pfeiffer. "That's what you said Bradwell's son claimed Greene said in the speakeasy. That's third hand hearsay. For all I know Greene was about to prove it was suicide and that's why he had to be killed."

Max looked at him with amazement. "You do have a suspicious mind."

"Occupational hazard. It comes from every two-bit bootlegger and would-be beer baron in the county trying to con me. God knows what their 'shine tastes like; they're not even good at lying."

"I find it's a lot easier to tell the truth," said Max. "You don't have to remember as much."

"Well, I'm all for the truth." Pfeiffer continued to smoke, eyeing Max critically. "So we're going to stay right here until we get it."

An hour later, Otto Pfeiffer was taking a break long enough to drink a cup of black coffee in his office. He was going over his notes and getting frustrated that Max's story seemed so logical and consistent. The more he thought about it, the more it looked like Max wasn't a very good suspect after all. As he ruminated, a clerk stuck his head in the door.

"Chief, Mrs. Hurlock is here. She wants to see you."

"Tell her I'm still investigating. I thought I made that clear this morning," Pfeiffer growled.

"I tried telling her that, but she says she has new information on the case. She's very persistent."

"For the love of.... Is <u>everybody</u> a damned detective now? Tell her...oh, there you are Mrs. Hurlock."

Allison was standing in the doorway, smiling innocently. "I just knew you'd want to see me right away," she said sweetly, "so I didn't wait for them to invite me in."

"How thoughtful of you," Pfeiffer muttered.

"I spoke to the lady across the street from the Greene house. She saw a man in a black Model T in front of the house around 7:30 last night. That's over three hours after Max was there. You find that man, Detective Pfeiffer, and you'll find the killer."

Pfeiffer almost jumped out of his chair. "At 7:30? Edwards! Get in here!"

A fresh-faced officer who looked as if he just got out of high school appeared in the doorway next to Allison.

"Didn't you question the lady across the street from the Greene place this morning?"

"Yes, sir. Right after I talked to the other neighbors. She didn't see Mr. Hurlock."

"Did you ask her if she saw anyone else?"

Edwards looked puzzled. "Well, no. I mean...we already had an eyewitness and the note from Mr. Hurlock, so I didn't think...."

With some effort, Pfeiffer controlled himself and told Edwards to get back to his duties. Finally, he addressed Allison.

"All right, Mrs. Hurlock. I'll have someone look into this; someone other than Edwards that is. But I can still hold your husband for another day."

Allison gave him what Max often called her "smile of sweet reason". "Oh, you know you shouldn't do that. You have an eyewitness identifying a far more likely suspect and he was seen hours after Max was there. The longer you hold Max now the harder it will be to explain why if some higher up should ask. You know how critical people can be. Besides, if Max is released, he'll be looking for the man as well, and so the case might get solved that much sooner."

Pfeiffer looked at her a moment. She was smiling the smile of an angel; an angel holding four aces. Without another word, Pfeiffer rose and walked back to the interrogation room. Max looked up, expecting another round of boring questions.

"All right, Hurlock. You're free to go. Your wife is waiting outside."

"Now you're talking." Max rose and grabbed his coat.

"All I can say, Hurlock," Pfeiffer grumbled, "is that your wife is one mighty persistent and persuasive woman."

Max chuckled and grinned. "Ain't that the truth."

"Max, are you all right?" said Allison as they drove away. "I expected to see you in a striped suit breaking rocks."

"Just a little misunderstanding with the local constabulary," Max assured her. "It shows the unreliability of circumstantial evidence."

"Well, you're the expert detective, not me," said Allison, "but in the future, wouldn't it be better to get someone else arrested for the crime you're investigating?"

"Thanks. I'll try to keep that in mind."

A few minutes later they were at the Bradwells'. Charlie was glad to see them.

"Max! You're out," he said. "Somehow I just knew Allison would pull it off. She is mighty persistent and persuasive."

"So I've heard. Why didn't you tell me about the insurance, Charlie?"

Charlie's face fell and his mouth hung open soundlessly for a moment. "I'm sorry, Max. I guess I was embarrassed to admit I needed the money. Besides, clearing Robert's name is what's really important, and I didn't want any other considerations to get in your way. I guess I just didn't want to complicate things."

"Well, it's a little late for that. Things have been complicated quite a bit, and the insurance is a big reason. How come Pfeiffer knows about it and I don't?"

"He found out during the investigation. They routinely check things like that when there's been a murder."

"Why would Robert even have a life insurance policy at his age?"

"Martha's cousin sells insurance and was just starting in the business. We all bought policies several years ago just to help him out. We were going to discontinue them when he got more established."

"But I thought you were a big real estate tycoon," Max insisted. "Pfeiffer says you need the money from that policy."

"The company was doing very well when I went into the navy, but it's been having some cash flow problems since the war ended," Charlie said. "A lot of our properties were leased to the government for the war. You know; offices, warehouses, and the like. Well, when the war ended those leases weren't renewed, so we have a lot of empty spaces that are costing us money instead of making it. We'll get it straightened out in time, but the bills for heat, maintenance, taxes and interest charges keep right on coming. That insurance money would be a big help to tide us over."

Max stood with his arms folded. "Any more secrets I should know about, or should I wait until Pfeiffer tells me?"

"That's it, Max. I swear. There's nothing else. Look; I'm sorry. I guess I was embarrassed."

"All right, Charlie, but no more secrets or we'll drop this whole thing and you can hire a local private eye. What you tell him is up to you."

"No more secrets, Max. I swear."

“Then tomorrow I need to talk to some people at your company, especially people Robert worked with.”

“I’ll make any arrangements you need, Max”

“And I have a boat to catch,” added Allison.

Chapter 10

Mrs. Greene remembers

Bradwell Properties operated out of an office on the second floor of a nondescript two story brick building on the outskirts of Philadelphia. Chan's Laundry on one side and Mel's Deli on the other shared the first floor. The heavy smell of corned beef and pastrami hung in the warm summer air.

"Hey, that smells good," said Max. "At least you won't go hungry here. But I envisioned your office a little differently."

Charlie smiled. "I started out here back in 1910. I figured I'd move to a bigger and better place once the company grew, but the fact is, this place suits me just fine. We invest and develop properties, you see. We don't have to attract the public or even clients, so why get overly fancy?"

Max nodded as they climbed the stairs to a glass-paneled door with the words "Bradwell Properties" painted on the glass. The letter w, Max noticed, was peeling and the glass looked as if it was last cleaned during the Wilson administration. Charlie opened the door to a cluttered office with three people at desks hunched over piles of real estate papers and one man talking on a telephone in the corner. On one wall were photos of various buildings, presumably owned or operated by Bradwell Properties. On the other wall was a large corkboard covered with scraps of paper that on closer examination proved to be advertisements and various real estate notices.

"Everyone, this is Max Hurlock," Charlie Bradwell announced. Everyone looked over and nodded. "He's investigating Robert's death and he's going to ask you some questions, so please help him all you can."

"Thanks," said Max.

"I'm going to take care of some work that's been piling up in the next room, so take your time and find out what you need to, Max. You can start with Doris here."

Doris Gentry was the secretary of Bradwell Properties. Sitting in front of a large black typewriter, she wore an old fashioned white shirtwaist blouse and a long black skirt with a border of gray at the bottom from dragging in the dust of the office floor. Large reading glasses hung suspended around her neck on a silver chain. As she talked, she constantly straightened her bun of gray-black hair, although Max couldn't see a hair out of place.

"Yes, Mr. Hurlock, there's a lot of noise and apparent activity in this place, but I'm the one who does all the real work. Why, except for Mr. Bradwell, nobody here can even write a coherent letter. It's always 'Doris, write to so and so and sign my name', or 'Doris, I need a report on the Smith Property by 5:00.' If I get run over by a trolley car one day, this place will have to close its doors."

Max tut-tutted sympathetically. "Did you work with Robert Bradwell when he was here?"

"Of course; though he mostly worked helping with the bookkeeping which is one of the few things I don't usually have to do. Oh, it was terrible what happened to Robert," she said, shaking her head. "He was such a nice boy, except...."

"Except what?" asked Max.

She pulled her chair closer. "Mr. Hurlock, I never thought he should have been running around with that Taylor girl. Why she was practically a flapper; out dancing the Charleston, smoking gaspers and drinking bathtub gin, I shouldn't wonder. She was just too worldly for him. But what's worse, that girl really pulled the rug out from under Robert when she broke off their engagement. He wasn't the same afterwards. He kept calling her on the phone and visiting her."

"I've heard how unhappy he was about being jilted."

Doris nodded knowingly. "Very unhappy. Believe me, Mr. Hurlock, a woman can tell. He just kept trying to get her to change her mind."

"So I guess if he hadn't died he'd still be trying," said Max. To his surprise, Doris shook her head.

"Oh, no. Robert was smitten, but he wasn't a fool. I think he must have come to his senses and was just about to give up."

"Why do you say that?"

Doris looked around, as if afraid of anyone else hearing, and lowered her voice still further. "The day before he was shot, Mr. Hurlock, Robert indicated to me that he was very close to dropping the whole matter."

Max was suddenly interested, and found himself looking around furtively as well. He felt like a conspirator. "Really? Why?"

"He told me he was going to give it one last try, and if she didn't take him back, then ....." She paused for dramatic effect.

Max leaned forward. "Then what?"

"Then," she said in almost a whisper, "that would be the end of it."

"The end of it?" Max repeated. "What did he mean by that?"

"Isn't it obvious?"

"No; not at all. Could it have meant he was going to give up and move on if she continued to reject him?"

She looked at him over the top of her glasses. "It could have, Mr. Hurlock, but in view of how things ended up, I think it's clear that it didn't."

"Then you think he killed her, then himself?"

"That's not for me to say, but he was certainly in the right frame of mind for it."

Bradwell's partner, Fred Madison regarded Max through thick round spectacles, no doubt worn for squinting at financial reports and ledgers. His bow tie and red suspenders made him look like an overdressed fireman. Madison had a small office of his own close to Bradwell's, where he sat behind a battered desk whose top was shaggy with papers.

"Well, Robert didn't actually work for me alone," Madison began. "He worked sort of 'at large', moving from one area to another. I did work with him part of the time, though. He helped with some of the bookkeeping. He had a degree in accounting after all, so it seemed a good fit. Robert was a bright lad, and could have had a good future. It's a damned shame what happened."

"Did he have any enemies or rivals that you know of?"

Madison laughed. "Robert? I doubt it. It would be hard to find anyone who didn't like him. Mind you, I've sometimes wondered if there might have been some romantic rival in the picture, but I never knew for sure."

"A romantic rival?"

"Exactly. Just consider the facts; a man is engaged to be married and the girl suddenly breaks it off. That seems to point to the girl's possible romantic interest in someone else. Miriam Taylor did have a reputation for being a bit fickle. I understand she was engaged to that Danny Greene at one time, so another flame is not unlikely."

"Do you know who?"

"No idea," said Madison shrugging his shoulders.

Max looked at his notes. "And if this rival found out about Robert's efforts to get Miriam to take him back, and about Miriam's tolerance of Robert's continued attentions, he might have lost his temper with both of them."

Madison raised his hands off the desk with his palms turned outward. "Well, it's all speculation, although...." Madison frowned as if he had just remembered something.

"Although what?" asked Max.

"Well, one day I heard him talking on the phone to Miriam and he said something like 'I don't care what he says. He doesn't scare me.'"

"Who was he talking about?"

"I don't know, but he seemed pretty unhappy about it afterward."

"I see. Anything else you can tell me?"

Madison looked at him uncertainly, as if unsure if he should say more. "Look, Robert was a great guy and everyone thinks the world of Charlie. Nobody knows the whole story for sure, but..."

"But what?"

"As an accountant, I know that when you do the books, the numbers either add up or they don't. It doesn't really matter what you think the bottom line should be, or might be; all that matters is what the numbers tell you."

"And what do the numbers tell you around here?"

"Nobody really wants to say it, because it's so painful to Charlie, but once you get past the personal feelings and look at the cold facts, well...I mean, it isn't certain of course, but.."

"Go on."

"It looks like the inquest had it right. Everything points to murder-suicide."

Allison stood at the ferry dock at the foot of Chestnut Street in Philadelphia glancing through the morning edition of the Enquirer. Max and Charlie had dropped her off and promised to pick her up again on the other side when they returned. She only glanced at the stories of President Harding's latest speech, the upcoming naval conference, Detroit's latest automobiles, and the rising unrest in Europe as the ferry opened its gates. Allison had calculated that Mrs. Greene would be using this ferry on her return from Florida, so she folded her newspaper, boarded and made her way among the passengers looking for her. It wasn't long before Allison spotted what she was looking for. As she expected, Mrs. Greene was somber and sitting alone, not happily crowding the rail with many of the others. She was in her 20s, dressed in black, and had a noticeable Florida tan.

"Mrs. Greene?" Allison asked.

An attractive, brown-haired woman turned towards her warily. She was wearing a black hat with a mesh veil that covered, but failed to hide her eyes, which Allison could tell were red from recent crying. She looked at Allison carefully, then nodded.

"Mrs. Greene. I want you to know how sorry I am about your loss. My husband is investigating Daniel's murder as well as the deaths of Miriam Taylor and Robert Bradwell. I got on this ferry so I could talk to you before you got to Moorestown and had to deal with the press and the police."

"Is your husband with the police?"

"He's an independent investigator. He has no ties to the police, or the press. In fact, we don't even live in New Jersey, so he has no axe to grind. He's just trying to find out the truth. He wanted to talk to your husband about the Taylor-Bradwell case, but didn't get the chance."

Mrs. Greene nodded dully. "Daniel knew both Miriam and Robert well. He was in college with Robert and was once engaged to Miriam himself."

"Did he ever mention what information he had about the case?"

"He talked about it from the beginning, but I didn't pay much attention. Danny was like that. He talked a lot, but didn't always have much substance behind it. I thought that was the case with the murders. That's what he said they were, you know; murders. He said Robert did not kill her and he certainly didn't kill himself."

"And why did he say that? Did he have any evidence?"

"None that I know of. It was just talk."

They looked at the green waters of the Delaware River passing by and the City of Philadelphia receding behind them. Mrs. Greene sighed deeply, daubed her eyes with a handkerchief she held in her hand, then spoke again.

“We got married shortly before Robert Bradwell died,” Danny was going to ask him to be an usher...”

“They were friends?” Allison asked. “I thought Danny had been Robert’s rival for Miriam Taylor.”

“No. That was well over a year ago. It didn’t work out, but they parted as friends as the saying goes. Danny and I met not long after he broke up with Miriam and were married a little over a year later. Danny and Robert were at school together, though Danny was two years ahead of Robert. They were both enrolled in the accounting program. I used to joke with Danny about it. I told him I wouldn’t marry him if he were going to wear a green eyeshade to bed. It seems such a long time ago now. *So wise, so young, they say do never live long*.”

“Richard III?” asked Allison.

Mrs. Greene smiled. “Yes. Sometimes I quote a line I remember from Shakespeare if it seems appropriate. It used to drive Danny crazy. He thought I was showing off, but I just sort of like old Will. He had a lot of wise things to say.”

“How did your husband react to Robert and Miriam’s deaths?”

“Danny was shocked. He said that Robert would never kill himself when he had such a good reason to live.”

“And Danny never said just what he meant?”

“No. When Robert died, Danny kept saying he knew it was murder. I told him if he knew it was murder why didn’t he tell the police? He said he didn’t want to tip his hand because the person that did it thought he got away clean. Danny said he would soon be able to get the evidence he needed to expose the killer."

"What evidence?"

"He never would say. If I asked him he would tell me he didn't want to burden me with it. But he insisted he had something. That was why he didn't go to Florida with me. He said he had some things he had to finish up and that it had something to do with the murder."

"Do you have any idea what things he was talking about or who he suspected?"

Mrs. Greene shook her head. "No, I'm afraid I don't."

The ferry was almost to Camden now, rocking slightly in the water and starting to slow as it approached to dock.

Allison patted Mrs. Greene's hand. "Mrs. Greene, I promise you my husband will do everything he can to find out what happened. If you think of anything else, my name is Allison Hurlock and I'm staying at Cole's Hotel."

"Hurlock?" Mrs. Greene looked stunned. "Didn't they arrest a man by that name?"

"That was my husband Max, but he's been released. Somebody saw him near your house and added two plus two and got five. It's all straightened out now."

"I see. Well, good day, Mrs. Hurlock. I'm afraid I have a train to catch."

"Now this is food that you can grab with both hands, so to speak," Max said over a dinner of Mrs. Bradwell's Hessian pot roast with sauerkraut that night. "When Allison and I eat crabs back home, I think we burn more energy getting the meat out than we gain by eating it. I like an animal with meat thick enough to slice."

Charlie Bradwell did not laugh, and Max noticed he hardly ate.

"Look, Charlie, I know it's a blow finding out Danny Greene might have been close to proving Robert was murdered, but if it's true, there has to be evidence elsewhere as well."

Bradwell looked at him sharply. "What do you mean, 'if it's true?'".

"I mean that a wife's recollection of the words of an admittedly bragging husband is not the sort of thing to bet the farm on."

"But she said...."

"Charlie, tomorrow I'm going to run down some of Danny's friends and see if he told them anything. If his talk in the Volstead Tavern is any indication, Danny Greene couldn't have resisted telling someone else. Maybe he left enough pieces for us to put together again."

"Like the roof and the house?"

Max smiled. "Now you're on the trolley. We started with the roof and now we have part of one wall, and maybe a column. We know the other walls and the floors and the foundation have to be here to support the roof. Now we just have to find them."

That night, Max and Allison returned to Cole's Hotel. The shadows seemed darker than they remembered and the creaks and groans of the old walls woke them several times. The next morning, Allison asked Max if they should order room service for breakfast again.

"Forget it. The last time we did that I wound up getting arrested, and spending the day with that charming Otto Pfeiffer. No thanks. We'll grab a bite at that soda fountain I saw down the street. I think it's called Conroy's."

Allison looked at him skeptically. "I see. Exactly what part of the breakfast was the cause of the trouble? Were the eggs too runny? The toast burned? Maybe the orange juice had a little too much pulp? You know, Max, I never realized such things could cause the police to come after you; maybe to come after the cook, but not you. I think that might make a good article for Reader's Digest: 'Is Your Breakfast Getting You in Trouble with the Law? Take our quick test and find out.' I'll start working on it as soon as we get back."

"Holy cats," said Max. "You really are persistent and persuasive."

"Come on, let's get going. You can wear the straw hat I just bought you. Unless of course you think that's unlucky as well."

"Not unlucky," Max grumbled, "just unattractive and uncomfortable."

As they neared Conroy's, they passed a newsstand on the corner.

"We should pick up a paper," said Allison. "I want to see if there's anything about Mrs. Greene.

Max fished a nickel from his pocket and took a paper. The headlines jumped out at them.

TAYLOR HAD BLOOD ON SHIRT BEFORE BODIES MOVED SAYS PATROLMAN

New evidence in Taylor Bradwell deaths

Presence of blood unexplained

Allison scanned the article. "Curiouser and curiouser. It seems Patrolman Mandrell was the first policeman to arrive and he helped Mr. Taylor move his daughter's body to the next room. But now he claims that Taylor's shirt was already bloody when he got there. So how did it get that way if the body was untouched?"

"Good question; one of many. That's what happens sometimes if you poke around enough," said Max. "Sooner or later you poke a hornet's nest."

Chapter 11

With friends like these...

Allison read the newspaper and shook her head. “This is sensational. Patrolman Mandrell told a reporter that he saw blood on William Taylor’s shirt when he first arrived at the house, even though no one had yet moved the bodies. He also hints of a cover up, saying he wasn’t allowed to testify as to what he saw.”

Max looked over her shoulder. “Yeah, this should get some more tongues wagging.”

“And now maybe everyone who has secret information will get in a lather about Danny Greene and start spilling the beans,” Allison said, excitedly. “Max, maybe you can crack this case after all.”

“If I can stay out of jail long enough,” he replied. He looked at his pocket watch. “All right. I’m going to see if I can run down the fellas that were pals with Danny Greene and see if he said anything to them.”

“Can I help?” Allison asked

“You’ve already done plenty. Mrs. Greene would never have told me what she told you. I’ll tell you what might help, though. If you could arrange to have lunch with Martha Bradwell and get her talking about Robert, maybe there might be something that helps tie this all together. I'm not sure what, exactly, but mothers often pick up things others miss."

"So do wives," said Allison.

They folded the paper and walked the rest of the way to Conroy's for breakfast, unaware of the man watching them from a car parked in the shade of a nearby Elm tree

Max and Allison went directly to the Bradwells' house after breakfast. Max knocked and a few seconds later, Charlie opened the door a crack, then told them to hurry inside.

"There have been three reporters here already," Charlie said, his voice trembling with exasperation. "I'm a prisoner in my own house. And you know the first thing they ask?"

"Well, I suppose..."

"They ask about the insurance! As if that's all I care about. I'm telling you Max, this thing is out of control. I never wanted this; I wanted you to do a nice quiet investigation and get to the bottom of things. You'll never be able to now."

"Charlie is very upset about this," said Martha, who sometimes had a talent for stating the obvious.

Max smiled soothingly and put his hand on Charlie's shoulder.

"Cheer up, Charlie, this is a good thing."

Charlie looked at Max incredulously. "A good thing? Are you nuts?"

"Sure, it's like a muddy pond," said Max.

"A what?" said Charlie.

"Here we go again," muttered Allison, who recognized an analogy coming.

"If you see a puddle, it usually has mud all settled to the bottom, so the water looks pretty clear."

Charlie turned to Allison. "Puddle? Mud? Do you know what he's talking about?"

Allison just smiled.

"So you know how to see the mud?" Max continued. "You throw in a rock to stir things up. That's what happened when Danny Greene was shot. Things are getting stirred up and we're starting to see the mud that was settled to the bottom."

"And just how does seeing mud make things clearer?" Charlie demanded, apparently taking Max literally.

"Well, it's not an exact analogy, I'll admit," said Max. "It's more like...like.."

"Stew," Martha interrupted. "If you want to see what vegetables are in it, you have to stir it up."

"Exactly!" said Allison. "Leave it to a woman."

Max, somewhat annoyed at this sudden detour into the kitchen, spoke up a bit more insistently. "The point is, all this churning is bringing things to the surface that have been hidden. It'll help us. You'll see."

"All right," said Charlie, wiping his forehead. "I hope you're right. Anyway, I hope the list of Robert's friends and their addresses you asked for will help."

"They've already helped," said Max. "I've also got a list of Danny Greene's friends. Allison got me a list from Mrs. Greene. Allison's been a big help, especially when I was in jail."

Allison laughed. "Martha, why don't we go out to lunch today and get your mind off things? How about Fulmer's Luncheonette? I hear it's the cat's pajamas."

Martha readily agreed and Max headed for the front door with Allison.

"Charlie, I'll call you later. I think Danny Greene's pals would talk more freely if you weren't there."

Charlie nodded and opened he front door for them.

Max and Allison stepped outside into the sunlight and were immediately accosted by a short man wearing a wrinkled brown suit with a derby, and carrying a notepad.

"Say, are you the Bradwell guy?"

"Bradwell? Actually..."

"Pettigrew's the name; Pete Pettigrew. But everybody calls me 'Pedigree Pettigrew'...on account of I'm so high class."

"I think the jury is still out on that question," said Allison, backing away slowly.

"I'm with the Chronicle. I wrote the article about Patrolman Mandrell and I need to ask you some questions."

"You may need to ask some questions," said Max, smiling, "but we don't need to answer them."

"Aw, don't be like that," Pettigrew protested. "I gotta make a living too, you know."

"Well, make it somewhere else," said Max. "We're in a bit of a hurry. Besides, I'm not Mr. Bradwell."

"Say, you must be that Hurlock fella what's been asking questions around town. What have you found out?"

"Really, Pettigrew. You know I can't reveal confidential information. I have to make a living, too," said Max.

"Well, how about you, young lady?" Pettigrew shifted his attention to Allison. "Or don't you talk to strange men?"

"On the contrary," said Allison, "they're almost the only kind I do talk to; but you really need to speak with Max here."

"I'll tell you what," said Max. "You can tell your readers this: My name is Max Hurlock. I am staying at Cole's Hotel and I am investigating the Taylor Bradwell killings. I'm going to find out the truth in this case and anybody who has anything to hide had better come clean while they still have the chance. If they do, I'll keep it as confidential as I can, but if I find out about it on my own, I'll tell the world."

"....tell the world," muttered Pettigrew as he wrote the words in his notepad. "Thanks, Mr. Hurlock. Here's my card. If there's anything else you can tell me, anything at all, you let me know."

Max took the card. "You'll be the first."

Pettigrew tipped his derby to Allison as he left. "Ma'am."

Allison watched him walk away. "An abrasive little man, but I suppose he has to be. I assume all the bragging about finding out the secrets was designed to loosen local tongues?"

"Of course; stirring up the mud. Or maybe the stew."

"Well, we'd better scram before another newspaper man starts nipping at our heels. I have some notes to make before I meet Martha Bradwell for lunch."

"And I have to get back to working on the names on my list."

They got in the car and drove away.

A minute later, a man sitting in nearby car finished his cigarette and threw it out the window before driving off in the same direction.

A little later, Max telephoned Danny Greene's friends Joe Bryant and Tim Walsh. Both suggested meeting at the Broken Axle, the restaurant containing the Volstead Tavern where Danny Greene had talked about the Taylor-Bradwell case just before he was murdered. As he approached the place, Max thought it looked so much like a speakeasy they might as well hang out a sign that said so. Still, it functioned as a restaurant during the day and he had heard the food was pretty good.

Joe Bryant and Tim Walsh were sitting at a table towards the back of the fairly busy room. Both had brilliantined hair parted in the middle and both wore tan suits with flared trouser legs. These two are walking posters for the latest in youth fashions, Max thought as he introduced himself and sat down. Since it was still morning they all ordered ham and eggs.

"Thanks for meeting me, fellas. I'm trying to find out what happened to Danny, as well as Robert Bradwell."

"Do you think the cases are related?" asked Bryant, surprised.

Max shrugged. "Well, what do you think? Did Danny ever say just what information he had about the Taylor Bradwell case?"

Walsh shook his head. "He talked about it once in a while, but never said exactly what the deal was. Whenever we would ask, he'd say he couldn't accuse anybody without proof."

"But he said it was murder and not a murder-suicide?"

"That's right. That was one thing he said and he seemed pretty sure about it."

"And he never mentioned just who the killer might be?"

"No, never. He wouldn't even hint. He claimed if he let the information out too soon it might spoil the case."

Max looked around the room. "Tell me about the night of the raid."

Bryant smiled. "That was a night! One minute everything is copacetic, and the next we're legging it out of here on the lam. I never did finish my drink."

"I know about all that," said Max. "What I want to know is what Danny talked about that night."

Joe lit a cigarette and Tim said "Butt me."

Joe handed him a cigarette and turned back to Max.

"It was the usual stuff; cars, sports, girls, and some kidding about the hootch."

"Yeah," added Tim, "but Danny seemed sort of out of it. You know; distracted. Finally he started talking about the Taylor-Bradwell thing. He said he was pretty sure he knew the real story and that it was murder, pure and simple."

"And he said pretty soon he'd be able to prove it, just as soon as he was finished looking over the dogs and cats."

Max made a note. "The dogs and cats? What did that mean?"

"Search me," said Joe. "Danny was all the time talking like that. He'd use a word that had the same first letter as the thing he wanted to say if it was something he didn't want an outsider to overhear. He said it was like a secret language only his friends could understand. Like when he wanted a beer he'd say he wanted a boot. That way if a Prohibition agent was listening, he wouldn't know what Danny really meant."

"Danny said it kept him out of trouble in case the wrong person was listening," added Tim. "Me, I just thought it was confusing."

"So if he wanted to see the dogs and cats he might have meant, say doctors and cooks?" said Max.

"Yeah," Tim nodded. "Something like that."

"Of course," said Joe, "It could just as well have meant ducks and cucumbers. The thing is, we'd heard most of his secret code words before. It was always boot for beer, goldfish for gin, Wilson for whiskey, and Wyoming for women. But we'd never heard him say dogs and cats before. That was something new."

"Didn't you ask him what it meant?" asked Max.

"Well, we were both a bit spifflicated at the time; you know, ossified."

"You mean drunk?" asked Max.

"Just a little. Anyway, we just kept telling him he was full of banana oil and Danny clamed up. Then he headed off to the john and in came the bulls and we all scattered. That's all we know."

"O.K. fellas," said Max, rising from the table, "If you think of anything else, let me know. Thanks for the information."

In the busy dining room of Fulmer's Luncheonette, Allison poked at her peach ice cream and listened to Martha Bradwell talking about Robert and his friends.

"Oh, Robert had his faults, of course. Who doesn't? But he was a good boy. When that Taylor girl threw him over, why it was just devastating."

"Did Robert's friends know how upset he was?" Allison asked.

"Oh, yes. Robert was very open about it," Martha assured her. "They were very supportive, especially Tim Walsh."

"Tim Walsh?"

Martha smiled, took a delicate sip of her tea and replaced the cup in the saucer with a slight clinking sound. "Tim was very interested and very sympathetic to Robert during the whole ordeal. He was always talking to Robert to get him to cheer up and even talked to Miriam Taylor on a number of occasions to try to get her to reconsider."

"That was certainly helpful of him," said Allison.

"Yes, although it was a little odd, really," said Martha. "I had always thought Tim seemed a little, well, self-centered; always thinking of himself first. In fact, in one uncharitable moment, I said to Charlie that I thought Tim Walsh probably carried his own picture around in his billfold. It was very unChristian of me, I know, but that's how it seemed."

Allison smiled to herself. "But he was supportive after Miriam broke up with Robert?"

"Oh, yes," said Martha, "especially considering Tim's own circumstances."

"What circumstances do you mean?"

Martha picked up her teacup again. "Oh, didn't you know? Tim used to be engaged to Miriam too."

"A popular girl," said Allison under her breath.

Chapter 12

The Most Popular Girl in Moorestown

Max had to do some fast talking to get Danny Greene's widow to see him, but for Allison's sake she finally agreed to meet at her place around 4:00. The rambling old house was comfortable and orderly, with a large picture window by the front door letting sunlight into the living room. Max noted a new throw rug had been placed over a section of the older rug near the back of the room. Mrs. Greene noticed Max looking at the throw rug.

"That's where they found Danny, Mr. Hurlock. I put that rug there to cover up the bloodstain. I'm having the rug replaced, but I couldn't bear to look at it in the meantime." Max nodded sympathetically. "Is it a big bloodstain?"

"*'tis not so deep as a well nor so big as a church door but 'tis enough; t'will serve*," she replied faintly.

Max nodded. "That's from Shakespeare, isn't it?"

"Mercutio said it when he was fatally wounded in Romeo and Juliet. It just seemed appropriate, somehow."

"Of course. Mrs. Greene, I understand Danny was working on getting the final proof he needed in the Taylor-Bradwell case."

"That's right, but as I told your wife, he never said just what he was doing."

"Yes, but you were on your way home when you told her that. I was wondering if you've come across anything now that you're back in the house. Did he leave any notes on his desk; anything like that?"

She shook her head. "Believe me, I've looked. Danny has a desk in the den off the living room. It has papers on it, but that was normal for Danny. He often had papers from work around. I didn't see anything out of the ordinary, but you're welcome to look if you'd like."

"If it wouldn't be too much trouble, I'd sure appreciate it."

She led Max into the next room and indicated a small roll top desk on one corner next to a potted plant. The desk was open, revealing several stacks of loose papers and two notebooks.

"The police have already been through Danny's papers. They couldn't find anything either."

Max started looking through the papers. "Did the police remove anything when they were here?"

"They messed the papers up a little, but left them when they were done."

"I take it Danny was a bookkeeper or an accountant?" Max asked, looking through the papers.

"That's right. Accountants do what they call a trial balance as a sort of preliminary to make sure everything is accounted for. Whenever one doesn't balance, they have to find out what was incorrectly entered or overlooked. Danny used to bring them home to go over them. He said he could concentrate better here. I thought it was pretty tedious work, but Danny thrived on it."

Max nodded as he thumbed through the papers. All he saw were page after page of balance sheets and more figures than he had seen in one place since engineering school.

"I don't see any company names here; only several letters written at the margin of each page. Is that some kind of a code?"

She laughed lightly. "Danny liked to have a good time and visit the speakeasies, but they were really his only vices. He didn't even smoke. When it came to his job, he was the height of responsibility. We entertained sometimes and Danny usually left his papers in plain view. Well, to protect the privacy of his clients, Danny never wrote their names on any working papers. He had some kind of code so no one would be able to snoop on private financial information."

"Did he have a list of what the codes meant?" Max asked.

"He didn't need to. It was all in his head. He said that made it even more secure."

Max looked at the notebooks and found only more letters and notes in accountant jargon. Each of the pages referenced the same letter codes as the ledger sheets. No wonder the police quickly lost interest in the papers.

"Could these papers document some sort of financial fraud or embezzlement that Danny discovered? Maybe Danny thought that was the behind the murders."

"I don't see how," Mrs. Greene sighed. "Danny never got involved in that sort of thing. I'm not at all sure he'd even know it if he saw it. His accounting was always strictly balancing books, computing depreciation, and the like, based on numbers his clients gave him. If those numbers were fraudulent, he'd have no way on knowing it as long as they balanced. He wouldn't have access to the kind of information that might indicate anything improper. No, Mr. Hurlock, I'm afraid that whatever Danny might have been working on regarding the Taylor-Bradwell case, it wasn't in these papers."

Max made a note of several of the letter codes then reluctantly agreed.

"Besides," Mrs. Greene added, "as far as I know, neither Miriam Taylor nor Robert Bradwell was ever in a position to commit any financial improprieties."

Max prepared to leave. "One more thing, Mrs. Greene. Was Danny shopping for pets?"

"Pets? No Danny couldn't stand animals."

"One of his friends told me he was talking about looking at some dogs and cats."

Mrs. Greene laughed. "That sounds like Danny. He was fond of word games and sometimes would use code words, especially when it was something he didn't want to spread around."

"So you don't know what he meant by dogs and cats?"

She just shook her head. "No idea. Sorry."

Allison and Max met at Cole's Hotel and took a stroll to discuss the latest developments. The air was balmy as they strolled along Main Street and wound up in Greenlawn Cemetery, an old burying ground just behind the hotel. Among the paths and trees were headstones dating back to the Revolution, their stone faces weathered and covered with moss. Between the trees, the sky was showing pink streaks as the sun set. There were only a few other strollers and the place was quiet except for the sound of birds and the occasional passing car on Main Street.

"So now we have Robert Bradwell, Danny Greene, and Tim Walsh all engaged to Miriam Taylor," said Max "Maybe I should just investigate everybody that wasn't engaged to her. It would save time."

"Yes," said Allison, "Miss Taylor certainly seemed to be the most popular girl in Moorestown, but what was really interesting is how solicitous Tim Walsh was when Robert Bradwell was jilted. It was against his character, so he must have had an angle."

"Sure," said Max. "Maybe he was trying to undermine Robert and weasel his way back into Miriam's good graces. Being a concerned friend would have given him great access to both of them, and it would have given him something even more important."

"Such as?"

"A motive," said Max. "What if Tim Walsh was working his concerned friend act and found it was backfiring? What if he went to console Miriam and found her with Robert, maybe even in bed with him? Walsh is self-centered. Maybe he's hot tempered, too. Maybe he shot them both."

Allison nodded slowly. "Well, maybe, but don't forget; it was done with a gun belonging to Robert's brother. Tim Walsh certainly wouldn't have that."

"I know, but what if Robert had the gun with him that night? What if he was really going to do something desperate, but was able to reconcile with Miriam at the last minute? Or maybe he was just taking the gun to a pawnshop and stopped to see her on the way. There could be a hundred reasons for Robert to have the gun with him that night. For that matter, Robert may have left the gun on a hall table for safekeeping while he was with Miriam. There are a lot of ways someone else might have gotten that gun. I may have to talk to Tim Walsh a bit more."

"And don't forget Patrolman Mandrell's claim that William Taylor had blood on his shirt when Mandrell arrived on the scene," Allison reminded him. "Maybe Taylor was involved. He could have returned home, found the gun and become enraged just as easily as Tim Walsh could have. In fact, he was more likely to have discovered the victims in a compromising position than Tim Walsh was. After all, it was his house."

"And what was the 'big thing' that Robert was apparently planning to rewin Miriam Taylor's heart?" asked Max. "Was that something significant, or just talk?"

They sat down on a stone bench and were silent for a moment. "It seems the more I investigate the more confusing it gets," said Max. "How's your article coming?"

"Spiffy," said Allison. "I had time to talk to two flappers in town today. At least I think they were flappers. They were certainly dressed that way. One was buying cigarettes and the other was shopping for a new cloche hat. I wrote some more of the article. Want to hear it?"

"Sure," said Max. "It probably makes a lot more sense than my investigation."

Allison took her notebook out of her purse and cleared her throat.

Although most people think of flappers as a big city phenomena, their influence is turning up in smaller towns as well. On a recent day in Moorestown, New Jersey, for example, several young women were openly sporting bobbed hair and skirts at knee level. A few were wearing silk stockings, or the more economical rayon variety.

"Not underwear again," Max groaned
"Hush up. There's more," said Allison.

When asked if she was a flapper, local girl Mary Barnhart just giggled, but Patty Louden said she sure was. Both ladies were looking forward to a party the next night and were going unescorted. "We'll find dates when we get there," they said. "My current boyfriend Tim canceled out on me," said Mary, "but I'm going anyway. It should be darb." Other young women in Moorestown express similar sentiments. They will turn up at the local nightspots with a date or without, but they will turn up.

"I assume darb is something good?" asked Max.

"Well, maybe not quite as good as the bee's knees or the elephant's elbows, but still pretty good," Allison explained.

"Thanks for clearing that up. I guess it's just as well you didn't try to research that article back in St Michaels," Max observed. "The only flappers around there are the ducks. Maybe that can be a follow up article 'The Flappers that fly south for the winter.'"

"I've got some more notes, but that's all I had a chance to write," said Allison, putting the notebook back in her bag. "I think it's coming along."

The sky was now blood red and the trees were getting darker, so they started back for the hotel. At the cemetery entrance, an opening in a surrounding stone wall, Max put his arm around Allison, leaned over and whispered in her ear.

"We're being followed," he said softly. "I noticed someone hanging around on the other side of the street when we left and now he's walking about a block behind us. Don't look around, just keep walking."

"Do you have your gun?" Allison asked.

"No, it's back at the hotel, but I don't think this guy is interested in jumping us. Otherwise he would have done so in the cemetery where it's private. No, I think someone's keeping track of our comings and goings."

"I suppose we should be flattered at the attention."

Their footsteps echoed down the empty street as they walked steadily towards Cole's. Although only a little over a block away, the hotel seemed very distant. Twice they stopped and the footsteps stopped, too. Max stole a glance behind and the figure was still there, but had stopped to light a cigarette. Their pursuer was tall and thin and was wearing a large fedora that obscured his face.

Finally they came to the front door of Cole's. When Allison was safely inside, Max turned to her.

"You wait in the room. I'm going to see just who our curious friend is."

"No, Max. Don't go out there. Stay here and call the police."

"And what do I tell them? Someone was on the street the same time we were and we're nervous about it? They'd just laugh at me. Besides, I'm getting a little tired of this. The people we want to talk to won't tell us anything and now someone we don't want to talk to is dogging us."

"Max, don't..."

But Max was gone. He slipped out the side door and carefully worked his way around towards the street by way of the side lawn. There were enough shrubs to give him good cover as he got closer to flanking whoever had been following them. There was a deeply shaded spot under some trees across the street and up a short distance from the hotel in front of the Quaker Meeting House, and Max thought that was a good place for whoever was tailing them to lay low. The street was almost completely dark now, with only a few widely spaced streetlights, so Max looked for the glow of the cigarette he remembered the man lighting.

Max was close to the clump of trees now. He strained his eyes and thought he saw...yes, he did. There in the darkest part of the clump, was the unmistakable glow of a lit cigarette. The figure was hunched over, as if hiding. Max listened and the figure was muttering to itself. "Come on, come on, will ya? I haven't got all night."

Max decided on the direct approach.

"You want to tell me what you're doing here?" he said sharply. To Max's satisfaction, the hunched figure let out a loud gasp and jumped in surprise.

"I...I...I was just..." the figure stammered.

"Go on," said Max. "You were just what?"

"I was just walking Bowser here," the figure said in a shaky voice. Max looked down and was surprised to see a small dog on a leash.

"Bowser always has his walkies after dinner. He was just a little slow tonight. You really startled me. Are you with the police?"

Max looked at the figure more carefully, The man was short, heavy set, and was wearing a porkpie hat. This was not the man who had been following them.

"Uhh, no, not the police," said Max. "I'm with the city. We've gotten complaints about people stepping in dog doo. Do you know anything about that?"

"No. Bowser is a small dog and I always take him where there are thick bushes so no one will step..."

"All right, all right," said Max. "You're free to go, but be careful with that dog in the future."

"Yes, sir," said the man, obviously relieved.

"Oh, by the way," said Max. "Have you seen anyone else around here in the last ten minutes or so?"

"There was one fellow here a minute ago. I don't see him now."

Somewhere farther down the block an automobile engine started up. Max looked around just in time to see a Buick pulling away from the curb under the dim glow of a street light.

By the time Max arrived back at the front door, Allison met him with an impromptu posse of three men she had gathered from the hotel staff.

"We were just coming to get you, Max."

"Thank you all, but the situation is under control. It was a false alarm."

Allison turned to the hotel staff, all of whom looked distinctly relieved.

"Thank you all so much," she smiled.

"Any time, Ma'am," they replied, and melted back towards their various duties in the hotel. Max and Allison sat in easy chairs in the deserted lobby.

"That wasn't the one following us. He got away," said Max.

"Lucky for you. That guy could have killed you. And if he didn't, I just might."

"I'm sorry, Allison, but I felt I had to go out there."

"Who could it have been?" said Allison after a pause... "Maybe another reporter?"

"Maybe," said Max slowly, "or maybe someone else who's very interested in what I might find out about the Taylor-Bradwell case."

"That could be a long list," Allison observed. "Max, you don't think it's the real killer, do you?"

"At this point I'm still not sure there is a killer other than Robert Bradwell and possibly some panicky burglar at the Greene household, but I'm afraid that is a possibility. In fact, the reason I talked to our friend Pedigree Pettigrew is to plant the notion that I'm about to blow the lid off in the hopes that it would flush someone out."

"I'd say you succeeded, except that the story hasn't come out yet," Allison replied. "Whoever that was must be associated with someone you've already talked to."

Back in their room, Max took out a pad of paper and made some notes.

"We have a girl engaged to three men. Two of them are now dead, and the other acts as if he might have something to hide. Danny Greene says he almost has proof the case is a double homicide and misses out on a Florida trip to pursue it, but is murdered. He either leaves no notes or notes that are encoded."

Max leaned back in his chair. "Well, before I get a headache, I think we should leave it until morning. We've gone as far as we can with what we've got; you with your article and me with the case. Maybe we should relax for a little while."

Allison kicked off her shoes and stretched out. "This place is very nice, but I'm starting to miss seeing geese overhead," she said.

"Me too," said Max. "And what I wouldn't give for a decent crab cake; the kind made from all backfin meat and big as a tennis ball."

"With coleslaw and hush puppies on the side," added Allison.

"Oh, yes," sighed Max. "The kind they have in that place in Cambridge down by the cannery. Well, we'll be able to crank up Gypsy and fly back before you know it."

Allison sighed. “That sounds great. I miss feeling the wind on my face, or swooping over treetops of golden autumn colors, or looking down on geese in flight, or seeing the morning sun turn the bay silver.”

Max gently squeezed her hand. “We’ll be back in the sky soon, I promise, but there are a lot of questions to answer first.”

“Just don’t get yourself killed trying to ask them,” Allison whispered.

As they were preparing for bed, Allison pulled back the curtain and looked out the window at the moonlit street below.

There was no one there.

Chapter 13

Stirring the stew

MANDRELL A LIAR SAYS TAYLOR
Denies blood was on shirt when patrolman arrived

Max read the screaming headlines and skimmed the article in the Morning Chronicle he picked up at the front desk. William Taylor vehemently denied patrolman Mandrell's sensational story of Taylor's bloody shirt. Taylor claimed he moved the body before Mandrell arrived, thus accounting for any blood. Further down in the article, Mandell reminded the reporter that Taylor's own inquest testimony was that Taylor and Mandrell had moved the body together.

"Yes," Max muttered, "That stew is getting stirred something fierce."

Allison read over Max's shoulder. "Yikes, Max. Could Taylor have anything to do with his daughter's murder?"

"I don't know. It seems far-fetched, but he does have a hot temper. He wouldn't be the first man driven to murder by the sight of the wrong woman in bed with the wrong man. Here's another article speculating about a mystery politician that supposedly told the coroner to back off. It quotes a number of citizens about who it could be and what should happen to him when his identity is discovered."

"I'll bet someone in Trenton is sweating right about now."

"No doubt," said Max, folding up the paper. "Well, while the stew stirs I'm off to the county offices to look at the autopsy reports. Maybe I can turn up something to make them sweat a little more. Care to come along?"

Allison wrinkled her nose. "No thanks. I prefer the living. I'm interviewing the owner of a local dress shop that caters to flappers. She should have some insights for my article. The place is in easy walking distance."

"All right, but keep an eye out for anyone following," said Max. "If someone is, duck into the nearest shop and see if you can get a good look at him, but stay out of sight."

"Can't I even kick him in the.."

"No."

The autopsy report confirmed what Max had heard already; each of the victims was shot with a .22 pistol. Miriam Taylor had been shot twice in the head and Robert Bradwell four times. The cartridges were the old weak black powder type. The answer to how a suicide could have shot himself four times in the head appeared plain. The first two shots lodged in the inner skull and didn't penetrate the brain at all. The third shot penetrated an area that did not control either thinking or motion. Only the fourth shot hit a vital area.

Max put the autopsy down, leaned back in his chair and thought about what he had just read. It seemed to make sense. A .22 bullet was smaller than a pencil eraser. Back home they were used for either target shooting or hunting small varmints like rats, ground hogs, or raccoons. Even so, it wouldn't always bring down a ground hog unless it hit a vital area, so it was entirely possible that a man could shoot himself in the head four times with such a bullet. The entry points of the bullets were also consistent with suicide, even to the close up powder burns. There was really only one curious aspect to the autopsy. The angles of the shots were all different, as if Robert Bradwell kept changing the position of his hand as he shot. Of course each subsequent shot was probably more shaky than the last, but still...Max also noted that the coroner seemed to have done a fairly thorough job despite his later claims of not being allowed to probe deeply by the mysterious influential politician.

Max made a few notes then strolled down the hall to Otto Pfeiffer's office. Max noticed that the police in the office looked at him with suspicion, but figured they probably did that with any murder suspect. Pfeiffer was in his office on the telephone, but quickly put it back in its cradle when he saw Max in his doorway.

"Well, Mr. Hurlock," Pfeiffer began. "Have you finally come to confess?"

Max chuckled. "I confess that I'm as far from a solution to who killed Danny Greene as you are. I'd like to see the police report on the Greene case."

Pfeiffer's eyes narrowed. "That's an ongoing investigation. The files are not available to the public."

Max was expecting this.

"Come on, Otto; how about a little professional courtesy? We're both interested in seeing the case solved. What harm could it do?"

"Professional courtesy? You told me you weren't a private dick. Now you want professional courtesy? Forget it."

"But...."

"I said forget it! You'll see the files once the guilty party has been convicted, and I'm still not convinced you didn't have anything to do with it."

Max sighed. "All right, Chief. I understand. I suppose there's a lot of sensitive stuff in there." Max rose as if to leave.

"Oh, by the way, I saw Mrs. Greene at her house yesterday. I assume your boys noticed the bloodstain on the rug in the far corner of the room?"

"Of course we did. We also noticed you went to her house yesterday. You leave that poor woman alone," Pfeiffer growled.

"Otto, please," said Max in an offended tone. "I am the very soul of discretion. We had a nice visit, but if she asks me to stay away I will certainly do so."

"Mighty big of you."

"Anyway, if your men noticed the blood, I'm sure they were puzzled at just how it got there."

Pfeiffer was beginning to turn slightly purple. His voice sounded like a small explosion. "Hurlock, a man was shot and died in that room. Has it occurred to you that that might possibly account for it?"

"Of course," said Max soothingly. "That would no doubt account for the blood's presence. I'm talking about the blood's location."

Pfeiffer's color deepened. "It was on the rug. Where did you expect it; on the ceiling?"

"It's clear on the other side of the living room, maybe 20 feet from the front door."

"That's where the body was found. Funny how those sort of things work out."

Max ignored the sarcasm. "So I heard. But here's the weird thing. Danny Greene was shot once in the chest at close range. The papers said it appeared he was shot when he answered the front door. If that was the case, he'd have left a trail of blood, or at least a few drops as he staggered to where he fell, but there was no blood found between the body and the front door."

"He could have been shot while trying to get away," suggested Pfeiffer, who immediately realized the fallacy of what he had just said. "No, wait. Then he would have been shot in the back instead."

"Exactly," nodded Max. "You see the dilemma. It seems that whoever shot Danny Greene was either someone he let into the house and who shot him once he was well inside, or...'

Pfeiffer leaned forward. "Or what?"

Max suddenly had a realization. "Chief, which way was the body facing?"

"The feet were towards the door and the head was towards the desk. He was face down," Pfeiffer replied. He reached into a desk drawer. "Here's the crime scene picture, if you're really interested."

Max looked intently and asked Pfeiffer for a magnifying glass.

"What do I look like, Sherlock Holmes?" asked Pfeiffer.

"Chief, please. Just for a minute."

"Oh, all right." He opened a desk drawer and rummaged around. "Here; you can use this one."

"Thank you, Chief." Max examined the photo with the glass. "Chief, was this picture taken before your men had disturbed anything?"

"Of course. We're not amateurs."

"Then did you notice how the papers on the desk were stacked?"

"How the papers were stacked?" Pfeiffer said in the tone of a man who couldn't take much more. "What are you looking for?"

Max shrugged. "I'm not really sure. I just wanted to get the picture straight."

Pfeiffer frowned. "Well here's something else you'd better get straight, Hurlock. I'm responsible for this investigation, and I won't allow any amateur interference. Just because you might have read Agatha Christie doesn't make you Hercule Poirot. I threw you in jail once and it won't take much to make me do it again."

"I admire your restraint," said Max, bowing slightly, "but I'm sure there's no harm in a concerned citizen asking around."

"Just don't ask the wrong things in the wrong places, Hurlock," Pfeiffer warned darkly. "This is my case and this is my town."

"But there might be a connection to the Taylor Bradwell case..." Max began.

"The Taylor Bradwell case," said Pfeiffer, opening the door, "is closed."

On his way out of police headquarters, Max asked the desk sergeant where he could find Patrolman Mandrell. Once the sergeant, a grizzled veteran of small town law enforcement, was convinced Max was not a reporter, he told him Mandrell was on foot patrol along South Church Street. A little while later, Max found Patrolman Mandrell by a light post along South Church Street observing the traffic and swinging his club in an easy practiced motion. Mandrell had an old fashioned handlebar mustache and a perpetual sour look .

"Good afternoon, Officer Mandrell." Max greeted him as he pulled his car to the curb.

Mandell looked at him suspiciously. "And who might you be? You're not another one of those newspaper fellas are you?"

"Absolutely not. My name is Max Hurlock and I'm investigating the Taylor-Bradwell case for Mr. Bradwell. I just want to talk about the night you were first on the scene at the Taylor house."

"What about it?" Mandrell looked at him warily.

"I'm just interested in what you observed. What did you see when you arrived?"

Mandrell hesitated, but his reluctance to talk to a stranger about a case soon gave way to his sense of importance at being the center of the biggest case to hit Moorestown in years.

"Well, Mr. Hurlock, I'll tell you. I was on motor patrol and called in to the station around 12:30 a.m. They told me they had just gotten a call from Mr. Taylor about a murder at his house. They were looking for the chief, but wanted me to get on over there as well. When I got there, every light in the house was on. I went up to the daughter's room. Mrs. Taylor was a wreck, but Mr. Taylor seemed to be calm and in control. Miriam Taylor and Robert Bradwell were stretched across the bed. Well, she was stretched across the bed, face down. He was slumped with his legs on the floor and the rest of him leaning on the bed; sort of like he was on the bed but slipped off."

"Where was the gun?"

"Oh, it was lying on the floor next to Robert Bradwell's hand."

"Now how about the blood on Mr. Taylor's shirt."

"Humph," Mandrell grumbled. "That Mr. Taylor has a mighty peculiar memory, saying I didn't help him remove Miriam to the other bedroom that night. Why, he even testified at the inquest that I helped him, then changed his story for the papers. He couldn't have moved her by himself. He's just trying to explain away the blood on his shirt."

"Where was the blood on the shirt?"

"Oh, it was mostly the upper front, but there was some on the front of the sleeves as well."

"Did it look splattered"

Mandrell frowned in thought a moment. "No, not splattered, really. I thought it seemed to look more like it was blotted; you know, as if he had used the shirt to mop up something."

"Did you tell them that at the inquest?"

"No, nobody asked me."

"Well, never mind. How do you think Mr. Taylor got the blood on his shirt if he didn't move the body himself?"

"I don't know for sure," Mandrell replied. "Maybe he was closer to the bodies than he wants people to think."

"Could it be," said Max, "that Robert Bradwell was originally lying next to or even on top of Miriam Taylor and her father grabbed Robert Bradwell's bloody head to drag him off his daughter before you or anyone else saw them like that? As a father, he would instinctively want to protect Miram's reputation. That would explain Robert Bradwell's position slumped to the floor and the blotted blood on William Taylor's shirt even though Miriam's body was moved later. Based on what you saw, does that sound possible?"

Mandrell frowned again and scratched his chin thoughtfully. "Why, yes; I suppose it does at that. Yes. Now that I think about it, I believe that's exactly what happened."

"Flappers? Oh, my dear, these days we see them in here all the time," said the surprisingly matronly lady in Phyllis's Dress Shop. "Of course we don't call them that, especially if they're here with their mothers. Most of them want to look like flappers without actually being one. To them it's less a way of life than a fashion trend. They like the comfort and freedom mostly. We hardly ever sell a corset or a shirtwaist any more, at least to anyone under 40. On the other hand, we're selling these straight dresses, cloche hats and artificial silk stockings like nobody's business. The big fashion houses send dresses with longer skirts and the customers don't want them. Either that or they'll shorten them as soon as they get them home."

Allison took a few notes and looked at the array of beaded multicolored short dresses on the racks, pulling out a shimmering red one and holding it up. "Ooooh, now this one's the berries! I guess the devil-may-care look doesn't come cheap," she remarked.

"Oh, no," the saleslady replied. "You should see some of them that come in here. It would break your heart to see how much they have to spend."

Allison was still looking at the red dress. "I'm surprised the flapper look is expensive. This dress looks pretty simple in design; with straight lines and hardly any hand stitching or fancywork."

"It's not just the dress," the saleslady said. "The flapper look is so different it requires a whole new wardrobe; new hat, stockings, necklaces. Everything is new, even down to the unmentionables."

Allison smiled and made a note. There was that underwear again. "Did Miriam Taylor ever shop here?"

The shop lady shook her head sadly. "Such a shame. She was a nice girl, but couldn't make up her mind as far as the men were concerned. She was engaged several times you know, and broke it off each time. But Miriam shopped here all the time. She was very fashion conscious, but she avoided the more extreme flapper dresses. Actually I think that wasn't so much her idea as it was her way to avoid antagonizing her father. He was very strict and bad tempered to boot."

"When did you see her last?" Allison asked.

"She was in here just a week before...well, you know. She wanted to know if we had anything suitable to wear while hunting."

Allison put down the dress she'd been holding. "Hunting?"

"She had a friend who wanted to shoot some squirrels that were making a nuisance of themselves. Miriam thought it would be a lot of fun."

"Not for the squirrels," murmured Allison. "Did she say who this friend was?"

"No, but I thought it might be that Tim Walsh. His family lives on the edge of town in a place that has several vegetable gardens and big old trees. I imagine the squirrels were a problem. Anyway, that was the last I heard about it."

The shop lady looked Allison up and down thoughtfully.

"You know, dear, that dress would really look wonderful on you. Why don't you try it on?"

Max called Mrs. Greene and asked to see her again briefly. Mrs. Greene was easier to persuade this time, and Max was soon back at her house. She answered the door in a long skirt and white blouse. Her makeup and hair were perfect.

"Well, Mr. Hurlock. To what do I owe your visit this time?"

"I'm really sorry to intrude again, but if I could see where Danny was found and look at his papers again, I have an idea I'd like to check."

"Certainly," she answered. "You know where they are."

"Thank you. Are the papers just as you found them?"

She nodded. "I thumbed through them looking for any clues about why Danny was killed, but I was careful to put them back the way I found them."

The desk was almost exactly as it appeared in the photo; a roll top secretary type affair. There were two piles of papers in two loose stacks, one on the writing surface of the desk and a bigger one on the top.

"Is this the way your husband usually organized his papers when he was working?" Max asked.

Mrs. Greene looked at the papers as if seeing them for the first time. "Why, no. Danny never stacked papers on the top of the secretary; he always had them on the desk itself. I assumed the police must have left them that way. Does it mean something?"

"The police claim they left the papers as they found them, so it could mean that the killer was going through the papers, probably before Danny got home. Listen, are the police finished with the papers on the desk?"

"Yes; they took some photos, then thumbed through them once or twice, but didn't take anything. They said they were releasing the crime scene."

"Could I borrow the ones in this short pile?"

"They're for clients and they're confidential," she answered. "You can look at them, since the names are encoded, but I think they should stay here in case someone comes to claim them."

"Fair enough," said Max, looking through the papers. "By the way, did Danny keep a client list?"

"I think he had their names in his phone book. You can have a look and copy anything you'd like. Here it is."

Max looked at the leather bound book and saw a list of 33 clients, but no names he recognized. He copied them down just in case. As he did so, he could hardly help thinking that with this case it seemed the more information he gathered, the less he really knew.

Chapter 14

The Bootlegger

Max was tired when he got back to the hotel, so the last person he wanted to see was Pedigree Pettigrew, the reporter, but that's who was waiting for him in the lobby.

"Mr. Hurlock. Just one minute."

Max groaned. "Hello, Pedigree. Still looking for a juicy quote?"

"I already got one," said Pedigree smoothly. "I just wanted to get your view on it. Folk'd be interested in your opinion."

"I'm not an authority on journalism."

Pedigree ignored the remark. "I talked to this feller who lives right down the street from the Taylor house. He claims on the night of the deaths he saw someone standing on the front lawn of the Taylor house looking up at the windows on the second floor."

Max was suddenly interested. "Does he know who?"

"Nope; 'fraid not. But he says the fellow was pacing back and forth like he was looking for something, or maybe trying to make up his mind."

"I don't suppose he had a description of this mysterious figure?"

"Well, it was hard to see from where he was, but it looked like a man of average height and build."

"That narrows it down to half the male population of Moorestown," Max said. "Good work."

"So do you have a comment?"

"Yes. Go tell it to Detective Pfeiffer."

Max sighed as he picked up the room key at the desk. Here was another clue that was absolutely no help.

"Has Mrs. Hurlock returned?" he asked the desk clerk.

"Not yet, Mr. Hurlock."

Max opened the door and flopped down on the bed to try once again to put the pieces together. He was staring at the ceiling half asleep from the strains of the day when he was conscious of the sound of a key in the lock. The door swung open and he heard a voice.

"Anybody home?"

He looked up and saw a beautiful flapper leaning up against one side of the doorway with her hand seductively on her hip. She wore a short red dress with a shimmering beaded fringe that barely reached the knees of two very shapely legs. The vision had a wide jeweled band around her head and tucked unto that band was a long fluffy white ostrich plume.

Max squinted at the apparition. His mouth fell open and he could only utter a single word.

"Allison?"

"Ain't we got fun?" she replied softly.

Max jerked up in bed. "Allison, what the...?"

"Couldn't resist, Max. I saw this little number in the dress shop and just had to have it. Isn't it the eel's eyebrows? It gives me a certain something, don't you think?"

"It certainly gets my attention," he replied, looking her up and down.

"Do you think it's too hot?"

"Hot isn't the word for it. That outfit could cause a riot in a monastery. I suppose this is part of your research. Do you plan on going under cover?"

She smiled and closed the door behind her. "Maybe if you play your cards right."

The rays of the morning sunrise reflected off the beads on the red flapper dress as it lay draped over the back of a chair. Max groaned as Allison tickled him with the white ostrich plume and told him to get up.

"Come on Sherlock," she said. "Fun time is over. There are crimes to solve. The game is afoot and you should be afoot, too."

"Will asleep do?" he muttered.

"Come on, Max. Aren't you anxious to see the scandal headlines of the day?"

Max yawned. "I suppose so. I guess you've got to put a few more miles on that article of yours."

"Oh, yes. In spite of the sales job, I got a lot of good insight from the dress lady yesterday. This is going to be a good effort."

"Fine," said Max. "At least one of us is making progress."

"Now, Max, it's not like you to let a problem get you down."

"I'm not down, exactly. It's just that the more I look into the case the more complicated it gets. I'm losing ground. Even when I get a new clue it doesn't help."

"A new clue?"

"Our newshound pal Pedigree Pettigrew told me he talked to someone who claimed to see a figure on the Taylor's lawn pacing and staring at the upstairs windows the night of the crime. But the description was so vague it could have been anybody."

"Did you get the name of this new witness?"

"He wouldn't tell me; claimed he had to protect his sources. So I'm back to my same problem. I just can't figure where the Danny Greene murder fits into this. I know he was investigating and was about to find out something important, but then he was killed. Assuming the killer was someone other than his wife or close friends, and that the killer did it to keep him quiet, how did the killer find out what he knew? And if he somehow knew that much about Danny Greene, how come he didn't know Danny never went to Florida?"

"Well," said Allison, "this is basically a small town like St Michaels, or Easton.. The killer could easily have heard about Danny's research, but not heard he was staying home from Florida. Then he could have broken into Danny's house to see what he could find and Danny came home and surprised him."

Max nodded. "Then the killer surprised Danny. Yes, that's the way it looks, and that would explain the papers."

Papers?"

"I'll tell you about that later," said Max. "Why don't we have breakfast first?"

"Hotcha," said Allison. "Now you're cooking with gas."

The hotel dining room was almost empty; the few business travelers having long since left. A waitress, looking almost as wilted as the potted plants by the front window brought Max and Allison some surprisingly good scrambled eggs, then disappeared. After a long drink of his orange juice, Max expanded on his theme.

"Now, about the papers on Danny's desk. Danny only told his wife and close friends about his supposed inside knowledge of the crime. I think we can eliminate the wife as a source of loose talk, and he wouldn't tell his friends if he thought one of them was the killer. So how would the killer know that Danny Greene was on to him?"

"Maybe one of the friends blabbed to the wrong person?" said Allison.

"Or maybe was overheard by the wrong person," said Max, "and with all the socializing at nightclubs and speakeasies, the opportunities for being overheard are endless."

Allison put some jelly on a piece of toast and looked thoughtful. "All of which begs the real question."

"What's that?"

Allison munched the piece of toast. "What evidence did Danny Greene find and did the killer get to it?"

"Well, if it's in the papers on Danny's desk, it'll be hard to find. Mrs. Greene won't let them out of her sight because of client privacy concerns and I can't figure out what I'm reading with only a brief glance. Based on what I've seen, though, they all look like normal accounting sheets. But then I don't really know what I'm looking for."

"Maybe you could ask Charlie Bradwell's partner, what's-his-name. Isn't he a bookkeeper or accountant of some sort?" Allison asked.

"Fred Madison? I suppose I could, but I don't even know enough to ask a coherent question at this point. Maybe I can run down Danny's client list again. The list had over 30 people or firms on it. It could be any one of them, but then what's the connection to the Taylor-Bradwell murders? Neither one of the victims had any connection with anyone on the client list as far as I can see."

"How about the Taylors or the Bradwells?" asked Allison. "Could they have had a connection with Greene?"

"I don't know yet, but neither Taylor nor Bradwell appear on the list and neither do their companies. No, I still think the connection must be some mutual acquaintance or friend."

Allison cocked her head slightly. "Wait a minute. I just remembered something." She fumbled in her bag and fished out her notebook and started flipping pages.

"Here it is. One of the girls I interviewed the other day said her boyfriend Tim had backed out on her that night and had done the same thing four days before. I wonder if that could have been Tim Walsh?"

"So what if it was?" said Max.

"Well, the night in question was the night Danny Greene was killed. So maybe Tim Walsh backed out because he had something more pressing he had to do; something that wouldn't wait," said Allison.

Max put down a forkful of eggs. "Like killing Danny Greene?"

"I didn't say that, but who knows at this point? Oh, and get a load of this; there's another thing the dress store lady told me. Miriam was going hunting for squirrels just a few days before she was killed and there's a good chance she went with none other than Tim Walsh."

Max sat up. " I wonder what gun they used? Funny how all roads seem to lead to Tim Walsh. Maybe I should get better acquainted with him."

Those who knew Otto Pfeiffer well could always tell when he was annoyed by the throbbing vein on the side of his forehead. Mrs. Greene did not know Pfeiffer well, but his annoyance was apparent even to her.

"You mean Max Hurlock was back to see you again yesterday?" he asked.

"Just for a few minutes. He had some more questions," she replied. "Is that a problem, detective?"

They were seated in the Greenes' living room, where Pfeiffer had stopped to visit the scene of the crime one more time. He especially wanted to take another look at the papers on the desk that annoying Hurlock guy thought were so significant, just in case he might have been on to something.

"Mrs. Greene, you are free to speak to anyone you'd like, of course. But Max Hurlock is an outsider and he's working for the father of the murderer in the Taylor-Bradwell case. I would recommend that you stay away from him, and his wife. It'll just confuse things. Leave it to the professionals."

"*Oh beware, my lord of jealousy. It is the green eyed monster which doth mock the meat it feeds upon*," said Mrs. Greene softly.

"I beg your pardon?" said Pfeiffer.

"Oh, nothing," she replied. "Just a little bit of Othello I picked up somewhere. You were saying?"

Pfeiffer looked at her sharply. "Never mind. I'd like to have another look at your husband's papers."

She nodded and Otto Pfeiffer went to the desk again. He shuffled through the papers for a moment, then turned to Mrs. Greene.

"I'm afraid I'm going to have to take these papers as evidence."

"Mr. Hurlock asked the same thing. I turned him down."

"I could get a warrant. You'll get them back when the case is solved."

"And how soon do you think that will be?" she asked.

"We're doing everything we can, Mrs. Greene. I've checked most of Danny's friends and his business acquaintances. Right now, though, we're acting on the theory that it was just a burglary gone bad."

"Extremely badly, I'd say," she remarked. "How do you think it happened?"

"The key seems to be the newspaper article about you going to Florida. We figure a burglar saw it and surmised the house would be empty and could be knocked over with no interference. We've had cases like that in the past. Some of these break-in men read the social columns as carefully as the debutantes do. So the burglar broke in, thinking no one would be home; Danny surprised him and the burglar panicked and shot him."

She nodded. "And how will you apprehend this social-column-reading burglar?"

"In addition to checking out Danny's friends and associates, we're questioning known burglars and ex-cons in the area. Unfortunately, the killer didn't leave us much to go on. He even gathered up the shell casing and took it with him."

"Really?" said Mrs. Greene. "That was pretty level headed for a panicking burglar, wasn't it?"

"The shot might have been in panic, but then the self-preservation reflexes kicked in," Pfeiffer replied. "I've seen it happen a hundred times. Of course if the gun was a revolver the shell casing wouldn't have been ejected in the first place, so this is all just conjecture. Well, good day, Mrs. Greene. I'll keep in touch."

He disappeared down the driveway with the papers under his arm.

Mrs. Greene watched him go and muttered to herself. "*There are more things in heaven and earth, Horatio, than are dreamt of in your philosophy.*"

Tim Walsh sounded surprised to hear from Max Hurlock again, but agreed to meet at the Broken Axle once more. Once again Max drove to the stretch of road near Trenton and walked into the somewhat down-at-heel restaurant. He was early this time and found a table where he could watch the rest of the place and spot Tim Walsh when he came in the front door. The patrons were average looking people, not like the adventurous types that frequented the speakeasy in the back room. Obviously the Volstead Tavern and the Broken Axle were very different operations with different clienteles. Max leaned back and tried to ignore the lingering smell of stale beer.

"Hey there, Mr. Hurlock. How are you?" came a voice behind him. Max turned and saw Tim Walsh approaching his table. He had somehow slipped in without being seen, a talent that could no doubt come in handy when the place was raided.

"Thanks for meeting me again, Tim," Max began. "I'm glad you were able to get away from work during the week."

"Oh, that's not a problem," Walsh replied. "My hours are sort of flexible. I run a small trucking company and can come and go when I like."

"A trucking company? A have a friend back home that has a truck for hire and has trouble getting enough business."

Walsh shrugged. "Oh, I do all right. What do you want to know?"

"I'm trying to put the facts together, but it's pretty confusing. When were you engaged to Miriam Taylor?"

Tim Walsh was unfazed. "Oh, about two years ago I guess. It only lasted about three months. We parted as friends."

"Is that why you were so helpful when Robert Bradwell was having similar troubles?"

Walsh looked slightly defensive. "Look, Bob Bradwell was having a bad time and I tried to help out, that's all. I mean, who better than someone who had gone through the same thing?"

"How about someone who wanted to take Robert's place with Miriam Taylor?"

Walsh laughed. "Is that what you think? You are whistling Dixie with that one. Miriam was through with me, no matter what. Her father saw to that."

"Her father? What's he got to do with it?' Max asked.

"He decided I wasn't suitable; wasn't respectable enough for Miriam."

"Not respectable? That seems odd. You come from a good family and run a business. Did he ever specify his objections to you?"

"Not to me, but I think he gave Miriam an earful. That's all she would say about it. He had some pretty firm ideas about what constituted a worthy boyfriend and I suppose I didn't measure up somehow. That's all I know."

"You knew Robert Bradwell pretty well, Tim. Do you think he could have murdered Miriam the way the inquest said?"

Tim slowly lit a cigarette and shook out the match. "It's hard to say. Robert wasn't hot tempered like her old man, and he wasn't violent. At least, I don't think he was. What's more, he really loved her. Still, he was pretty upset about getting dumped so who knows? Problems like that can make a man do crazy things."

"How about her father? Could he have had anything to do with it?"

Walsh nodded. "Now there's a good suspect. He was always flying off the handle and going into a red-faced rage about something. I know he was pretty cheesed off about Robert pestering Miriam, so if he had come home and found them in the sack together, there's no telling what he would do. Yeah, I could see him doing it. I really could."

"His own daughter?" Max was skeptical.

"Yes, I think so. Oh, he'd probably feel real bad about it later, once he calmed down and all," Walsh replied, "but in the heat of the moment, something comes over him and he just sees red, so who knows?"

As Walsh spoke, another man materialized at the table, excused himself and handed Walsh a note. Walsh looked at it quickly, wrote something brief on it, and handed it back. Out of the corner of his eye, Max watched the man walk away. An idea had been forming in his mind and Max decided to try it out.

"So Tim, how long have you been involved in bootlegging?"

Walsh went pale. "Bootlegging? What makes you think I'm involved in bootlegging?"

"I'm an investigator, remember? Finding things out is my business and lately business has been good. So answer my question; how long have you been involved in bootlegging?"

"It was Joe Bryant, wasn't it?" Walsh grumbled. "Joe could never keep his mouth shut. Wait until I get hold of him, I'll...."

"No, Tim," said Max soothingly. "It wasn't Joe Bryant. You tell me about the bootlegging and I'll tell you how I knew."

Walsh hesitated.

"Look, I'm not a cop, Tim, and I'm certainly not a Prohibition agent. You might be the biggest rum runner on the East Coast, but that's not why I'm here. I'm investigating three deaths, and I need all the facts. Even a small detail could be crucial. Now spill it."

"You won't report me?"

"No."

"All right." Walsh pulled his chair closer and lowered his voice. "My trucking company is small, only three trucks, and we were just getting by until about a couple of years ago. A new client asked us to transport thirty boxes of machine parts from a dock on the Rancocas River to a warehouse in Trenton. I thought it was a pretty isolated place to be landing machine parts, but the money was good and I jumped at it. Well, we delivered the boxes and got paid in cash. The customer was so pleased he gave us some more shipments, and we were on velvet, until one crate fell off the back of a truck and started leaking beer. That let the cat out of the bag; we were shipping bootleg hootch. Pretty soon after that, we started making deliveries directly to speakeasies. We've been doing it ever since. That's why I work at night so much."

Max nodded. "I'm guessing that's the real reason that William Taylor made his daughter break the engagement with you?"

"Probably. He had someone looking into my background and must have found out, or at least suspected. But how did you know?"

Max smiled. "I heard that your present girlfriend complained of you suddenly breaking nighttime appointments for more urgent business. That suggested something unstructured and secretive was going on. Then when I came here to meet you today, I noticed you did not enter by the front door. I was watching it.

The only other door in the place leads to the Volstead Tavern in the back, which is closed during the day. Only someone having business there would be allowed in at this hour, and other than employees, the only people having business there would be suppliers. My suspicions were confirmed a few minutes ago when your friend came out of that same door with a note for you, a note that was obviously of a business nature, since you wrote a reply. Then when you said Miriam's father thought you unsuitable son in law material, some sort of unsavory or illegal activity was indicated. Finally, when you said you ran a trucking company and apparently had plenty of business, the conclusion was obvious."

Walsh's eyes were wide. "Jeez. No wonder they call you Sherlock Hurlock."

Max grinned. "It was elementary. Now a few more questions. Did Danny Greene know anything about your business?"

"Sure. Danny did my books. I tried to cover it up by calling the bootleg runs something else, but he knew."

"How about Robert Bradwell? Did he know about it too?"

"Probably. I mean, I never told him and he never mentioned it, but I figured Miriam probably told him at some point. Say, am I in trouble?"

"I told you, I'm not with the police," said Max, "but with all the people that know about your bootlegging, you're only a phone call away from jail. If you don't want someone to make that call, you'd better consider another line of work."

"All right, all right," said Walsh, wiping his forehead with a large handkerchief.

Max frowned at him. "But that's not your biggest problem, Tim. You see, I know about the gun."

"Gun?" Walsh stammered. "What do you mean?"

Max decided to bluff Tim Walsh out with some speculation. "A week before Miriam Taylor died, you took her hunting. How did you get hold of Peter Bradwell's pistol?"

"Peter Bradwell's pistol?" Walsh replied hoarsely, "How do you know about that?"

Max leaned closer to Walsh and gave him a menacing look. "I'm Sherlock Hurlock, remember? Now out with it; what's the story? I want the truth and if I don't get it, I'll know. Then you really will be in trouble."

Tim Walsh was silent a long time, weighing his options. Finally, he spoke in a low voice. "Look, I didn't know it was Peter's gun. I thought it belonged to Robert. He called me a couple of weeks before he died and asked if I wanted to go and shoot some target practice with him in the woods. It sounded like a hoot, so I said I would. The gun was only a .22 revolver, nothing big. We just shot up some beer bottles in the woods behind the frog pond; that's all. Anyway, Robert remembered me complaining about the squirrels at my parents' place and offered to lend me the gun to get rid of them; the squirrels that is, not my parents."

"Thanks for clearing that up," remarked Max dryly. "So how did the gun wind up killing two people, and where were you when it happened?"

"How would I know? I didn't have it then." If Walsh was nervous, he didn't show it. "I asked Miriam to come with me to shoot the squirrels, and ..."

"Why did you ask Miriam?" snapped Max.

"Actually, that was Robert's idea. He said Miriam liked any kind of sport, so he said she'd jump at the chance."

"Very noble of him," said Max.

"Naw, he thought it would be a chance for me to talk to Miriam alone about taking him back. That's the real reason."

"I see. But how did the gun wind up on the floor of Miriam's room?"

Tim Walsh shrugged. "I don't know, but I sure didn't put it there. Robert said to give the gun to Miriam when we were finished shooting and he would get it back the next time he saw her. That would give him another excuse for visiting her. So that's exactly what I did and that's the last I saw of that gun. I swear that's all I know."

Max looked skeptical. "Come on, Tim. It's only your word that you gave that gun to Miriam. Maybe you never gave her the gun at all. Maybe you held on to it and used it to kill them both when you found them in bed. That way you could get your revenge on both of them and throw the blame on Robert in the bargain."

Tim looked horrified. "Absolutely not. It was just like I told you; I gave the gun to Miriam. That's the last I saw of it."

Suddenly, Max shifted gears. "When you went hunting the squirrels, how many shots did you fire?"

"I never fired the gun at all. The squirrels never showed themselves."

"So when you gave it to Miriam it was fully loaded?"

"That's right, but I had the safety on and I told her to be careful. She had fired guns before, so I didn't think anything of it."

"Revolvers don't have safeties," Max remarked.

"Oh, you know what I mean; the halfcocked position," Walsh replied. "When you pull back the hammer it's on the halfcocked position on the first click. If you pull the trigger then, nothing will happen, and the hammer isn't resting on the primer of the round in the chamber, so there's no chance of firing accidentally if you drop it. You're right, it's not a safety, exactly, but it's practically the same thing."

Max made a mental note that Tim Walsh was no novice when it came to firearms.

"And when was the next time Robert went to see her?" asked Max, though he was pretty sure he knew the answer already.

"A few days later as far as I know; the night they were both killed. Look, I know Bradwell is paying you to prove Robert was murdered, and for all I know, maybe he was, but don't try to pin this on me. It'll never stick."

Max picked up his hat, threw a couple of dollars on the table and stood up to leave.

"When I'm ready to conclude who is to blame, Tim, rest assured that I will see to it that it sticks to that person like glue."

Chapter 15

Read all about it

In the lobby of Cole's Hotel, Allison settled into a large overstuffed mohair chair nestled between two shaggy potted palms. She took her notebook out of her bag to write more of her article on the small town flapper. At this time of day the sun came through the front windows throwing bright highlights on the potted plants, the blue oriental type rugs, and the overstuffed furniture. Hotel lobbies, Allison thought, are often so much better than hotel rooms for writing because they were bigger, better lit, and had more comfortable furniture. Turning her gaze away from the pleasant surroundings, Allison began to write.

The small town flapper looks, talks, and acts as much like her big city counterpart as she can, but differs in some fundamental ways. She seldom spends her nights roaming from nightclub to nightclub, for instance, if only because there are not many available in small towns. In a small town, too, a would-be flapper cannot depend on the anonymity she would have in a big city. This potential for scandal puts a damper on overly outrageous behavior that can quickly make a girl an outcast in town.

Probably the biggest difference, however, is that a small town flapper is far less likely to be financially self-sufficient than her Gotham sisters. Living at home with Mom and Dad acts as a powerful brake on a would-be flapper's possible excesses, so the small town flapper concentrates more on the outward appearances of flapperdom. Lots of flapper clothing and public displays are the rule, and not so much drunkenness and promiscuity. Like so many other things, flapperdom has been refined for small town sensibilities.

Allison placed the cap back on her red fountain pen and reread what she had written with satisfaction.

"It's getting there," she murmured. "Just a few more interviews and it should be aces."

Allison ordered a cup of tea from the bellhop and settled back to read the evening paper while waiting for Max to return. The tea soon came, hot and steaming in a china cup and saucer. She took a sip and sighed contentedly.

The paper was full of the usual booster articles about the opening of a new hardware store or the appointment of a new school principal, but Allison hurried past until she found an article about the Taylor-Bradwell murder, written by Pedigree Pettigrew.

DIDN'T TRY TO HINDER TAYLOR-BRADWELL INVESTIGATION SAYS CONRAD

State Treasurer claims only concern was for Taylor family

In a statement issued this morning, New Jersey State treasurer Jason Conrad admitted intervening to avoid an inquest into the Taylor-Bradwell killings, but claimed he did not apply any pressure and was merely trying to protect the Taylors from further heartache. "I have known the Taylor's for years and my heart went out to them," Conrad said. "I believed the case was clear cut and there was no need to drag the details before the public. When the decision was made to hold an inquest, however, I made no further requests and took no further action. At no time did I make any attempt to hinder the investigation."

Dr. Carstairs, the county coroner has claimed that "a highly placed state political official" pressured him to refrain from holding an inquest into the case. The official was later revealed to be state treasurer Jason Conrad. The inquest was held regardless, and the case was determined to be a murder/suicide. Charles Bradwell, father of Robert Bradwell, the accused killer in the case, has questioned the inquest's findings, believing his son was murdered. He has retained a private investigator, Max Hurlock from Maryland, to make inquiries.

The recent murder of a Taylor family ex-neighbor, Daniel Greene has given rise to public speculation that the official verdict in the case might not have told the whole story. Feeling Greene was killed to keep him from revealing information he claimed to have about the case, many people believe that others were involved in the killings and are still at large.

Not everyone is convinced, however. When asked about the alternate theories being discussed and the possibility of holding another inquest to resolve them, chief county detective Otto Pfeiffer stated "The case was investigated and the case is closed. We don't need another inquest. We need a sanity hearing so all these people can be locked up in the same asylum."

Allison giggled as she read Pfeiffer's remarks. Based on her brief contact with the chief, she could easily picture him saying them.

When Max returned, they had a light supper and were soon back in their room. Allison sat on the bed with her legs crossed while Max sat back in a chair with his shoes off and his feet up on a table. Outside the moon was rising and streetlights were coming on around Moorestown.

"Oh, Max, I forgot to tell you," Allison said, "Martha Bradwell invited us to lunch and tennis at their country club tomorrow."

"Lunch and tennis at their country club? Why?"

"She says we've been working too hard and need a few hours to relax," said Allison. "It's hard to argue with that."

Max sighed. "Sure; why not? Maybe a few hours off will help clear our heads. Unfortunately, it doesn't get us any closer to who killed Robert Bradwell."

Allison raised her eyebrows. "Oh? Do we know for a fact that Robert's death was murder and not suicide at this point?"

"Oh, he was murdered all right," said Max, matter-of-factly. "What's more, whoever killed Robert killed Danny Greene as well."

"Well, that's just ducky. I was thinking the same thing, but how do you know?"

"Where do you want me to start?" said Max. "We have a man who somehow shoots himself four times in the head; a gun that seems to have been in everyone's' possession at one time or another; a close friend and neighbor who claims to know who really killed Robert then winds up dead; a supposedly panicky burglar/killer who doesn't steal anything, but takes the time to systematically go through Danny Greene's papers...."

"Wait," Allison interrupted. "That's all nifty reasoning, but how do you know Danny Greene's killer was going through his papers?"

"Well, the location of the blood stain indicates the killer was in that area when he shot Danny," Max explained, "plus, there were two piles of papers on the roll top desk, one on the writing surface and another on the top of the desk. Mrs. Greene said Danny never left papers on the top of the desk, so the killer must have done it."

"O.K., but why couldn't he have just been rifling through the papers looking for money or negotiable bonds to cash?"

Max shook his head. "A real burglar wouldn't be that neat; he'd either dump the papers on the floor or simply take them all with him to go through later. This burglar was going through the papers one by one and making two neat stacks; one he was finished with and one he was still going through. The only reason to do that...."

Allison jumped up off the bed. "...is to be able to replace the papers the way he found them so no one would know anyone had been going through them, or any of them were missing. No burglar would do that, only someone who wanted to remove certain selected papers without anyone knowing he'd been there."

"Exactly," said Max.

Allison was now pacing the room. " The intruder reads the article about the Greenes going to Florida and sees a chance to go through Danny's papers at leisure to remove incriminating evidence. So he breaks in and starts to do just that, but halfway through, Danny shows up and the intruder shoots him. He doesn't finish going through the papers because he's afraid someone heard the shots and maybe called the police. He just grabs the shell casing and beats it."

"That's the way it looks," said Max. "The real question is who are we looking for? There's no real evidence pointing to anyone in particular."

Allison looked out the window thoughtfully. "The answer seems to be in those papers. Didn't you say they were accounting ledgers of some sort?"

"That's what they looked like."

"Max, could Robert have been mixed up in some sort of swindle or scam that Greene was trying to track down?"

"You mean he might have been a con man of some sort?"

Allison shook her head. "Not necessarily. Maybe he was a victim of a con and Greene was trying to prove it somehow."

Max frowned thoughtfully. "Maybe. Or maybe he just borrowed money from a loan shark for a gambling bet or something, and..."

"And he couldn't pay it back so the mob bumped him off," said Allison excitedly. "It happens all the time. Why, Moorestown is just a hop skip and a jump from Philadelphia, Trenton, and even New York. He could have had his pick of loan sharks."

"I suppose it's possible," Max admitted, "although an enforcer for a loan shark will usually just beat up a client, not kill him. After all, you can't get money from a dead man. Besides, what ledgers could Greene have? Loan sharks don't leave written records lying around."

"Well, maybe they were <u>Robert's</u> records," said Allison. "Maybe they showed what he had borrowed and who he had borrowed from. The loan shark/killer certainly wouldn't want that to get out."

"Jilted lovers, bootleggers, and now a loan shark," Max shook his head. "This case has everything."

"Everything except a solution," said Allison.

Chapter 16

The Moorestown Field Club

The late summer sun shone down on the green lawns of the Moorestown Field Club the next morning, promising another hot day. As the Bradwells and the Hurlocks turned into the entrance off of Chester Avenue, Allison noted the sign, which featured a flying mallard duck.

"Well, we should feel right at home here," she remarked.

As they drove up the drive towards the clubhouse, Max and Allison noticed several tennis courts and, of all things, a cricket pitch. Charlie explained that cricket was still a popular game in the area among some Anglophiles.

"Have you ever played cricket, Max?" he asked.

"No," Max replied, "but I've been in more than a few sticky wickets."

Lunch in the clubhouse was every bit as lush as they had expected, with the conversation mostly concerning Max and Charlie's adventures in the navy.

"I'll never forget coming ashore after my first convoy," Charlie laughed. "I could still feel the ship moving for days, even on dry land."

"Shiver me timbers," Allison remarked to Martha Bradwell, "I'm glad I didn't order the fish."

"And remember Charlie Noble?" Charlie laughed.

"Who was that?" Allison asked. "Another one of your mateys?"

"Don't encourage him, dear," said Martha Bradwell.

"Charlie Noble was the stovepipe from the galley," Charlie explained. "It's called that after some British naval guy. Anyway, new sailors usually didn't know the term, so older salts would tell them to go find Charlie Noble because the captain wanted to see him and the poor guys would be running all around the ship on a wild goose chase."

Allison turned to Martha. "Isn't it reassuring that even in the middle of a war men can still find time for some schoolboy humor?"

"I suppose it's how they kept the world safe for democracy," said Martha Bradwell rising from her chair. "Allison, how about a little tennis while the boys talk about old times? You do play, don't you?"

"I did once," said Allison.

"Then come along. I think we have something that would fit you. Maybe the sort of outfit Suzanne Lenglen wears?"

"Who?"

"That French tennis player who's been wowing them at Wimbledon the last several years. She beat Lambert Chambers in the most thrilling match anyone has ever seen. She wears the most marvelous creations; all pleated silk and the like. Scandalously tight fitting."

"It doesn't sound very athletic, but I'll give it a try," said Allison as they left the room.

Max and Charlie slowly strolled outside and made their way towards the tennis courts.

"I'm not a very good tennis player myself," said Charlie. "Last week I twisted my knee and it's still sore. I'll have to sit this one out."

Max nodded. "Fine by me. We can watch the ladies."

"So how's the investigation going, Max?" Charlie asked, lighting a cigarette. "I didn't want to ask during lunch."

"Well, I'm pretty sure Robert did not commit suicide," said Max cautiously, "but I really can't prove anything yet."

"That means someone shot Robert, but who?"

"I don't know yet," said Max. "Charlie, did Robert ever gamble?"

Charlie looked at him. "Gamble? Well, he'd play the hay burners once in a while over at Monmouth Park. I think he also went to Saratoga once with some friends, but he wasn't really a serious better as far as I know. Why do you ask?"

"I'm just covering all the bases, Charlie. Could Robert have owed anyone money?"

"He was always hard up for cash; his income hadn't caught up with his tastes yet. But I'm not aware of any loans he took out. What's all this about anyway?"

They had reached the tennis courts and were standing by the fence. "Danny Greene had some papers on his desk that might have something to do with the case, but I'm not sure what they mean. They're ledgers of financial information."

"Financial information?" said Charlie. "Well, why don't you ask my partner Fred? He knows the financial stuff inside and out. Robert worked with him, so Fred might actually know more about any of Robert's possible financial problems than I would."

Max nodded. "That's not a bad idea. I'll talk to him this afternoon. Is there some place in the office that's private? I'd rather the others didn't hear."

"Good idea," said Charlie. "You can catch him at his house around six or so. He has a big place over in Palmyra he inherited when his father died a few years ago. I'll give you the address. That way nobody in the office can eavesdrop. I'll call him and let him know you're coming."

"Thanks, Charlie. It is a bit delicate."

"Hey, there are the ladies!"

Martha and Allison had emerged from the door to the ladies' locker room. They were wearing white tennis dresses of the latest style, with a tight sleeveless top and skirts just below the knee. Even so, Max thought the outfits featured far more material than needed for comfort. Allison swung her racquet and pirouetted.

"Max," she shouted. "How do you like this outfit? Isn't it the ocelot's elbows?"

"It's the berries, all right," replied Max. "I can't tell if you're going to play tennis or dance in Swan Lake."

"I'd probably do either one equally well," she laughed. "Get ready to duck."

Martha prepared to serve.

"This doesn't look so hard," said Allison, still talking to Max. "When someone hits it to you, you just hit it back. It's just like... Yeooow!"

Martha's serve whistled past Allison's ear and slammed into the fence behind.

"Sorry, dear, I can slow it down a little," Martha said evenly.

Allison planted her feet apart and set herself with her racquet ready. "That's O.K. Next time I'll try whacking the ball instead of beating my gums. I'm ready now."

This time Allison smacked the ball back sharply and the game was on. The volleys continued as Max and Charlie cheered encouragement. Ten minutes later, Martha had won by a single point. Both women were tired from the exertion and headed for the locker room.

"Allison did pretty well," Max remarked.

"I'll say," Charlie nodded. "Martha was club champion last year."

"Then I guess Allison did really well," said Max, "She only..."

"She only what?" said Charlie.

Max was looking back towards the entrance on Chester Avenue. "Charlie, was that car there when we came in?"

"What car?"

"There on the road by the entrance. There's a brown Buick parked there, under the shade of that maple tree."

Charlie Bradwell squinted in the sun. "I see it, Max. So what?"

"There's nothing along that road; no reason for anyone to stop. It's just a country road. It's like parking in the middle of a cornfield. Not only that but it looks like someone is sitting inside. What's he doing there?"

Charlie shrugged. "Search me. Is it important?"

"I don't know, but I'm going to find out."

"I'll go with you, Max."

As they got closer, Max and Charlie could see a figure in the car parked on Chester Avenue, but when they got within sight, the occupant started the car and drove away.

Just as Charlie Bradwell had said, Fred Madison's house was a rambling old Victorian place that somehow managed to be both roomy and somewhat claustrophobic at the same time. Madison greeted Max at the door and showed him into a parlor done in dark wood and full of overstuffed furniture. An oak stairway led to the second floor and a grandfather clock ticked loudly in the hall.

"Quite a place you have here," said Max.

"It was my parents' house," Madison replied. "They left it to me two years ago. It's way more than I need, but I haven't had the heart to sell it. The place has a sentimental hold on me I suppose."

Max looked around and nodded.

"Charlie said you wanted to talk some more about Robert and about financial papers?" said Madison. He wasn't wearing a bow tie now, but still had the glasses and suspenders.

"Yes. You worked with Robert and I was wondering if he ever mentioned that he might have been having financial problems."

Madison shrugged. "Well, he was always somewhat short of cash, but I don't recall anything really spectacular. Excuse me; I hope you don't mind if I light this?" He produced a large cigar and a lighter.

"This is a Partagas Lusitania straight from Cuba. It's my only real vice," Madison explained, "but I can't smoke it in the office or they'd run me out. Would you like to try one?"

"No thanks," said Max.

"Suit yourself." Madison lit the end and blew out a long puff of smoke that slowly rolled up towards the high ceiling. "Ah, that's better. After staring at numbers all day this is as close as I come to being eccentric and daring. Now, you were saying?"

"Did Robert ever mention gambling debts; like maybe from playing the ponies?"

"Oh, he was known to place a bet now and again," said Madison, "but it seemed casual enough as far as I could see. He did talk about it occasionally. You know the type; they brag about their wins, but never mention when they lose."

"Did he ever borrow any money from anyone as far as you knew?"

"I loaned him a $20 once, but he paid it back. What are you getting at?"

"Well, one possibility is that Robert was in debt to a loan shark and was killed as a result."

Madison let out a low whistle. "Wow. You think you know a person..."

"So he never mentioned any loan shark to you?"

"No, but then I wouldn't have expected him to. Still...." Madison looked thoughtful.

"What?"

"Well, do you remember that phone conversation I overheard? I told you about it the last time we talked."

Max nodded. "Something about not being afraid of somebody?"

"Right. I overheard Robert on the phone with Miriam and he said 'I don't care what he says. I'm not afraid of him.' Well, I thought he was talking about another of Miriam's suitors, you know; a romantic rival of some sort, but now that you mention it, he could just as well have been talking about a loan shark."

"He never mentioned a name?"

Madison shook his head. "No, that's all I heard. Just goes to show you how dangerous it is to jump to conclusions."

Max leaned forward in his chair. "Now, there's another possibility I wanted to talk to you about; one I haven't even mentioned to Charlie Bradwell. Could

Robert have been embezzling from Bradwell Properties to pay off his debt?"

Madison looked shocked. "What? Are you serious? Robert stealing from his own father? Impossible."

"Oh, I'm sure he intended to pay it back. If he did, he probably considered it a loan."

"Even so, why steal at all?" Madison protested. "If he was in trouble he could have simply asked Charlie to bail him out. Hell, I would have bailed him out myself if I had known."

"To do that, though, he'd have to admit he owed gambling money to a bookie," said Max. "Next to that, a little temporary embezzling might have looked like the lesser of the evils, especially if he intended to pay it back."

"I guess so," said Madison, sounding less than convinced. "Well, as you say you have to look into every possibility, no matter how painful."

"If Robert had been embezzling somehow, would it have shown up on the books?"

Madison frowned in thought. "Well, theoretically, sure, but.."

"But what?"

Madison squirmed. "Look, I'm really not comfortable talking about this. It's like defaming the dead."

"If it makes you feel any better," said Max, "you're just being an expert witness about accounting. Leave the suspicions and wild accusations to me. Now you were saying about embezzling showing up in the books?"

"It's really hard to say. The fact is, there are a lot of ways to cheat and Robert did have access to the books from time to time. Of course he could have come to the office after hours and work on them as well. No one would have seen him, so I suppose it is possible to embezzle and cover it up."

"Would you have caught it if the books had been altered?"

Madison sighed heavily. "I don't know. Of course I should have. I mean, keeping the books straight is part of my job, but quite honestly, it never occurred to me to check behind Robert except for math errors or something obvious like that. Why would I? The fact is, I trusted him."

"If Robert had wanted to embezzle from Bradwell Properties, how would he do it so it wouldn't show up on the books?"

"Well auditing is sort of a specialty in itself, and I'm not really an expert, but I suppose the easiest way is simply altering the income from accounts receivable."

"You mean if someone owes you $200, you change the entry in the book to say $100 and keep the difference?"

"Something like that," Madison agreed. "Then you mark that the debt was paid in cash and you pocket the other $100. If anyone looks at the book he sees a $100 accounts receivable item matched with a $100 payment, so the deception isn't obvious. Of course it's not really that simple. There have to be records of receipts issued and the receipt would have to say $200 or the tenant would protest. Plus the canceled check would have to be endorsed. There are plenty of ways a would-be embezzler would get tripped up. I doubt that Robert could have pulled it off even if he wanted to."

"But maybe he only did it a short time and the audit was still months off," said Max. "Maybe he figured on replacing the money and making it all right before anybody found out, but the loan shark's torpedoes got him first."

Madison nodded slowly. "It's possible, of course. The audit is done every year, but it isn't scheduled for another month. If the books have been altered, no one would have found it yet."

Max thought about it. "Then how does Danny Greene fit into this? What papers could he have been examining?"

"Well, he wouldn't have papers from our books because I would have noticed if any had been removed. That much I'm sure of," said Madison, "but I guess he might have had Robert's personal papers."

"Personal papers?"

"Look, I'm not accusing Robert of anything, you understand. This is just hypothetical, and pretty far-fetched at that. You raised the possibility, not me."

"Understood," said Max.

"Well, if Robert was really doing what you say he was, he'd have to keep a careful record of things so he could cover his tracks later. He'd have to have books of his own. You've heard the expression about keeping two sets of books? Well, that's what it means. Maybe that's what Danny Greene was working on."

"But if they were Robert's own books and secret, how would Danny Greene have gotten hold of them?"

"Only one way I can think of," said Madison. "Somebody gave them to him."

"Yes, but who? And why?"

Fred Madison shrugged. "Don't ask me; I'm just a pencil pusher. You're the detective."

The next morning, Allison was already up and making some notes for her article when Max got up.

"You know, Max, I could write a whole chapter on women's tennis alone. It's like a primeval battle between members of the fair sex; a way for women to work out their hostilities."

"I thought they worked out their hostilities on men," said Max dryly, and was immediately struck by a pillow thrown with deadly accuracy.

"Well, who can blame us?" said Allison. "Tennis as female aggression therapy. It sounds like the kind of thing Freud would say."

"Sure, if his wife would let him."

Just then, there was a knock at the door.

"If that's Pfeiffer coming to arrest me again, tell him I'm busy," said Max.

But when the door was opened, Charlie Bradwell was standing there.

"Max, I just got a call from the office; someone broke in last night."

Chapter 17

A case of burglary

Otto Pfeiffer and Detective Edwards were at the office of Bradwell Properties when Max and Charlie Bradwell arrived. Since the office was in Philadelphia, the Philadelphia Police had been first on the scene, but had already left. The front door stood ajar, its doorjamb splintered. Detective Edwards had just finished taking a statement from Doris Gentry when Pfeiffer turned to see who had entered.

"Well," said Pfeiffer when he saw Max, "first a murder and now a burglary. Trouble just seems to follow you everywhere doesn't it?"

"I don't know about trouble," replied Max, "but you certainly seem to. What are you doing in Philadelphia? Isn't this out of your jurisdiction? It's not even in the same state."

"This act is related to a case I'm investigating, wise guy. The Philadelphia Police are cooperating."

Max nodded. "So you can cooperate when you want to. That's encouraging."

"Do we know what was taken?" asked Charlie Bradwell. "We never keep anything valuable around here except maybe $100 or so in petty cash. The eatery downstairs probably keeps a lot more cash on hand than we ever do."

"They took the books!" said Fred Madison incredulously. "Somebody made off with all our account books. This is unbelievable. What would anybody want with our books?" Madison, now with his bow tie back on, stood with his hands outstretched like an Old Testament martyr in a stained glass window. "All that work! All the records! All gone! How can I put it all back together?"

Max started to examine the empty file cabinet that had held the books.

"Hold it," snapped Pfeiffer. "That's evidence. You stay away. Besides, I've got a few questions for the two of you. Where were you last night?"

"For God's sake, Otto," said Max, "You don't mean that you suspect Charlie here of breaking into his own place, do you?"

"Well, why not?" said Pfeiffer. "What better way to make evidence disappear than to claim it was stolen?"

"Oh, for the love of…."

"You could have staged the burglary to make it look like some mysterious killer was still roaming around and working behind the scenes," said Pfeiffer, pointing at Bradwell. "That way you'd have a better case for collecting the insurance money, seeing as Mr. Hurlock here doesn't seem to be able to prove it for you."

"Damn it, Pfeiffer. You're going too far," shouted Bradwell. "This is outrageous. A man's business is ransacked and the police blame him. Come to think of it, maybe it does make sense; after all, you blamed Robert for his own murder."

"So did the coroner and the inquest," Pfeiffer retorted. "But this is a new crime and you and Sherlock here have a good motive for committing it. In fact, it makes a lot more sense than the idea of burglars who go to all the trouble and all the risk of a break in just to steal some dusty old ledger books. So I'm thinking you boys have a pretty good motive and that makes you prime suspects. Well, if you did stage this little caper, I'm going to find out, and when I do, I'm going to find out why."

"While you're at it, maybe you can find out who killed Danny Greene," said Max, "or maybe you think we did that too."

Pfeiffer glared at him. "Ed, get in here." Detective Edwards appeared from the hallway.

"Get some fingerprints from Mr. Hurlock here so we can compare them to prints we find around the crime scene."

"How about from Mr. Bradwell?" Edwards asked eagerly.

"Of course. We'll need comparison prints to eliminate his prints when we find them here. It's his office. His prints will be everywhere."

"Oh, right," said Edwards, fumbling with the fingerprint kit. "Just let me get this roller thing and.....oh, nuts."

"Now what?" snarled Pfeiffer.

"Uh, I forgot to ink the pad. It's all dried up."

"Oh, for Pete's sake! Well get some ink from your fountain pen until we get back."

As Pfeiffer simmered, he telephone rang and someone asked for Pfeiffer. He listened silently, then replaced the phone on its cradle.

"We can't seem to find Peter Bradwell. Nobody's seen him. You want to help us out?"

Bradwell looked amazed. "My God, Pfeiffer; do you mean to tell me you think Peter broke into the office too? No wonder the door jamb was broken with so many people trying to get through at once."

Pfeiffer's expression was suddenly one of self-satisfaction. "I don't know what he did, but I have a pretty good idea he's mixed up in this as well."

"Peter?" Max asked. "Just what makes you think Peter had anything to do with it? Are you guessing again?"

Pfeiffer smiled a knowing smile. "I don't need to guess, Hurlock; I have the evidence! I went back to see Mrs. Greene and I grabbed the papers that I think Danny Greene's killer was looking for. When we went through them, we found that one of them had the initials R.B. at the top. That's Robert Bradwell unless I miss my guess. We checked the papers for prints. Now normally it's hard to get decent fingerprints from paper unless someone has greasy hands or something like that because the surface of most paper is too rough and absorbent. As it happens, though, I know of a lab up in Trenton that can detect prints on paper chemically by using silver nitrate. They found two sets we couldn't identify until I thought of something; we had taken prints from everyone involved in the Taylor–Bradwell case. So we compared with those prints."

"You don't mean...."

"Peter Bradwell's prints were on that paper."

The sky was dark with the promise of rain that afternoon as Max and Allison drove in the borrowed Packard towards New Brunswick, home of Rutgers University and the last known whereabouts of Peter Bradwell.

"You know, Max, sometimes I wish Miriam Taylor had just married Robert Bradwell and lived happily ever after. Then we could be back in St Michaels doing the same. Or maybe we could be up in Gypsy, soaring through the sky."

"Something I'm having a very hard time doing here," grumbled Max.

"Do you think Pfeiffer really suspects you and Charlie of staging that burglary?"

"I don't think so," Max replied. "Pfeiffer blusters a lot, but he's a good cop. He throws outrageous statements around then sits back to see if anything sticks. That's just his version of stirring the stew."

"Maybe so, but he seemed pretty sincere when he arrested you for the murder of Danny Greene."

"Yeah, it sort of seemed that way to me, too," Max agreed.

"What's the story with that Edwards guy?"

Max chuckled. "Edwards? He's fresh out of school and very eager, but he has a lot to learn. He'll probably be a good cop someday, but meanwhile, he's driving Pfieffer nuts."

"I like him already," Allison remarked.

They arrived on the main campus and pulled to the curb along College Avenue near Ford Residence Hall, a four story brick building set on a slight rise.

"This is where Charlie said we'd find Peter's room," said Max, consulting a piece of paper Bradwell had given him.

"Max, isn't this a state school?" asked Allison as they got out of the car. "Why do they call it Rutgers?"

"Charlie says it was called Queens College but was renamed for some benefactor. You have to admit it sounds better than the University of New Jersey," said Max. "Now let's see if we can find out what happened to Peter."

Max convinced the Ford Hall faculty resident to allow a woman to visit, but only on the condition that they warn the students on the floor. Since most of them were in class, this was not hard to do.

Peter Bradwell's room was on the third floor and had a raccoon coat hanging behind the door, a red megaphone emblazoned with a black letter R in the corner, and several red Rutgers pennants on the walls.

"Sis boom bah," said Allison. "It looks like my old room at Goucher, only without the pictures of Rudolph Valentino."

Max moved over to Peter's desk and started looking through the papers.

"Nothing here but some homework, a copy of Colliers, and a bill from the cleaners. It looks like dull and routine stuff for the most part."

"Well, you could hardly have expected him to leave a copy of his itinerary," said Allison, poking through some books on a shelf. "Hey, who's the hot number?"

Max looked around and saw Allison holding up a framed photo of what looked like a smiling co-ed.

"Now, I wonder who that is?" said Max, putting down a notebook he had been examining.

"More to the point," said Allison, squinting at the photo, "I wonder if she's missing as well?"

At that moment a voice behind them said, "Who are you?" They turned around to see a short sandy-haired student standing in the doorway with several books under his arm.

"You must be Peter's roommate Ben Daniels," said Max. "We're looking for Peter. His father sent us. Do you know where he is?"

Ben looked a little suspicious, but Allison smiled at him and he softened.

"Gee, no. I haven't seen him since yesterday morning." His voice squeaked slightly as if it hadn't quite changed completely yet.

"Is this his girlfriend?" Allison asked, holding up the picture.

"That's Emma Manelli. They're just good friends. Peter sort of plays the field."

"Did he say anything that indicated he was going somewhere?" Max asked.

"No, not a thing. Well, of course he's been balled up since Robert died, but he didn't say he was going anywhere."

"Balled up?" asked Max.

"You know; confused; upset; out of sorts. I can't really blame him, of course. He was real pals with Robert, except near the end."

Max looked at Ben sharply. "What do you mean?"

"Well, just before Robert was killed, Peter sort of grumbled about him. I'm not sure what the problem was, but once I heard him on the hall phone arguing with him about not wanting to do something. Of course brothers argue a lot. I've got a brother myself and he's a real bird. One time he took all my socks and...."

"How is Peter doing in his classes?" Max interrupted the flow of sibling reminiscences.

"Swell. Peter's a smart guy and always does pretty good." Ben paused a moment and remembered something.

"You know, Peter had one class he really talked about a lot. He even liked to go and talk to Professor Enwright after hours. Enwright was sort of a faculty advisor to Peter. Of course the class seemed pretty dull to me, but Peter seemed to like it.

"What class was that?" Max asked.

"Auditing."

"Max I know you're in a hurry to see Professor Enwright, but you should have let Ben finish his story. I wanted to know what his brother did to his socks."

"Forget the socks," said Max. "What about Emma Manelli?"

"What about her?"

"Well, do you really think that Peter plays the field as his roommate said?"

"Max, you know how much baseball expressions applied to romance annoy me. They're so trite. Do you know what happens to men who use terms like play the field, get to first base, and make a pitch to describe their love life?"

"Well..."

"They usually wind up striking out."

"Point taken, so let me put it another way. Do you think Peter and Emma Manelli are just casual friends as Ben said?"

"No." Allison sounded positive.

"Really? Why do you say that?"

"People don't display framed formal pictures of casual friends," Allison replied. "They might have a group photo of a sports team or school class, or maybe a snapshot of some event they were both involved in, but that's it. Besides, there was a lock of her hair in the corner under the glass. Casual friends certainly don't do that. Whoever Emma Manelli might be, she's not a casual friend."

"Are you sure?"

"Of course, but there's more. On the back of the photo, written in a delicate feminine hand was the inscription, "To Peter, and all those wonderful times at the Raritan. Love, Emma."

"How do you know that?

“I snuck a peek while you were having that fascinating conversation about Ben’s socks. Sometimes it pays to be nosy. Of course, the Raritan is the river that flows through New Brunswick, so that doesn’t really tell us anything.”

“Maybe it does,” said Max. “It said at the Raritan. If you’re talking about a river, wouldn’t you say by the Raritan, or, if you’re boating, on the Raritan? I think she’s referring to a place; maybe a park or a hotel or something. Maybe Enwright will know.”

Professor Enwright’s office was a small room crammed with papers and books, and smelling of cherry pipe tobacco. On one wall was his doctorate from Princeton, and on the opposite wall was a series of stick figure drawings done in crayon, evidence of small children at home. Max and Allison were happy to see he was in, seated behind a cluttered desk grading papers. Enwright had thick glasses and thinning hair. If people had been asked at random to guess what Emerson did for a living, at least half of them would have guessed he was an accountant.

The professor was outgoing and cheerful, however, and readily agreed to provide any information he could.

“Peter is a bright student. I have no idea where he could have gotten to, but I know he was despondent about his brother’s death, so maybe he just went to be alone for a while.”

“Do you know a friend of his named Emma Manelli?” Max asked.

“I remember Peter mentioning her, but I never met her. She’s not in any of my classes. In fact, I’m not even sure if she goes to Rutgers at all.”

Max made a note. No one seemed to know much about Emma Manelli.

"How about the Raritan?"

"The river?"

"Not the river," said Max. "Is there a hotel or a theater or something by that name; some place that two students who were romantically inclined might go?"

"There's the Raritan Road House on George's Road south of town. It's a rundown sort of place, but a lot of students hang out there when they can get away. Rumor has it that the place is a speakeasy, but then rumor has it that almost every place is a speakeasy these days, what with Prohibition and everything."

"His roommate said Peter was having some sort of dispute with his brother just before Robert was killed," said Max. "Do you know anything about that?"

Enwright lit a pipe and looked even more like an accounting professor. "I'm not really sure if this means anything, but about a month or two before Robert was killed, Peter came to me to ask about fraud and how to detect it."

"You mean embezzlement?" Max asked.

"Well, let's just say any sort of intentional irregularity in the books. He never said if he had any specific case in mind, but from his questions, I suspect he did. But what was most disturbing was his occasional references to his brother."

"Like what?"

"Again, there was nothing really specific, but Peter would grumble almost under his breath about how his brother was trying to drag him into something and was headed for trouble. Apparently Peter had tried to talk him out of it, but hadn't been successful."

Max digested this for a moment.

"Professor, I'm investigating the possibility that Robert might have been embezzling from his father's company, possibly to pay off gambling debts. From what Peter told you, does that seem possible?"

Enwight took the pipe from his mouth and gaped a moment.

"From what Peter said, I'd say it's more than possible; it's damned likely."

"So Robert was embezzling from Bradwell Properties to pay off gambling debts and was trying to get Peter involved?" Allison asked as they drove back to Moorestown.

"It sure seems to look that way," said Max, "but then how does Danny Greene fit into this? If Robert was embezzling he certainly wouldn't give Danny Greene his books to examine."

"But Robert didn't give the papers to Danny Greene," Allison reminded him. "Remember; Peter's prints were on the papers. Maybe Peter got Robert's papers and gave them to Danny Greene to find out exactly what Robert was doing and to convince Robert to stop, or make restitution."

"Maybe. Then let's say Robert did stop and some torpedo shot him along with Miriam because he couldn't pay the money back."

"Right; and Danny Greene figured it all out and then he got the business to keep him quiet."

"All right, but then how did a loan shark get Peter's gun?" Max asked.

Allison's face fell. "Well, the theory does have a few loose ends."

Chapter 18

Small town girls

Allison's voice rose slightly in frustration as she stood talking on the telephone in the lobby of Cole's Hotel while pacing back and forth as far as the cord would allow. The acquisitions editor of Modern Girls Magazine was being difficult.

"But Mary, I have the article on the small town flapper almost written," Allison was arguing. "I can't just change the whole slant at this point."

"Nonsense, Allison. It's just a few alterations- like repainting a birdhouse."

"More like changing it into a table, you mean."

"Look, I know you've done a lot of work, but we here at Modern Girls are looking for articles that are more, well, sensational," the editor insisted. "That's what readers want; a little spice. What you've described about your small town flapper article is all very informative, but some might think it sounds a bit dull."

"Dull? I've got bathtub gin, speakeasies, scandalously short skirts, family friction, and parties. If it got any more sensational, I'd get arrested."

"Yes," the editor continued, "that's all the bee's knees of course, but there's also all that blab about how small town girls are more inhibited than the big city ones and about how constrained they are because of living at home."

"Well, that's all true," Allison insisted. "I can't just make up things to jazz up the article."

"No one's asking you to make up things. We want the truth as much as you do. All we are saying is that the tone of the article can be shifted in a very positive direction without sacrificing accuracy. That way the article will be true, but will also be, well, sensational enough to attract readers."

"So you don't want me to lie, but just to pound on the sensational parts?" Allison said.

"Exactly, my dear," Mary's voice rose in delight. "Just put a little more emphasis on the scandalous aspects of the small town flapper and a little less about the traditional ones. Get a few more human-interest stories about wild parties and necking and what goes on in the rumble seat, or struggle buggy as I believe they're calling it now. I'm sure with a little reworking the article will be one that Modern Girls Monthly will be proud of. The emphasis shouldn't be on how small town girls are different than their big city counterparts, but how they're similar."

"It sounds more like something modern boys would be reading," Allison observed. "Are girls really looking for scandal?"

"Allison," Mary sighed, "the fact is that people read magazines for many reasons; becoming informed is only one of them, and way down the list at that. People like to peek at how others live. Well, there's not much point in that if the other people live the same way they do. Also, readers like to be able to feel more in control than those they read about. They even like to feel superior. They want to hear about the more sensational aspects. I'm sorry dear. Modern Girls Magazine didn't invent human nature; we just have to appeal to it to stay in business."

Allison sighed. "All right, Mary. You sell magazines for a living and I don't, so I'm sure you know what's what. I'll look over my notes and see what I can do."

"Artistic differences?" Max asked when she had hung up. He had been standing nearby.

"No, just a difference in how to satisfy public tastes," said Allison. "I'll figure it out, but I may have to stay here to get more interviews, I'm afraid. Do you really need me today?"

"No, you just do what you need to do here," Max reassured her. "One of us can stumble around in New Brunswick just as well as two."

"Are you sure, Max?"

"Of course. Now get going. I'm on my way north to find the elusive Emma Manelli."

Peter Bradwell's roommate Ben Daniels was apparently in class when Max arrived at Ford Hall once again, but the room showed no sign of any unexpected return by Peter Bradwell. Max went to the Registrar's office to check out student records. The office was in semi gothic brick building with ivy crawling all over the walls, and window frames that were a bit overdue for the attentions of a paintbrush. Inside were dark offices smelling faintly of age, wood and floor wax. The secretary in the student records section confirmed that there was no student by the name of Emma Manelli currently registered at Rutgers. A subsequent visit to the New Brunswick Post Office, Police Department, and telephone exchange yielded similar results.

Before returning to Ford Hall to look for Ben Daniels again, Max stopped by the school cafeteria for a quick lunch. As he watched the crowds of students start to fill up the place, he heard a familiar voice.

"Hey, Mr. Hurlock. Over here!"

Max looked and saw Ben Daniels and another student sitting at a nearby table. Max picked up his plate and sat down between them. Both students were wearing black sweaters, but Ben's friend had a big red varsity R on his.

"Hey, Mr. Hurlock," said Ben. "Are you enrolling? Where's your wife?"

"No, I'm not enrolling, Ben, and Allison had to stay back in Moorestown today."

"That's too bad," said Ben, obviously disappointed. "Oh, Ozzie, this is Mr. Hurlock. He's some sort of a detective and he's looking for Peter. Mr. Hurlock, this is Ozzie, Ozzie Nelson. He's the quarterback for the Rutgers football team."

"How are you?" said Nelson, who looked a bit undersized for a football player, but who had a broad and friendly grin. "A detective, eh? Do you have any idea what happened to Peter?"

Max shook Ozzie's hand and noted a particularly strong grip. "I'm not a detective, exactly, just an investigator. I was hoping one of you fellows could help me."

"Sure. Mr. Hurlock. Ozzie here knows everybody. He draws cartoons for the school magazine, directs the band, and is in the debate club, so he gets around, but he hasn't seen Peter either. We were just talking about him."

Nelson grinned again. "Well, I don't really know everybody. After all there are about 800 students here."

Max noticed that most of the students greeted Nelson as they passed by the table. Several more pulled up chairs. Ozzie Nelson was obviously a big man on campus. Maybe he knew something about Peter and the mysterious Emma.

"Listen, fellas, I know you're all at sea about Peter, but what can you tell me about Emma Manelli? Do any of you know her?"

"Sure," said Ben. "I met her a couple of times. Nice girl. Lives over towards Monmouth Beach somewhere. Funny story; Peter went to Monmouth Park one day to meet his brother and he met Emma somehow."

"I saw her with Peter at a couple of band concerts and once or twice near the football practice field," said Ozzie. "I talked to them once. Gee, do you think that maybe he's with her?"

"It's a possibility," said Max. "Say, you mentioned Monmouth Park. Does Peter play the horses?"

"Not really," said Ben, "but his brother did. He used to offer to place bets for Peter, but Peter never wanted him to."

Ozzie Nelson shook his head in disapproval. "Horse racing is a mug's game. The odds are terrible, not to mention the possibility of inside betting, or a jockey throwing the race."

"Any idea where Emma Manelli might be found?" Max asked. "Monmouth Beach is a pretty big place."

"She lives on Etting Avenue," said Nelson.

Max and Peter looked at him in amazement.

"How do you know that?" said Max.

"Well, I told you I spoke with them once," said Nelson. "It was after a band concert and Peter Bradwell was with her and stopped to say hello. We got to talking about music and I said something about Ruth Etting; you know, the girl, who sings 'If I could be with you'?

Well Emma said she liked her and said what a coincidence it was that she lived on Etting Avenue. I didn't know it was in Monmouth Beach, though."

Max made a note. Etting Avenue in Monmouth Beach.

"Well, fellas, I thank you for the help," he said. "I'm staying at Cole's Hotel in Moorestown. If any of you think of anything else, or if Peter shows up, please give me a call. Reverse the charges."

"So, girls, tell me about the parties around here."

Allison stood near a Main Street soda fountain talking to a group of four young women that had just left. They wore fashionable but fairly modest dresses with skirts well below the knee. Their hair was somewhat short, but not extremely so. Two wore cloche hats and one was smoking a cigarette.

"Parties?" One of them seemed to have trouble understanding the question.

"Yes, parties. You know; boys and girls; bathtub gin; petting; dancing the Charleston till dawn; Hotcha cha."

"My Mom would kill me," one said. "I have to be in by 11:00."

"And who makes bathtub gin, anyway?" another added. "You can get a pretty good near-beer down at the White Horse, and nobody'll put you in jail for it."

"I do dance the Charleston sometimes," another volunteered, "as long as the music isn't too fast. If it is, I get out of step."

"The last time I tried it I twisted my ankle," said another.

Allison, seeing her story slipping away, began to get somewhat exasperated.

"So I don't suppose you girls would call yourselves flappers then?"

The girls looked at each other and giggled.

"Well, I guess we're sort of flappers," one said. "...in a way that is."

"Sort of flappers?" Allison asked. She suddenly had a vision of her article being renamed The Small Town Sort-of Flapper.

"Well, I mean we want to look like flappers sometimes, and listen to Jazz and all, but that doesn't mean we go crazy."

"So where are you all planning on going this Saturday night?" Allison bravely carried on in hopes of teasing out some more salable answers.

The girls looked at each other. "We'll probably go to the White Horse."

This was more like it, Allison thought. "Is the White Horse a speakeasy?"

"No, it's sort of a restaurant," the girl with the cigarette said, "but it's really darb. We go there a lot."

"Do they have bootleg hootch there?" Allison asked.

"Not bootleg. They still sell Neuweiler Beer sometimes, but not if you're underage. It's illegal, but the place is small and I guess the Prohibition cops haven't gotten around to it yet."

"So why do you go there?"

"It's a good place to meet, especially after dances or other events."

"Ah," said Allison hopefully, "what event are you going to first this week; a dance; a wild party?"

"I'm going to a wild party," one girl named Dory said quietly. She didn't look like a pioneer. In fact, Allison had thought Dory was the most average looking girl she had ever seen. You never could tell.

The others looked at her. Allison found hope springing forth once more.

“I’m going to a petting party. You know, a bunch of guys and girls get together and pitch a little woo.”

Now we’re getting somewhere, Allison thought.

“The thing is,” Dory continued, “if you know a guy with a passion buggy, you can go where you don’t have to worry about prying eyes. A bunch of us find someone’s house where their parents are away, put on some jazz, break out the gin and let nature take its course.”

“Meaning what?” Allison asked, though she thought she had a pretty good idea.

“Hugging, kissing, maybe some grappling here and there.”

“But why?” Allison couldn’t help asking. “Why let some fella grope you if you’re not even engaged?”

Dory giggled. “It’s fun and it keeps them interested. Besides, if you get a guy in the right condition, he’ll give you anything you ask for.”

Or maybe something you didn’t ask for, Allison thought. “So exactly how far do these parties go?” Allison asked, fascinated and repelled at the same time.

“It doesn’t go all the way, if that’s what you mean; although I know a few girls who have.”

Allison felt as if she had just stepped off her porch and found someone had removed the stairs. Although she knew the article just might be saved, she suddenly felt very old.

Chapter 19

Rum runners

Cole's Hotel was washed in the red and orange tones of the sunset outside its windows. A few guests sat scattered around the stuffed chairs reading newspapers, chatting, or just waiting to go into the adjoining restaurant to investigate the intriguing dinner time cooking smells in the air.

Allison sat slumped in a chair near the front door. Her arms were on the arms of the chair, but her hands hung down limply and her head lolled back as if she were asleep. After a half hour or so, Max dragged himself in the front door and collapsed into the chair next to her and took a similar posture. For a few seconds, neither spoke, but finally, Max broke the ice.

"So how was your day?" he mumbled.

"Mmmmph," came the reply.

"That bad, huh?"

"Worse. How did you do at Rutgers?"

"Mmmmph."

After another pause, Allison spoke again, her eyes still closed. "I found that most small town flappers aren't wild at all, certainly not wild enough to merit the attention of Modern Girls Magazine, but the few that are almost make up for the others."

Max nodded slowly. "Well at least you made progress. I just wasted an entire day tracking down Emma Manelli."

"You didn't find her?" said Allison, her eyes opening slightly.

"Oh, I found her, all right," Max replied wearily. "That's not the problem. I found out where she lives and called the house. He mother answered and put her on the phone. Not only is she not with Peter, she didn't even know he was missing. She was half hysterical about it. He never said anything to her either."

"How about the Raritan?"

"That was a little better. I dropped by the place. It's a shabby roadhouse that would close its doors if it weren't for the college students that frequent the place. Anyway, things are slow during the day so the bartender had time to talk. He said Peter and Emma came in a lot, but two days ago he saw Peter by himself."

"By himself? So did he say where he was going?"

"As a matter of fact, he did," Max replied. "He said he was going on a camping trip."

"A camping trip? Where?"

"He didn't say. Big help, huh?"

"So now what?"

"If he really is camping somewhere, it could be to just get away for a few days, or..."

"Or what?"

"Or maybe he really isn't camping at all. Tomorrow morning I'll send telegrams to see if state park officials and maybe forest rangers can look for him, but I'm not optimistic. If he's really in the woods somewhere, and that's a big if, he won't be found if he doesn't want to be. We may just have to wait for Peter to show up on his own, if he ever does. I can't drop everything to do a missing persons investigation. I have to check out things here about the murders. What about you?"

"I'm finding out," said Allison, "that the term 'small town flapper' is an oxymoron. Most of these babies make the ones in Easton look wild. They couldn't even name a proper juice joint around here. On the other hand, a few are such bearcats that I'm not sure what they're talking about sometimes. I think with a few more interviews I'll be able to salvage the article though."

"Well, you're doing better than I am," said Max. "Sometimes it seems that I knew more about this case the day we arrived than I do now."

"Mmmmph," said Allison.

"Mr. Hurlock?"

Max opened one eye to see Tim Walsh advancing across the lobby towards him.

"Hi, Mr. Hurlock, Mrs. Hurlock," said Tim as he approached. "Gee, you both look pretty tired."

"Not at all," said Max. "Our room hasn't been made up yet so we decided to sleep down here." He heard Allison giggle softly.

Tim was understandably confused. "Your room hasn't...."

"Never mind," said Max, sitting up straight for the first time. "It was just a dumb joke. What can I do for you?"

Tim Walsh sat down in an opposite chair and looked around the room before continuing.

"I hear Peter Bradwell is missing," he said quietly.

"Bad news travels fast," said Max.

"Well, I was thinking, I might be able to help."

"I'm listening."

"Well, you know I've done some er... confidential shipping from time to time," he began.

"You mean the rumrunning?" said Max.

"Shhh! You never know who's listening," said Walsh, looking over his shoulder. "Anyway, in the course of these shipments, I've made a few, shall we say, 'unconventional' contacts."

"You mean you've met a lot of bootleggers?" said Max.

"Tim," said Allison, "why don't you just come right out and tell us what you mean. It'll save a lot of time if Max doesn't have to translate everything into English from the original Euphemism."

Tim nodded, then looked around again. "All right. The thing is, I know a few bootleggers from my deliveries, and these guys know a lot of other people who aren't exactly the country club set, if you know what I mean. So I thought I'd see if they would ask around and see if they could find out anything about Peter and where he might have gotten to. I'm not saying Peter's involved in anything he shouldn't be, but just in case..."

Max looked at him sharply. "Tim, didn't I tell you to get out of rum running?"

"I will, honest, but I can't just yet," he replied. "I'm committed to make one last run later tonight to help haul almost $150,000 worth of hootch. If I don't show up, I could wind up on the bottom of the river."

"If you do show up, you could wind up in jail," Max reminded him.

"I have to go through with this. I'm committed. After this, I swear I'll lay off."

Allison shook her head. "What was it St. Augustine was supposed to have said? 'Oh Lord, give me chastity, but not yet.'"

"Well, I..."

"But what about the revenue agents?" Max asked.

"Not to mention the local police," Allison added.

Tim smiled knowingly. "The truth is, there are very few agents around the area. They're all in Philly or New York. Oh, they swing by once in a while, usually to pull off a big raid like the one at the Volstead Tavern, but not very often. Yes, there is a chance of getting caught. It does happen sometimes on the bigger shipments where too many people know about it, but it hasn't happened to me yet."

Max and Allison looked at each other in surprise.

"Look," said Tim. "I know Prohibition is the law, and booze is illegal, but most people don't see it that way. They figure 'Why should I suffer just because a few people get drunk and neglect their families? I don't do that. I'm not an alcoholic, so why shouldn't I have a drink once in a while when I want to?' Of course the side effect of making booze illegal is making it expensive, and all that money attracts the crooks. The crooks wind up fighting and killing over territories and that's pretty dangerous, but the drinking itself is harmless for most people. Bootleggers are just giving the people what they demand. The public doesn't see it as a real crime."

"Unfortunately, though, law enforcement does," said Max.

"So how does it all work?" Allison asked.

"Well, the booze itself comes from several sources," Tim began. He was talking faster now, warming to his theme. "Some of it's shipped from Canada; that's the good stuff; much more expensive. Some of it comes from Europe or the Caribbean in 'Rum Fleets', ships that hang around in international waters until they see a chance to run the stuff ashore. Some of it's brewed in homemade stills here and there. The Sourland Mountain area around Hopewell is full of 'em. Some of it comes from local breweries that were converted over to make medicinal alcohol or industrial alcohol. Some of these breweries are run by the mob now, and secretly make booze while pretending to make industrial alcohol."

"You seem to have learned quite a bit in your short time running rum," Max observed.

Tim smiled modestly. "Let's just say I had some good teachers. You have to learn the ropes whatever business you're in, don't you?"

"So where do you come in?" Allison asked. She was sitting up now, and leaning forward to hear this extraordinary story.

"Well, the money men make the arrangements and put up the dough to buy the booze and get it to a warehouse or a speakeasy. It gets delivered to some drop off point, usually a pier or a smaller boat, and that's where my trucks are waiting. We load and take it away and deliver it to the speakeasies. The whole thing takes an hour or less. We use covered trucks, but the stuff is usually in crates or barrels marked as something else, so we're pretty safe."

"But what if you do get caught?" Max asked.

"They give us each a roll of bills in case we have to buy our way out. Usually it works, but you can't depend on it."

Max and Allison looked at each other.

"Good old American enterprise," she remarked. "Supply and demand in action. Planning, production, financing, transportation and distribution, and all so someone can get pie-faced on a Saturday night. You almost have to admire the spirit of public service."

"Oh, yes; they're real humanitarians," Max said sarcastically. "Salt of the earth. So what's this shindig that's so important?"

"We're supposed to pick up a shipment from a barge on Rancocas Creek," Tim continued. "I think the barge was towed up the Delaware from the Rum Fleet offshore, or possibly a distillery across the river in Philly. Anyway, we load it and run it to a warehouse outside of Trenton. Simple."

"Right; simple," Max repeated. "Just like finding out who killed Danny Greene. But you're not doing rum running any more, remember?"

"Mr. Hurlock; tonight I have to," Tim almost pleaded. "You know I didn't have to even tell you about it, but I want to help Peter."

"Well, I think you're taking a crazy and unnecessary chance, but that's up to you. If you can spread the word about Peter and get some leads, I suppose it might be worth it, but get out the minute you can."

Tim grinned. "Just leave it to me."

As Tim walked away, Max shook his head and turned to Allison.

"I really don't like this one bit," he said. "I'm not a big booster of Prohibition, but I'm not in the habit of condoning law breaking either."

Allison took a more practical view. "You heard what he said, Max. He promised a bunch of hoods he'd do the job. He has to. When you break a promise to those creeps it can cause very unpleasant or even fatal results. We've got enough bodies in this case already. Anyway, it's not like he's going to be an accessory to murder or anything."

"We hope," said Max. "I'm going to call Charlie and let him know what I found out. Then I think I'll go and pay a visit to my good friend Otto Pfeiffer."

"Pfeiffer?" said Allison. "And I thought Tim Walsh was taking chances."

"Max," Charlie Bradwell said when Max had told him of his progress. "You've got to help me find Peter. That's more important than the other stuff. There must be something else you can do."

"Well, Charlie, I can inform the local police, forest rangers and the like, but wandering the woods would be a waste of time. Peter might not even be there."

"Maybe you could take your airplane up and look for him." said Charlie. "You know; a search from the air. You could cover a lot of ground in a hurry."

"Maybe if he was lost at sea, or in a desert, but he's in a wooded state full of buildings and people. I could fly right over him and not know it. Besides, I wouldn't know where to even start. Look, Charlie, I've already talked to his friends, professors, his girlfriend, and the guy at the Raritan. Nobody knows anything except that Peter said he was going camping."

"Did you talk to Emma Manelli face to face?"

"No. Just on the phone," Max replied. "I'll tell you what. Maybe I can send Allison up to talk to her. You know; woman to woman. Maybe Emma will open up to her and give us some hint about what Peter was thinking, something she wouldn't tell me. Meanwhile, I can keep operating down here."

"All right, Max. I'll make some calls as well. I've already lost one son and that's enough."

Max hung up the lobby phone and went back to ask Allison to drive up to Monmouth Breach and talk to Emma Manelli.

"Sure, Max," she said. "It'll be a chance to get away for a day and clear my head of the elusive small town almost-flappers."

"Thanks. I have a feeling she'll tell all when confronted with the mysterious Allison Hurlock charm, although that seems to work better on men."

She smiled. The strands of brown hair fell over her forehead once again. "Flattery will get you everywhere. Come on upstairs. I have a feeling you'll need your rest before seeing Pfeiffer tomorrow."

The next morning, Otto Pfeiffer looked up from his desk and scowled.

"Well, well. If it isn't Mr. Hurlock, the man from Maryland. Have you come to tell me you solved the case?"

"Which one?" asked Max, "the Taylor Bradwell case, the Danny Greene case, the Bradwell Properties break-in case, or the Peter Bradwell missing person case?"

"Take your pick," said Pfeiffer.

"To tell the truth, Otto, I'm not quite at a solution to any of them yet."

"I'm shocked."

"I'm really here to help us both," said Max. "I ran into Pedigree Pettigrew a day or two ago and he told me there were reports of someone pacing on the front lawn of the Taylor house the night of the Taylor Bradwell killings."

To Max's surprise, Pfeiffer laughed.

"Oh, brother; not that one again," said Pfeiffer. "A barber heard that from one of his customers and has been blabbing about it ever since. That's probably where Pettigrew heard it. We checked it the first time it came up and there's nothing to it. We even tracked it back to its source, an old lady with a vivid imagination. She was probably talking about a different night anyway. If that's what you're here for, you're wasting your time and mine."

"Well, actually, there's another matter," said Max, glad to change the subject. "I'd like to look at the papers you took from the Greenes' house; the one with Robert Bradwell's initials on it."

"This isn't the public library," said Pfeiffer. "Those papers are evidence."

"Otto, I just want to look at them, not start a fire with them."

"You ever heard of 'chain of custody', smart guy?" Pfeiffer retorted.

"I don't even need to touch it," Max insisted. "I just want to look at it for a few minutes. You can stand next to me and hold it if you'd like."

"Well..."

"Look, at the Greenes' house I didn't have a chance to go through the papers long enough to catch the fact that one had Robert Bradwell's initials on it. Your guys did that. Of course I had no way of finding the fingerprints either, but now that I know about it, I can see how important the paper would be. So what do you say?"

"Why should I help you?" Pfeiffer asked. "So you can make me look bad?"

"Otto, I'm trying to do the same thing you are;" Max insisted, "find out who killed Robert Bradwell, Miriam Taylor and Danny Greene. I don't plan to make any dramatic statements to the press to show you up. Why would I? I'm not running for office. If you'd like, I'll even keep you up to date on whatever I find. I'm working for Charlie Bradwell and I don't much care who gets the credit for solving the cases as long as Charlie gets the answers he needs."

Pfeiffer regarded him suspiciously, and then thought of the phone call he had gotten from the county prosecutor, George Hillsborough, earlier. The governor was leaning on the prosecutor and the prosecutor was leaning on the chief detective. Crap runs downhill, as Pfeiffer liked to say. Their message had been clear; make the rumors and whispering about conspiracy go away. The only way to do that, Pfeiffer knew, was to crack the cases once and for all, and having a sharp guy like Hurlock on his side might be a big help. This time, Pfeiffer realized, his desire to protect his turf would have to take a back seat to his desire to protect his job.

"All right, Hurlock," he said smoothly. "I'll make a deal with you. I'll let you see the papers, but in turn, you have to let me know whatever you find out within a day of when you find it out. That goes for your wife, too. You can't talk to the press about this case either. Do we have a deal?"

"It's a deal," Max said. "Now where are those papers?"

The papers were a disappointment. They were encased in cellophane to avoid more fingerprints, so Max was allowed to handle them. There were three that had Robert Bradwell's initials, all standard lined ledger sheets covered with rows of figures. To Max's untrained eye, they looked pretty routine, with entries for rent payments, maintenance items, supplies, and all the other expenses that go with operating a number of commercial properties. Then he noticed something else. Next to many of the items were pencil notations written in freehand. Beside each item was a check or an X. Occasionally he saw a question mark as well.

To Max it looked like Danny Greene was checking the figures for routine entry or arithmetic errors, hardly the sort of thing to kill someone about. Another curious feature of the papers was the fact that the question mark notations occurred not next to numbers, but next to words, specifically entries explaining expenses. Most of the question marks, Max noted, were next to entries of bills and payments to Eagle Property Maintenance.

"Well, see anything that names the killer?" Pfeiffer asked, looking over his shoulder.

"Not exactly," Max replied. "but one thing is interesting; a lot of question marks next to Eagle Property Maintenance."

Pfeiffer nodded. "We're way ahead of you, Hurlock. We already checked them out. They're a legit firm in Philadelphia. We talked to the owner and he confirmed that they've been doing property work for Bradwell for years."

"Then why the question marks?" Max asked.

"Who knows? Maybe Danny Greene found out the same thing we did and was just about to erase the question marks," said Pfeiffer.

"Except somebody erased him first," said Max.

Allison drove the Packard slowly down Etting Avenue in Monmouth Beach looking for Emma Manelli's address. She pulled up in front of a comfortable white clapboard bungalow with several pine trees in the front yard and a long front porch. Emma Manelli appeared in a long green, slightly old fashioned dress, as if she was on her way to town, or even to church. She was a pleasantly attractive blonde with an infectious smile and an easy laugh. They sat on the front porch on white wicker furniture while Emma's mother brought them lemonades.

"Thanks for talking to me," Allison began.

"Mrs. Hurlock, I'd do anything to get Peter back safely."

"He didn't tell you where he was going?"

Emma shook her head. "Not a word. It isn't like him. I sure hope he's all right."

"Someone at the Raritan said he stopped by and said he was going camping."

Emma looked up sharply. "Camping? He said that?"

"That's what the man at the Raritan said. Why?"

Emma took a long sip of her lemonade and frowned thoughtfully. "Peter and I are close. Sometimes he told me things."

Allison nodded sympathetically. "What sort of things, Emma?"

"Well, he really misses his brother, in spite of their differences. Sometimes he really got down about it. He talked about getting away."

"Away where?"

"He never really said any specific place; just that it would be good to get away."

Allison took a sip of lemonade and noticed a large gray cat sleeping on a nearby swing. At least he knew how to get away.

"You said Peter had differences with his brother. What sort of differences, exactly?"

"I'm not really sure." Emma shifted in her seat, tucking one leg under and smoothing her skirt over it as she did so. "He wouldn't tell me any details, but he said Robert was going to get himself in trouble if he wasn't careful. I got the impression that Robert had asked him to do something he didn't want to do. This was going on at the same time Robert was so upset about Miriam rejecting him. I think Peter thought it affected Robert's judgment; that Robert might not be doing whatever he was doing otherwise."

"Why did he think that?" Allison asked.

"It was something Robert said to him one day. Peter was telling Robert to give up whatever it was that he was doing, and Robert kept telling him it would all come out right in the end. In fact, he told Peter something like 'If this works out the way I think it will, Miriam will be so impressed she'll beg to get engaged again."

"What could he have been talking about?"

Emma shook her head. "I don't know, but it seemed to involve money."

Max returned to the hotel around 5:30 and had dinner with Allison, who had just returned a few minutes earlier.

"So that's what Emma Manelli said," Allison concluded when she had finished telling Max about her earlier interview. "It sounds like Robert was counting on whatever he was doing to impress Miriam."

"The problem is," said Max, "that embezzlement fits in to that scenario very nicely. With the money, Robert could pay off gambling debts and impress Miriam. It's a pretty good motive. But how does all that fit in with what I found out today?" He told her about the financial papers and wondered about what role, if any was played by Eagle Property Maintenance.

"Maybe Robert was skimming money from their payments somehow," Allison suggested. "If he was, maybe Peter got hold of Robert's papers and gave them to Danny Greene to get him to analyze them."

"Why?"

"Maybe to take back to Robert to convince him that he would get caught and get him to stop."

"Then who killed Robert and why?" said Max.

"Someone he owed money to but couldn't repay?"

"Whew," said Max, "Eagle is one more complication in a case that already had more than it could handle."

They sat silently for a few minutes.

"Say," said Allison. "Isn't Tim Walsh making his last run tonight?"

"That's what he said."

"I just hope he's careful," said Allison.

"Nice of you to be thinking of Tim's well-being," said Max.

"I'm mostly thinking of yours. He won't do you much good if he's in jail."

Long after Max and Allison had gone to bed, Tim Walsh's truck swayed, squeaked and rattled as he slowly drove it down an unlighted dirt road near Bridgeboro. As he turned the final bend in the road, he came to a clearing where a dozen other trucks were pulled up at the head of a pier stretching into the black and silent waters of Rancocas Creek. At the end of the pier was a sand barge sitting low in the water with at least a dozen men standing on its deck. Even at that distance in the dim light, Tim could see that several of the men were carrying Thompson sub machine guns, known among gangsters as "choppers", or "Chicago typewriters". Nervously, Tim pulled up next to the last truck and waited. Presently a big man in a slouch hat and dark raincoat came up to him and verified who he was.

"Wait here until it's your turn, then back your truck down the pier for loading," the man said. "We'll be unloading when we get the hatches open. As soon as you're got your shipment, get out of here and get on the road. Don't stop for anything. You know where to deliver the goods?"

Tim nodded.

"Good. Now remember, if anybody comes around or any cops show up, let me do the talking. You don't know from nothin'. As far as you're concerned, you're picking up farm equipment."

Tim nodded again. The man disappeared towards the barge and everything was quiet except for the clunking wooden sounds of the men on the barge opening the hatches and starting down the ladders to the interior. The other trucks were silent silhouettes beside him, receding into the murky darkness. Tim looked nervously at the blackness of the tree line around him, praying for the loading to get finished quickly so he could get out.

Barrels and wooden crates were emerging from the barge now, as the men steadily stacked them on the end of the pier. Men with wheelbarrows and hand trucks started to load barrels and crates into the first truck that had backed up to receive them. The process seemed maddeningly slow to Tim, as he fought back a rising sense of panic. This was bigger than any shipment he had ever seen. All these trucks. All these people down a narrow dirt road to the creek. Someone must have seen them. They must have. The first truck was almost loaded now. More barrels and crates were hauled up from inside the barge and stockpiled on the pier. Tim Walsh took out a handkerchief and silently wiped a line of sweat from over his upper lip.

He heard the tailgate of the first truck close and the engine start up. Good; one down and five more to go.

"Come on; come on!" he whispered.

He froze. Somewhere in the very limits of his peripheral vision, he thought he detected movement. He looked again. Nothing.

"Jeez," he said softly. "This is the last time I'll ever do something like this."

"New Jersey State Police. Everybody freeze!" The voice shattered the night air like a glass pitcher dropping on a stone floor. Headlights came on from cars concealed in the brush, flooding the area with a yellow glare and freezing the startled bootleggers in their places as the pier came alive with running uniformed policemen shouting orders. One by one the bootleggers hesitantly put their hands in the air. Police rounded up scores of men and herded them towards three paddy wagons that had appeared seemingly from nowhere.

Instinctively, Tim Walsh fumbled with the ignition switch. He had to get out of there. He just had to.

"Just relax, son," came a voice. Tim spun his head to the left and looked beside the truck. "You ain't goin' nowhere," said a state trooper with a shotgun.

Chapter 20

Doris Gentry tells all

The next morning, Max returned to Bradwell Properties to discuss the papers he had seen in Pfeiffer's office with Charlie Bradwell and Fred Madison.

The three men sat in the small conference area at a table that was piled with neat stacks of papers.

"You'll have to excuse the mess," said Charlie. "Fred here is trying to recreate the papers we lost using other records."

"Can you do that?" Max asked.

"Not entirely, I'm afraid," Fred answered gloomily, "but I think I can put enough back together to keep it from seriously hurting our ability to do business. I've already been to the bank to get whatever duplicate records they have, but it isn't that much. Still, what else can we do? We have to keep going and I doubt that the police will show up one day with the missing records in their hands."

"No, probably not," Max had to agree.

"The worst part," Charlie said, "is putting back together a record of who owes us what. Accounts payable isn't a problem because creditors will happily remind you, but when people who owe us money hear we lost our records of their debts, they'll suddenly get amnesia."

"Well, speaking of records, I visited Pfeiffer yesterday and saw what looked like some financial sheets Danny Greene was checking regarding Robert."

"Robert?" Charlie said, surprised. "What financial sheets would Robert have?"

"Until the break in, none were missing," Fred Madison added.

"I know," said Max. "It appears they were some sort of financial records Robert kept on his own. Danny Greene seemed to be going over the figures and marking checks or Xs next to them. Any idea what that could have been about?"

"Probably checking the math at least," said Fred Madison. "You know, making sure the debits equal the credits."

"Of course!" said Max, striking his forehead with the palm of his hand. "Debits and credits; dogs and cats. That's what Danny Greene was talking about at the Volstead Tavern. I should have figured it out sooner. He was also checking, or at least looking at the names of creditors, especially Eagle Property Maintenance."

"I don't know what he could have been checking," said Charlie Bradwell. "We've used them for repairs and upkeep on our buildings for years."

"That's right," said Fred. "They're one of the biggest firms around."

Max thought about it some more. "Did Robert have charge of any payments or accounts having to do with Eagle?"

"I think he made up a check or two," said Fred, "Maybe a few hundred dollars worth as near as I can remember, but that's about it. What are you getting at?"

"I'm not really sure," said Max, "but I believe those papers hold the answer to who killed Danny Greene and to who killed Robert as well."

As he was leaving, Max ran into Doris Gentry. Secretaries, of course, often know all the inside information of a company, so Max decided to talk to her once more.

"Hi, Doris," he said. "Got time for a coffee?"

She smiled. "Sure, Mr. Hurlock."

"Max."

"All right. Sure, Max."

The deli downstairs had a couple of small wooden tables in a corner, so they got a place where the smells of coffee blended with the smells of hot Pastrami.

"You hardly have to even eat here," Max observed. "Just inhale."

Doris laughed. "I'll have a coffee with cream and two sugars."

The coffee came and Doris smiled without drinking it. She looked more like a librarian than ever. "Mr. Hurlo...Max. I know you want to ask me about things in the office, so go ahead."

"I guess subtlety is not my long suit," Max admitted. "You're pretty perceptive, Doris, so I'll get right to it. I think Robert Bradwell was murdered and I think it had something to do with events at this office. I don't know exactly what yet, but it seems to somehow involve something financial. Now my question to you is a simple one. When I want to know what's going on in an office, I go to the people closest to the action. I don't think much escapes you in this place, so I want you to think back to when Robert was working here and tell me anything you remember that was unusual."

"Unusual?"

"Yes. Anything he did one way but then changed; anything he said that seemed strange; anything he did that seemed out of character."

Doris took a sip of her coffee, as if taking on fuel for revelations to come...

"Well, as I said, Robert was a good boy; everyone liked him. I suppose the biggest change was when that Taylor girl jilted him, but I already told you about that."

"Yes, but other than despondency, did he act peculiar after that?" Max pressed.

Doris frowned. "Actually, there was one thing, other than the despondency I mean. I suppose it was really a natural reaction to occupy his mind, but Robert threw himself into his work."

"What do you mean?" Max was interested.

"Well, he was a good worker when he was here, but he was always out the door at 5:00. You could set your watch by him."

Max nodded. "And afterwards?"

"As I say, he threw himself into his work. He started staying late and on several occasions I noticed he was actually taking work home with him."

"What sort of work?" Max asked.

"I don't know, really. I just saw him put some papers into a big manila envelope on several occasions. I'm sure no one else saw it because I was the only one who had a clear view of where he sat."

"Did you say anything to him about it?"

"Oh, no," she sighed. "I thought he was just trying to get his mind off of things by burying himself in his work. I couldn't really blame him. Is it important?"

Max put his coffee cup down and placed some money on the table. “Probably not, Doris. Thank you for the information. I have to get back.”

“I’d better get back as well, Max,” she said, rising, “If I’m gone too long the office suffers.”

Max smiled. “I can believe that.”

Allison was optimistic about her article, but was still finding the going slow. She looked up several of the customers of the dress shop she had visited earlier, thinking that at least these girls were interested in flapper fashion, so they might be involved in the kind of activities the editors of Modern Girls were looking for. One of them, Moreen Simpson, sounded like a good prospect over the telephone and agreed to meet Allison at a Main Street soda fountain.

The soda fountain at Style’s had started the way most drugstore soda fountains had started; as a service provided by the drugstores to make it easier for customers to ingest their often-bitter tasting medicine. With time the drugstores learned to make the concoctions more and more flavorful, and people started asking for them even when they didn’t have medicine to wash down. Soon every drug store had a busy and profitable soda fountain attached. The fountain at Style’s featured a long counter with stools and several booths on the opposite wall.

Moreen turned up outfitted in the latest flapper style, with a fringed green and gold dress and a wide headband around her close bobbed blond hair. A long strand of pearls hung around her neck and swayed as she walked. Allison introduced herself.

“Pleased to meetcha,” Moreen giggled. She seemed to chirp in a high pitched, squeaky voice, like some bird that had somehow developed the ability to speak. Allison noticed she was noisily chewing gum as well.

"Same here," Allison replied as they slid into a booth near the rear. "Can I order you anything?"

"Not unless they got Canadian," Moreen sniggered.

"I'm afraid the only Canadian they're likely to have here is Canadian bacon," said Allison. "How about a Phosphate?"

"No, I think I'll have a White Cow."

"A White Cow?"

"Vanilla milkshake," Moreen translated, then waved to girl at another table. "Hey, Diana! I'm telling you, since Prohibition you see everyone in here."

"Yes," Allison agreed. "Now that thc bars are closed, the corner soda fountain is the new gathering place for a lot of people, at least people who aren't comfortable in nightclubs. Speaking of which..."

"Do I go to nightclubs?" Moreen finished the question for her. "And how! Of course, there aren't many nearby. You have to go all the way to Philly for the really good ones, although Camden has a few and so does Trenton."

"Have you ever been in a raid?"

Moreen shook her head. "No, not once, but I heard about a few. It's all a lot of bushwa, really. They take your name and let you go. If I get caught, I'm going to tell them my name is Clara Bow. Won't that be a hoot?"

"Hysterical," agreed Allison. "So you consider yourself a modern woman, a flapper?"

"I guess so. I never really thought about it. All I know is that my mother and my grandmother were chained to the kitchen, the children, and whatever their husband wanted. That's not for me; not yet anyway."

"What do you want, then?" Allison asked.

"Ah, here's my White Cow." Moreen clapped her hands eagerly as the tall foaming glass was placed in front of her. She tasted it and sat back with a look of ecstasy on her face, along with a white milk mustache. "That's the stuff! Times like this, I'm glad I don't have to wear a corset."

"You were saying what you wanted that was different than your mother?" Allison tried to turn the conversation away from white cows.

Moreen took another sip and looked serious. "The thing is, I love my mother, but I have freedoms and choices she never had. I go to nightclubs and smoke and flirt with fellows, and maybe even get blotto once in a while because I can. I know the newspapers and magazines go on about how crazy flappers act, and make us out to be dumb Doras, but the way I see it, I'd be crazy not to be a flapper."

Allison smiled as she took down the quote. The article was coming back to life before her eyes.

Returning to Cole's Hotel, Allison plopped down in her favorite overstuffed chair in the lobby and smiled. She was pleased with her day's work. In addition to a very good interview with Moreen Simpson, she had talked to several of Moreen's friends at Style's where so many of them congregated. The information she got, while not exactly sensational, was something that could more easily be worked into a form suitable for Modern Girls Magazine.

"Yes," she said, "it looks like I might be able to salvage this article after all. Now let's see...."

Small Town Girls having Big Time Fun:
The Rise of the Small Town Flapper
By Allison Hurlock

She may not be on every street corner yet, but you can bet she's in every nightclub. She wears her hair short and her skirt shorter. She drinks, smokes, listens to jazz music and hangs out with the boys, though she's also been seen indulging in such wholesome activities as golfing, bicycling, and playing tennis. She's America's newest sensation; the flapper, and she's not just in the big cities any more.

"I want more than my mother and grandmother had," said one young bearcat at a small town watering hole recently, "I go to nightclubs and smoke and flirt with fellows, and maybe even get blotto once in a while because I can. The world is more open to someone like me than it ever has been, so why waste it?...The way I see it, I'd be crazy <u>*not*</u> *to be a flapper."*

"Nifty," said Allison. "Now we're cooking with gas! All I have to do is work in the stuff I got from my other sources. That ought to be enough Tabasco for them."

"Mrs. Hurlock? Is Max here?"

Allison looked up from her notes and saw the figure approaching her from the other side of the hotel lobby. She couldn't make out the figure because the light was behind him, but there was no mistaking the voice.

"Tim Walsh? Is that you?"

He sat down heavily beside her in a wrinkled suit that looked as if it had been slept in. His eyes were sunken and his unshaven face was the color of old bed sheets.

"You look like you're not hitting on all sixes, Tim. What happened to you?"

"Is Max around?" he repeated. "I have to see Max."

"No. Max is in Philadelphia at Bradwell Properties. Now I want you to tell me what happened."

Tim wiped his hand over his forehead. The hand, she noticed, was shaking.

"I was arrested last night...at the pickup point."

"Arrested? Trying to run liquor?" Allison was only partly surprised.

"I should have known it was too hot from the first. That operation was way too big to cover up. The state police found out somehow and raided it. They were everywhere. They herded us into paddy wagons packed like sardines and took us to Trenton. They pushed all of us, maybe 50 men, before the magistrate in Trenton. I thought I was a goner. I saw myself going to prison and I saw everything I've worked for going down the drain."

Allison put her hand on his shoulder soothingly. "So what happened then?"

"Then one of the guys standing next to me said that everyone was going to give phony names and try to get out on bail. I could see everyone that went before the judge was getting released on $50 bail, so when my turn came, I did the same. I got a ride back to Moorestown with one of the others. They said they'll never show up for trial and the police will be left holding the bag. I got back but was afraid to go home in case they were waiting for me. I've been looking for Max all day."

"Well I think you're all right now, Tim. It looks like you got away," said Allison.

"I got away, but Mrs. Hurlock, that was too close for comfort. They could have thrown us all in the slammer until trial and I could be heading for the state prison. The money isn't worth that kind of risk. I'm really getting out. Max was right."

He reached into his coat and pulled out a small address book.

"You see this?" he said, flipping the pages. "This is my secret client list. I carry it on me all the time so it won't get lost. Well, I'm taking it home and burning it. That's it for me."

"Tim, Max will be back soon, I'm sure," Allison said in a voice that was somehow both soothing and authoritative. "Why don't you settle back, close your eyes and take a little nap. You'll feel better. I have to finish up some notes, so I'll stay right here and wake you up just as soon as Max gets back."

Tim relaxed a little. "Gee, Mrs. Hurlock; you're aces. I feel better already, and I guess I could use some rest. I've been afraid to close my eyes in case I woke up in jail."

"Don't worry," Allison said smiling. "I'll be right here to yell 'Cheese it; the cops!' if need be. So you can relax. Oh, and Tim? That address book of yours is fascinating. Could I look at it again?"

He took it out of his coat and handed it to her. "Sure. I'm going to get rid of it anyway."

As Tim drifted off into an exhausted sleep, Allison flipped through the address book to an entry she thought she had seen briefly. There on the third page, she found it;

Eagle Prop. Maint......2909 Whitney, Phil.

Chapter 21

Mr. Eagle

Max stopped off briefly at the Bradwells' on his way back, and noticed that Charlie was looking worn and haggard by his ordeal. He assured Charlie as best he could and drove back towards the hotel. He was late, but satisfied that his time that day had not been wasted. The streetlights were just coming on, although it was still light out when he noticed a familiar looking car in his rear view mirror. No doubt about it, he was being followed, and probably by the same guy that had followed them before. The car wasn't close enough for Max to read the license number, so he continued on his way, keeping an eye on the rear view mirror. There was no sense trying to shake this guy, Max figured; he had nothing to hide. Let the palooka follow him.

Max pulled the car into a space in front of the hotel and looked in the mirror just in time to see the brown Buick turn off at the previous street.

"Another complication," he muttered.

Allison was half-asleep on a chair in the lobby as Max walked in.

"I know I'm late," he began, "but I had to run down a lead and I couldn't get hold of you."

"Never mind that," she cut him off short. "Tim Walsh was here looking for you, but after a short nap he got tired of waiting and went to have a bite in the restaurant."

"Tim Walsh? What did he..."

"He was arrested last night but got away on a phony name and light bail. The experience shook him up so much he decided to get out of rum running once and for all. He's even going to burn his address book of his bootlegger customers, but I persuaded him to let me see it first."

She took out the book with a flourish. And opened it so Max could see the names on page two.

"That's nice, Allison, but what do we want with a.....Wait a minute. Does that say Eagle Property Maintenance?"

"It sure does."

"Eagle Property Maintenance is in the bootlegging business?" Max was amazed.

"So it would seem."

"Mr. Hurlock!" Tim Walsh had returned from the dining room.

"Hello, Tim," said Max. "You're looking a little frayed around the edges. Allison told me what happened."

"I'm out of the rum running business for good. You were right."

"That's great, Tim, but maybe you could help me out, too."

Tim brightened up. "Sure thing, Mr. Hurlock. What do you want?"

"I'm interested in one of your customers. Tell me about Eagle Property Maintenance."

"Eagle? Oh, that guy. That was strange, but his money was good."

"What was his real name?" Max asked.

"I don't know. I always called him Mr. Eagle. That was nothing unusual; most of my customers used aliases. Anyway, I never saw him face to face. He called me one day on the telephone and said he heard about me and wanted me to run a shipment for him. His regular guy had been arrested I suppose."

"When was this?"

"Maybe two years ago. Anyway, the deal was, if he wanted to call me it would always be at 9:00 sharp on a Thursday night. Some weeks he'd call and some he wouldn't. And it was always the same thing. He'd tell me what to pick up, where to pick it up, where to deliver it, and how much to collect from the customer. But it was always by telephone. I never met him face to face."

"So you don't know who he was?"

"He never said, and I knew enough not to ask that kind of question. Besides, he sounded like he was disguising his voice by talking through a tin can or something.

"Wait a minute," Max asked. "If you never met him, how did he pay you, and how did you get the customer's payment back to him? Did he mail you the money?"

"No. There was too much risk sending money through the mail. It could get lost or stolen, not to mention postmarks and such. No, the transactions were through a drop."

"You mean a place where he left the money for you or you left money for him?

"Right. There's this ratty storefront on Whitney Avenue in Philly. It had a sign on the door that said Eagle Property Maintenance. I thought it was sort of funny seeing as how that place needed so much maintenance itself."

"What about the money?" Max insisted.

"When we started, he sent me a key in the mail; unmarked, or course. The key opened the front door to Eagle. There were some loose bricks in one wall inside and the money would always be left behind one."

Max nodded. "Simple and almost foolproof."

"Sure, as long as I was home at 9:00 on Thursday night for assignments, which I always was, except for once."

"What happened that time?" Max asked.

"Aw, that was the night the Volstead Tavern got raided. I didn't get home until late that night and I missed his call. He called the next Thursday and was hopping mad. I told him what had happened and he calmed down."

Max and Allison looked at each other. They both had the same thought.

"Tim, what exactly did you tell him?"

"Oh, you know. I told him I was out with my friends and how we were all talking when the place was raided."

"Tim, did you tell Mr. Eagle about Danny Greene and what he was saying that night; about how he knew the real story behind Robert's death?"

"Uh, yeah, I guess I did."

"That's how the killer knew Danny Greene was looking into Robert Bradwell's murder," Max whispered to Allison.

"So I suppose now you'll have to tell Mr. Eagle you're out of the business," Max suggested.

"I don't have to," Tim replied. "I haven't heard from Mr. Eagle since Danny Greene was killed."

The next morning Max was at the Philadelphia Department of Records looking through property information in a room filled with racks of bulky canvas bound books of deeds and mortgages. Various property developers, prospective buyers and simply curious people hunched over opened books on long tables looking up information and taking notes on pads. After some difficulty, Max found a somewhat sour looking clerk who took time off from entering mortgage information in the records to guide him to the tax records. There he found the owner of 2909 Whitney Avenue, the Benski Company. The clerk said that the Benski Company was a commercial real estate firm in Camden, but that they had extensive holdings of commercial property in Philadelphia. Max wrote down the address of the Benski Company, and turned to thank the clerk, but he had already returned to his entries.

The Benski Company's offices in Camden were on the second floor of a bank in a neat, but dull looking suburban street. Max walked in the door to the outer office and felt his eyes stinging. Struggling to breathe normally, he saw the cause. The receptionist, whom Max interrupted while she was doing her nails, was a young lady who apparently believed that if a drop of perfume was pleasant, a cup full would be sensational. Trying not to choke, Max told her he was looking for information about 2909 Whitney Avenue. To his surprise, he was immediately ushered into the office of the president, Sol Benski. Benski was a large man with a bald head and a full gray beard. He sat behind a large, but ancient looking desk and wore a white shirt open at the neck. He peered at Max behind large black rimmed glasses.

"So, you interested in renting 2909 Whitney?" Sol asked.

"I thought it was already rented," said Max.

"Feh! I have a tenant there for almost eight years," Sol began. "Suddenly he stops paying the rent. No explanation, no how-are-you, no nothing."

"Has he vacated?"

"Vacated, schmacated; the putz never really moved into the place. Eight years he pays rent, but there's never any furniture and nobody ever sees anybody working there. If you ask me, the whole thing was phony baloney"

"Phony?"

"The tenant is supposed to be in the property maintenance business, right? So I ask him if he wants to maybe do some work for us. We're always on the lookout for reliable people to take care of our properties. So he tells me his client list is full, so he can't take on any new work!"

"Is that unusual?"

"Unusual he says. Mister, that's unheard of. Property maintenance is a cutthroat business; very high turnover in companies and clients. A fixed client list? They should be so lucky."

"Maybe he had all the work he could handle?" suggested Max.

"For eight years? So hire more people, already." Sol Benski shook his head then shrugged. "Anyway, he always paid his rent, so why should I care? It's just that the whole thing seemed a little meshugana to me. But now I've got that space to rent and it hasn't been fixed up for years so nobody wants it and it's earning me bupkis."

"Look, Mr. Benski, I'll level with you. I'm trying to track down the guy who rented that property."

"So does he owe you money too?"

"No, but he might be involved in some underhanded dealings I'm investigating. What can you tell me about him?"

"I never met the man," said Sol. "He said his name was John Smith, an obvious alias if you ask me. He called one day asking about the space and asked me to leave a copy of the lease for him to sign on the hall table outside the office. It was weird, but I was having a hard time renting that space and he offered six months in advance, so I should care? After that, I received the rent checks every month, but never talked to him or saw him. The rent checks were from Eagle Properties and signed with a stamp. Since the rent stopped I looked at the lease again and found that all the information is phony, but as long as he was paying, it didn't matter."

"All right, Mr. Benski," said Max. "I guess finding him won't be so easy. Here's my card. Will you let me know if he contacts you or starts paying rent again?"

Sol rolled his eyes heavenward. "Oy! I should be so lucky."

Max went from Benski Properties directly to see Charlie Bradwell at his office. He brought him up to date on the mysterious Mr. Eagle and on what he had learned at Benski Properties.

"Sol Benski?" Charlie said. "I've been knocking heads with that guy for years. Every time there's a good property coming on the market, he seems to know about it ahead of time and swoops in. I've lost a lot of business to him over the years. Could Sol Benski be behind all this somehow? Is he Mr. Eagle?"

Max shook his head. "I don't see how, but I'll keep on looking. One thing seems certain; there are two

Eagle Property Maintenance Companies. One seems on the up and up, but the other is a storefront/mail drop operation of some kind that uses the same name and is mixed up in bootlegging. Could any of Bradwell Properties checks for services to Eagle have been going to the mail drop in Philadelphia?"

"I doubt it," said Charlie. "Hey, Fred."

Fred Madison looked up then came to Charlie's office.

"Fred did you know there's another Eagle Properties in Philadelphia?"

"You mean a branch office?" Fred asked.

"No; an entirely different operation with the same name and only a mail drop as an office. I never heard of them. I don't think they're in the phone directory or I'd have noticed."

"No, they're not," said Max. "I already checked."

"Fred, could any of our payments to Eagle have been diverted to the mail drop Eagle in Philadelphia somehow?"

Madison frowned and shook his head slowly. "I don't see how. I write all the checks except for the ones that Robert did. Besides, if the Eagle we deal with didn't receive a payment they were expecting, they'd be on the telephone in a minute."

Charlie nodded. "That's true. If any of their payments were diverted somewhere else they'd scream to the high heavens. Max, I don't know what to tell you."

"Maybe they're not in the property maintenance business at all," said Max. "Maybe it's a front for bootlegging and the name is just a coincidence. It wouldn't be the first one. Well, I'll keep on working on it. It's still pretty fuzzy, but I'm getting closer."

"Fine," said Charlie. "Now what about Peter?"

"Nothing yet. The police are working on it and I've talked to his friends and professors; they all promised to call me up. I'll make some more calls today, but I think Peter's disappearance could have something to do with this Eagle Property."

Max went from Bradwell's office to see Otto Pfeiffer, partly to keep his promise about keeping the police informed and partly to enlist his help. Pfeiffer was out so Max talked to Detective Edwards.

"Sure, I'll tell him," Edwards said. His brown necktie was tightly tied in spite of the heat in the room. He looked like a high school student that had somehow found himself behind a desk at the police station. "The chief's over to Palmyra on business. He'll be back this afternoon. He'll appreciate the information."

"Fine," said Max. "Oh, and one more thing; I need to have a look at Robert and Peter's bank accounts to see if any large deposits or withdrawals have taken place. I can't access them myself. The police, however, could easily get a warrant based on the information I've given you."

Edwards got up from the desk and walked over to a nearby file cabinet and removed a folder.

"We've already done it," he said, placing the folder in front of Max.

Sure enough, Max opened the folder to see copies of the last two years transactions of both bank accounts.

"You can look through it if you want," Edwards continued, "but you won't find any big withdrawals or deposits for either one of them."

Max nodded. He could already see that. "This is very impressive, How did you get the warrant?"

"We didn't. Last year the head teller's car was stolen and Chief Pfeiffer got it back for her. She was happy to return the favor; unofficially, of course."

"Of course," said Max. "Well, I've seen enough. Thanks. Oh, by the way, weren't you the first officer on the scene when Danny Greene was murdered?"

Edwards nodded. "Yes. I responded to a call about a shooting. The door of the house was locked and there was no answer, so I went around back. The back door was open, so I went in."

"Did you notice anything unusual about the place when you first went in?"

Edwards pushed his chair back, clearly happy to be of use in a murder investigation. "Not really. The kitchen was a little cluttered and smelled like someone had burned some coffee recently. The room with the body looked like the dining room; it had a table and chairs and a desk on one side with two stacks of papers. Danny Greene's body was lying in the living room like he'd been walking towards the room with the desk when he was shot. Danny Greene was already dead. He'd been shot in the heart. I'd never seen a dead body before, and I guess it surprised me."

"Surprised?"

"Somehow I always thought a body would have a distinctive smell. You know how they talk about the smell of death? But all I could smell was the gunpowder, along with a little cigar smoke and the burned coffee I already mentioned. I also noticed that the only light that was on was the one in the room with the desk. There were no footprints visible because the rug wasn't thick enough. The weather had been pretty dry so there was no trace of mud or outside footprints either."

"There was no murder weapon found?" Max asked.

"No. The killer took it with him, along with the shell casing. When the chief got there we both searched for any sign of another bullet and didn't find any. We looked through the papers on the desk until the chief told us we were wasting our time. That was about it."

"Thanks," said Max, turning to leave.

"Mr. Hurlock," Edwards called after him. "Did that help?"

"Everything helps. Thanks."

Allison realized she needed one more perspective to include in her article; the thoughts of mothers on how their daughters were behaving. A few pithy quotes from that quarter and the article could be finished. She decided to contact Martha Bradwell, thinking she could recommend some of her friends. Martha was delighted to see Allison again, and invited her to sit and have some tea. The sitting room of the Bradwell house was cheerily sunlit when Allison dropped by that afternoon and Martha Bradwell quickly produced a silver tea service.

"I'm so glad you decided to come by, dear," she cooed.

"Just so long as we don't play tennis again," Allison remarked. "I'm still sore."

"Now, dear, you really did very well. You have a natural athletic ability. Why, with a little practice, I think you could easily beat anyone at the club. Now, I understand you wanted to talk to some mothers of young women?"

"Yes. I thought their perspective would round out my article."

"I do know a few, of course, and I'll give you their names and addresses. They all have concerns the way modern girls seem to be behaving these days, and I think what they have to say would be most interesting to your readers."

"Great. That's just the stuff I need,' said Allison.

"Of course it's a shame you can't talk to Ruth Taylor. Miriam was something of a flapper herself, you know. Ruth could tell you tales, but she's no longer speaking to me. As far as she is concerned, I'm the mother of a murderer and the wife of a fortune seeker."

"You used to be friends with Ruth Taylor?"

"Oh, yes. Well, not close friends, you understand, but we spoke at the club off and on. You know how it is; prospective in-laws pretending to be perhaps more compatible than they really are. Anyway, Ruth always thought Miriam was a handful, what with her engagements and so on. I think she was surprised when Miriam broke off the engagement with our Robert. She was optimistic about Robert's prospects, even after the breakup, and it seemed to me that she hoped Miriam would change her mind."

"Did she say that?" Allison asked.

Martha Bradwell took a long sip of tea and daintily patted her lips with her lace napkin. "Not in so many words, of course, but shortly after the breakup she told me, in the strictest confidence, mind you, that Miriam had shown her one of Robert's letters. Robert said he was involved in something that would assure his place in the world. He hinted that once he completed doing whatever it was, he and Miriam would be able to live happily ever after. Martha Taylor asked me what he meant. Of course I had no idea."

"Did you ever ask Robert about it?"

"Oh, no. I couldn't let him know I had been discussing his private letters with Mrs. Taylor, could I?"

"No, I suppose not."

"Robert could be very secretive sometimes," said Martha Bradwell, staring into her teacup. "I'm afraid now we'll never know what he meant."

Max and Allison had just gotten dressed to leave the hotel the next morning when someone started knocking on their door. The desk clerk was outside calling to them.

"Mr. and Mrs. Hurlock? Mr. and Mrs. Hurlock? I'm sorry to disturb you, but Mr. Bradwell's on the telephone. He says it's important."

Hey went downstairs and Max picked up the telephone. Charlie Bradwell's voice came through loud and clear.

"We found Peter."

Chapter 22-

Peter Bradwell comes clean

"He called us from school a few minutes ago," Charlie Bradwell continued. "He really had been camping. He was feeling down about Robert and decided to get lost for a few days. He's been camping out in the Adirondacks. He called us ahead of time to let us know, but we were out, so he sent a note but it got returned for insufficient postage after he left so we never saw it. Can you beat that?"

"That's great news, Charlie," said Max. "Does he know Pfeiffer is looking for him?"

"No, not yet."

"Well, tell him to stay there until I can talk to him. Before Pfeiffer gets hold of him, I have some questions for him."

"I'll call him and tell him to stay put right now, Max."

Max hung up the phone and turned to Allison.

"Peter came back to Rutgers."

"What? Where was he?"

"Camping, just as he said. He was down about Robert. I'm going up there to find out about his fingerprints on the papers Danny Greene was working on."

"I'd like to hear the answer to that," Allison commented, pulling a cloche hat down on her head, "but I've got a mother to interview at noon."

"That's fine. I should be back before dark., but I want to hear Peter's explanation of how his fingerprints got on those papers and what he was arguing about with Robert."

"And why he didn't tell anyone about it."

When they emerged from the hotel, Max turned toward Allison.

"Can I drop you off?"

Allison shook her head. "No, I'm not interviewing Mrs. Denton for over an hour. It's nearby; I can easily walk. It's you I'm worried about."

Max reached out and grasped her hands.

"It's not like you to worry. What's the matter?"

"I guess I just realized that you might be closer to the answer in this case than you think. You have so many pieces you're bound to put them together."

"So? That's good isn't it?"

She frowned in a worried way that Max hadn't seen before. "Max, consider. If I think you're close to finding the answers, then the killer might have come to the same conclusion. Whoever it is has already killed three people apparently, so I don't see any reason they would hesitate to kill one more if they think they're about to be exposed."

Max nodded. "Don't worry. I'll be on the lookout. Besides, I'm carrying my trusty Mauser pistol with me just in case."

She grasped his hand. Her voice was a whisper. "The killer is no stranger to pistols himself. And don't forget about whoever has been following us. Promise me you won't let anything happen to you."

"Of course."

They embraced and Max thought that Allison was holding him unusually tightly. She seemed reluctant to let him go, but finally he was able to break free. With one last goodbye, Max got in the Packard and started off towards New Brunswick. Allison stood in front of the hotel watching him until he disappeared from sight.

The drive up to Rutgers took Max along winding country roads passing small towns and gently rolling farmland. As he drove, with the Packard running smoothly on the uneven roads, Max reviewed the cases in his mind and kept coming to the same dead ends. Thinking of the mysterious Mr. Eagle, one uncomfortable possibility kept nagging at him. What if none of the people he had talked to was the murderer? What if the killer, lurking silent and unseen, was someone else altogether? What if the killer was someone Max had never even met? And what if Allison was right; what if he was starting to feel threatened? With that disturbing thought in mind, Max approached the New Brunswick campus once again.

Back in Moorestown, sunlight filtered through the front window and cast speckled shadows on the blue mohair furniture inside Mrs. Denton's parlor as Allison prepared for what she hoped would be her final interview. Mrs. Denton brought in a silver tray with two cups of tea and a plate of cookies.

"Mrs. Denton," Allison began, "I asked to speak with you because I spoke with your daughter and I'm working on a magazine article about flappers in smaller towns as opposed to the big cities. So what can you tell me about your daughter's social life and her friends?"

Mrs. Denton put down the teacup, set herself comfortably in the chair, and took a deep breath. "The young girl of today is beset with grave temptations on all sides as she traverses the forest of life. Our leaders, both civic and religious, have failed to properly prepare them for the world's..."

"Er, Mrs. Denton?" Allison interrupted. "We can talk about the rest of the world a little later. Right now I just want to know about Constance and her friends."

"Constance and her friends are a part of the great social milieu of our times, and as such, they must continually find a way to avoid the excesses of their fellows. As my husband, Mr. Denton said only last Tuesday,..."

"Mrs. Denton?" Allison interrupted the flow of reason before Mr. Denton could be added to it. "Maybe it would be easier if I just ask some more specific questions. Would you consider your daughter Constance a flapper?"

Mrs. Denton looked disappointed. "Well, as I said, my daughter Constance encounters such issues daily. On one hand, every girl wants to be independent, but on the other hand, they want to belong, to conform to the norm of their social peer group."

"You mean they want to fit in?" Allison asked.

"Well, yes."

"Tell me about this desire to fit in."

"The desire to conform to the social peer group norm manifests itself in a number of ways," said Mrs. Denton, "most notably in the areas of clothing, articulation, and social acclimatization."

"You mean they try to dress, talk and act like everyone else?" Allison could see that it might be necessary to translate Mrs. Denton's pronouncements into English.

"Exactly."

"Do you think they are all seeking independence?" Allison asked.

"Oh, yes. They wish to enjoy parental support systems without the attendant parental controls and oversight."

"I'll take that as a yes," Allison said. "What about her dating practices?"

"Dating practices? Well, you just make yourself comfortable, young lady. I have a great deal to say about dating habits."

Allison sighed. It was going to be a long interview.

Peter Bradwell greeted Max at the door to his Rutgers dormitory room and readily agreed to a walk outside for some measure of privacy since several residents of the floor were conducting an impromptu, and very loud, poker game in the next room.

"Gosh, Mr. Hurlock. I'm sorry for the trouble I caused. I thought I had let Mom and Dad know with the note I sent. "

"So why did you take off like that, Peter?"

Peter sighed. "I guess I was just down about Robert. Usually I'm all right, but sometimes it really hits me hard...about him being gone and all. When that happens I just want to get away someplace and clear my mind. You know; just be alone for a while. That's why I didn't tell anyone at school."

They walked a little farther, then sat on a bench under a tree.

"Peter, you and Robert quarreled just before he died, didn't you?"

Peter looked evasive. "No...well, not really."

"It's all right, Peter. Brothers often fight."

Peter was silent a while longer, then spoke in a hushed tone. "Not just before one of them dies they don't. Not when the last memory he had was of our fighting. That's one of the reasons it hits me so hard sometimes. Now we'll never have the chance to make it right. It's frozen forever."

Max was sympathetic. "Peter, no one knows when someone is going to die. We have to just live our lives and not worry about the timing. Wherever Robert is, I'm sure he understands. I'm sure the good memories will easily crowd out the bad ones."

"I suppose." Peter didn't sound entirely convinced .

"Peter, I need to know about your fight with your brother. It may be painful or even embarrassing, but it may also have a bearing on Robert's murder."

"Did you say murder?"

"That's what I believe happened, Peter. But I need more information to find out the rest, so you need to tell me everything."

"I can't."

"Peter, you have to. It's something you can do for Robert. It's something you must do for Robert."

Peter was still sullen. He sat staring at the ground moodily.

"Look," said Max, "I think Robert was mixed up in something you didn't want him to be involved in. I also think that he tried to get you involved in it somehow."

Peter looked up. "How do you know that?"

"Never mind how I know. The fact is you don't want to tell me for the same reason you didn't tell your father and the same reason the only person you could even give a hint about it was Professor Enwright. Peter, I promise that no one will know who doesn't have to know. Robert's memory will not be soiled."

Peter thought about it, looked around to see if anyone was in earshot, then took a deep breath. "It started a few months before Robert's death. He was real broken up about how Miriam dumped him. He'd mope around and complain about how she didn't appreciate him or his talents. I told him he should forget her and get on with things, but he just kept it up. Sometimes I felt sorry for him, and sometimes I just wanted to hit him."

Max nodded. So far, there was nothing new. Peter's story fit in with what everyone said about Robert.

"Robert had been working at the company for several months by this time, but he seldom talked much about it. I mean, he liked it well enough; he just didn't have a lot of enthusiasm. Then one day, he suddenly seemed to get really interested, especially in the money part of it. He talked about how the checks were written, and where the rent money was deposited, and how contractors were handled, and just about everything that had anything to do with the money. He used to talk about cash flow and accounts payable, and all that financial stuff. The funny thing was that he never talked about it with Dad. I kept telling Robert to talk to him, but he only talked to me about it. That made me a little uncomfortable, but when he started talking about embezzling and how it could be done and how it could be covered up, I really got concerned. Oh, he always said it was just theoretical, that he was interested because he thought it was a good thing for a businessman to know to protect himself, but I could tell he had something more practical in mind. I knew him pretty well, you see. Ever since we were kids I could tell when he was covering up something."

"But you still didn't tell anyone?" Max asked.

"Tell them what? Nobody would ever believe it. Robert never gave any specifics. He made it all sound theoretical. Besides, he was still mooning for Miriam, so anyone would have thought he was acting strange for that reason. Well, this went on for some time, and Robert started talking about how he was going to do something to really impress Miriam and get her to change her mind; something that would make him set for good."

"Was that related to the financial comments, do you think?"

"I'm sure it was," said Peter. "One day Robert asked me if I would take some papers to Danny Greene. I asked him what kind of papers and he said they were just some financial figures he wanted Danny Greene to check for him. Well, that sounded pretty suspicious to me. Robert was always good at math, so why would he want someone else to check his figures? I looked at the papers and saw a lot of hand notations with checks and question marks next to a lot of the figures. It didn't look like any financial paper I'd ever seen; it looked like, well, like maybe he was trying to get Danny Greene to give him some fine points to help alter the books to embezzle money."

Max let out a low whistle. "So did you take the papers to Danny Greene?"

"No. That's what the big beef was about, you see. I told him to take them himself and he said he didn't want anyone to see him taking anything to Danny Greene, but that nobody really knew me. I told him to mail the papers, but he was afraid the papers might get lost or maybe a mailman would notice them."

"So what happened?"

"I told him I wasn't going to be a part of helping him steal from Dad's company. He just laughed and said I didn't understand how important it was. He kept telling me there was nothing wrong and that I had to do it; I wouldn't get in any trouble. He also wanted me to pick up any papers Danny Greene wanted to send back to him for the same reason. To me that just meant he and Danny Greene were in it together. We went back and forth arguing about it for weeks until a week or so before he died."

Back in Moorestown, Allison was finally finishing up her interview with Mrs. Denton, who felt her daughter was out of control as a flapper. Allison couldn't help thinking that Mrs. Denton was a bit out of control herself, and could feel a headache coming on.

"Yes, my dear. I feel that modern young ladies have certain proclivities that are, shall we say, somewhat suspect. Of course, I'm sure that her social peer group reinforces and extends these practices, but it seems to me that the mores of society should be upheld."

And so on. Mrs. Denton had actually provided some useful insights, but they were sandwiched between so much intellectual boilerplate that Allison was beginning to feel like she was not so much interviewing as mining. Allison stole a glance at a clock and wondered what Max was doing up at Rutgers.

"So Robert asked you to deliver his papers to Danny Greene, but you refused, and that's what the disagreement was about," said Max. "Then if you didn't deliver the papers how did Danny Greene wind up with them?"

Peter shrugged. "Search me. I guess Robert must have mailed them after all. Or he may have delivered them himself; maybe at night or something."

"Peter, so why didn't you tell anyone any of this before?"

Peter shook his head slowly. "I didn't see how it had anything to do with Robert's death, so why smear his memory? Why make everyone suspicious of him and maybe start more rumors? No, I just wanted to forget it and let people remember Robert as the upright and honest guy everyone always thought he was. I was concerned about Mom and Dad, too. Losing a child is bad enough, but losing a child and then find he was stealing from you has to be a lot worse."

"Peter, did Robert ever mention the Eagle Property Maintenance Company, or anyone called Mr. Eagle?"

"No. Robert didn't give me any specifics."

"How about bootlegging? Did he ever talk about bootlegging or rumrunning?"

"Of course. Everybody talks about bootlegging these days, but Robert never said anything unusual about it. He certainly never mentioned it as relating to whatever he was doing at the company."

Max sat back on the bench.

"Peter, I'm trying to get to the bottom of Robert's death, and I think the murder of Danny Greene has something to do with it. Anything else you can tell me or anything else you remember might be a big help."

"I can tell you one thing, Mr. Hurlock; a lot of people have said a lot of things about Robert and Danny Greene and all the rest, but they all have their own axes to grind. Everyone in my family has had a lot of sleepless nights worrying that we would never know the truth. Then you came along, and some people were complaining that you were an outsider and didn't know anything about the place. The way I see it, though, you're the only chance we've got to find out what really happened. You will find out, won't you?"

Max felt both touched and on the spot. Finally, he patted Peter on the shoulder. “I’ll find out. I promise.”

“That’s good enough for me,” said Peter. “Say, I have some letters Robert sent me over the last year or so. I don’t think there’s much in there that would help, but you could look through them if you’d like.”

“Sure,” said Max. “At this point we can’t afford to ignore anything.”

A few minutes later they were back in Peter’s room going through a pile of letters Peter had received from his brother over the last year before his death.

“It’s like I told you, Mr. Hurlock,” Peter said as he watched Max sift through the letters one by one, “Peter wrote about a lot of things, but I didn’t see anything that would give any hint about what he was up to.”

Max flipped another letter onto the pile of ones he had finished. “It does seem to look that way, but there’s just a few more.”

Although finally away from Mrs. Denton and back at the hotel, Allison was restless. She went down to the lobby and tried working on the article, but her mind kept coming back to Max. She had never been a believer in women’s intuition, but couldn’t shake the strong feeling that Max needed her somehow. As time passed, she grew more and more uneasy. Sitting in the hotel lobby, Allison looked at the article again. She had managed to write a few paragraphs, but with the worry over Max, Allison was experiencing a case of writer’s block. Around five thirty, the bell clerk approached.

“Mrs. Hurlock? There’s a call for you.”

Allison flew to the phone.

“Allison? It’s me!”

“Max. Where are you? Are you all right?”

"I'm fine, but it took longer than I thought. I'm still at Rutgers, but I'm getting ready to leave. Why don't you have dinner without me? I'll grab something at a campus place and be back around eight or so."

"Max, I don't want you driving around after dark. It just doesn't feel right somehow. The killer might be watching."

"I'll try to get back sooner then. Don't worry. I have more information from Peter. It looks like Robert might have been involved in some sort of embezzlement or swindle at Bradwell Properties after all, but I still have a lot of loose ends to deal with."

"Yes, Max," said Allison sternly, "and one of those 'loose ends' is that killer wandering around somewhere. Now you get yourself back here as soon as you can."

"All right. I'll skip dinner."

Allison hung up the phone and sat restlessly trying to get back to her article.

The sun was lowering in the late afternoon sky as Max drove along the tree-shaded road from New Brunswick, turning the case over in his mind. The facts still seemed to drift in a meaningless confusion of things and people that didn't quite fit.

Max pulled into a Flying A garage to gas up for the trip back to Moorestown. As the garage owner started filling the tank, Max got out of the car and idly watched the amber liquid fill the glass cylinder on the top of the pump, noting the graduations on the glass indicating how many gallons had been pumped. The pump was a slow one, so Max started to look through his notebook, reading about his interviews with William Taylor, Mrs. Greene, Tim Walsh, Doris Gentry, Fred Madison, Otto Pfeiffer, Patrolman Mandrell, Detective Edwards....

He stopped. When he saw the name Edwards, something faintly stirred in the back of his mind, like the rustle of dry leaves far away. What was it that Edwards had said? He flipped through the pages. Where did he see...?

"That'll be $2.25, mister," the attendant said, suddenly appearing and wiping his hands on a rag. Max fumbled with the money then returned to his notebook. Page after page of contradictory and fragmented notes stared back at him, but where .....There it was. One casual remark recorded in the notebook suddenly seemed to jump out at Max.

"But that can't be," he murmured to himself, "because if that's true, then that means..."

He closed the notebook and started counting off points on his fingers. Everything he had learned was finally beginning to fall into place. All the crazy and conflicting pieces were actually starting to fit together. As each piece fit into place, the house that Max always talked about began to appear in his mind.

Right down to the foundation.

"Of course," he muttered to himself. "That's what happened. That's the only way it all makes sense. Why didn't I see it before?"

Max jumped from the car and ran into the small station building. The attendant was leaning over the engine of a Model T replacing spark plugs.

"I need to use your phone," Max blurted out.

The attendant, who had somehow managed to get a streak of black grease across his nose looked up and shook his head.

"Don't got no phone. Been thinking of getting one, though."

"Where's the nearest phone I could use?"

The attendant scratched his head. “Oh, couple of folks in town have phones, but along the road, I couldn’t tell you. The way you’re heading, you might ask at the next garage.”

Max winced. He remembered from his trip up to New Brunswick that the next garage was almost in Moorestown.

Chapter 23

The house of shadows

In the lobby of the hotel, Allison looked at what she had written in the last two hours. It wasn't much, but she had other things on her mind.

The great gap between parents and young adult children has been worsened by the flapper craze, as daughters flirt with new ways of doing things and new standards of behavior.

"They have their own secret codes," said one Moorestown mother recently. Sometimes it is difficult to fully comprehend exactly what ideas she is expounding."

Her daughter's way of expressing the same thought shows just how far apart their views really are.

"Oh, Mom's swell, but we don't really speak the same language sometimes. When I say something is the berries, she thinks it's a lot of applesauce, and I have to tell her that means good. Of course my friends are on the trolley, but sometimes Mom acts like she

isn't hitting on all sixes. She's really a little like Mrs. Grundy."

Even with all this confusion and friction, however, it is clear that both generations are struggling to keep up with the times as best they can, and that the small town flapper, unlike her big city sister, has her feet planted firmly on both sides. She is a small town girl who has seen the big city and likes what she sees. She wants the parties, the fast cars, the late nights, the scandalous behavior, and most of all, the freedom and independence. In the end, the small town flapper is looking for glamour and excitement combined with the solid foundation of life in a small town. All things considered, that's a pretty ambitious goal.

Allison frowned at the papers, then packed them in a small valise she carried.

"That's it. I can't concentrate...can't look at it anymore; not until Max gets back. Where is he, anyway?"

She glanced at the clock over the reception desk and made a mental calculation. Max should be back in less than an hour. It was still light, so there was time.

"Oh, drat!" she said, rummaging through her purse. "Where's my compact? I must have left it over at Mrs. Denton's. Max'll be back soon, but Mrs. Denton's house is only a few blocks away. Do I have time to go get it?"

She decided that she did. After a quick call to Mrs. Denton, she stepped outside and started to walk the five blocks to Mrs. Denton's house.

"Finally! There's a garage with a telephone sign," said Max as he spotted the blue and white sign with the picture of the bell in the distance. He pulled in and found a telephone inside. He dialed the hotel and asked for Allison.

"I'm sorry, Mr. Hurlock," came the voice of the desk clerk, "but I'm afraid she's gone out. You just missed her."

"Gone out? Where?"

"She didn't say, but she said she would be back before you arrived. She had some minor errand to attend to."

"For the love of.... All right; listen. When she comes back tell her I called. Tell her I know who Mr. Eagle is. That's right; Mr. Eagle. She'll understand what that means. Tell her I'm going to get the final piece of evidence we need, and I'm calling chief Pfeiffer to go with me. Tell her I'm going to the following address...."

The desk clerk wrote down the message and Max hung up to dial Chief Pfeiffer. A cheerful secretary answered.

"I'm sorry, sir. Chief Pfeiffer is out on a burglary investigation. Detective Edwards is with him. No one else is here right now."

"Does his car have a radio?" Max asked.

"No, I'm afraid it doesn't. We're a small town, and really don't need it."

"Maybe you don't need it, but it would sure come in handy for me right now," Max grumbled. "All right, but when he returns, give him this message. It's very important."

Max hung up and scratched his chin thoughtfully. Allison had said she'd be back soon, but Chief Pfeiffer could be out for hours. Every minute he waited meant that much more chance of the killer figuring out Max was getting close and destroying the evidence.

Max decided to go alone. With any luck, Pfeiffer would get the message and show up later.

With any luck.

He got back into the Packard and sped off towards the south.

Long shadows from the lowering sun fell across the street as Max pulled up at the address. There was a garage in the back, but the door was open, showing it was empty. Apparently, no one was home. Max waited another ten minutes, and seeing no signs of life in the house, walked up to the front door. The doorbell climes rang hollowly somewhere inside, but no one answered. The door was a heavy wooden one. Max fished around in his pocket for a skeleton key he usually carried, and found it. After several attempts, the lock clicked.

The door swung open silently. The brass hinges were obviously well oiled, Max thought, grateful for the lack of any creaking. He stepped inside and waited as he closed the door behind him. A dark paneled entrance hall seemed to engulf him, like some great beast devouring its prey. Still there was silence. He pulled out his Mauser pistol, checked it to make sure the clip was full, and then replaced it in the belt holster. He took a deep breath, and then slowly started for the staircase. The evidence he was looking for would most likely be upstairs in a bedroom or a study.

The house was still except for the soft creak of the bare wood of the stairs under Max's feet as he ascended one careful step at a time. The weakness of the dying outside light made the house seem sinister and almost alive. Sofas, chairs, tables and even curtains became dark masses that took on unsettling and threatening shapes in the dimming light and long shadows. Somewhere downstairs, a clock chimed loudly, causing Max a momentary chill.

At the top of the stairs was a room that looked like a den or a study. In the center of the opposite wall was a desk and nearby, a tall cabinet with a glass front. Several mounted deer heads hung on the walls, adding to the eerie feel of the room. As he got closer and details became visible in the dim light, Max could see the cabinet was for storing and displaying rifles and pistols.

He also noticed that one of the pistols was missing.

Conscious of his own heartbeat, Max slowly opened the desk drawer by drawer. Turning, he bumped into a tall metal desk lamp that tottered as he tried to stop it, but fell to the floor with a loud metallic clatter that filled the room with noise. Max stood still listening as the echo died away, but there was no other sound from within the house, so he resumed his search. He found papers and a few personal items, but not what he was looking for. One thing seemed odd. The owner obviously collected guns, but there was no pistol in any of the drawers. If the missing pistol was the one used to murder Danny Greene, Max thought, it had probably been ditched, or at least hidden elsewhere...unless the killer carried it with him.

"Now where could he be keeping them?" Max muttered to himself. He looked around the room, trying not to look at the deer heads that seemed to stare down at him accusingly.

Max crept over to some bookshelves on the other side of the room. He wanted to turn on a light, but didn't want to alert any nosy neighbors. The shelves were lined with books, but not what he was looking for.

Max froze. He thought he heard a creak. He knew these old houses made all sorts of noises as they cooled when the sun went down, and he was sure that was all it was, but didn't want to take any chances. He drew his pistol and waited, but the sound did not repeat. He put the Mauser back in the belt holster. He was beginning to sweat, increasingly aware of the passing of time and the possibility of someone returning.

Max spun around and froze in place. Was that another creak? Silence.

He wiped his forehead. The place was getting to him. He had to find what he came for then get out.

Still the search continued, shelf after shelf, drawer after drawer. The clock downstairs chimed once more, telling Max he had been in the house more than 15 minutes, much too long. He had to hurry. He was really pressing his luck. Looking around, he saw there was only one other place to look, a small closet in the corner of the room. He walked over and turned the handle cautiously.

In the interior of the closet were the dark forms of clothes on hangers and a box on the floor. Max pulled out the box, cringing as it made a loud scraping noise along the wood floor.

The box was full of shoes.

Max sighed. This was not going to work. It would take hours to search the whole house, and he had looked in the most likely places already. He was not going to get the evidence he needed this way.

The room was darker now, its shadows merging into an all-encompassing grayness of vague and barely defined masses. Max carefully slid the box back and closed the closet door. The clicking of the door latch seemed to echo off the walls. He turned towards the back of the room.

"Looking for something?" A voice split the silence and Max felt his heart leap.

Max spun around to see a figure standing in the doorway. The figure was just a silhouette in the failing light, only slightly blacker than the darkness around it, but Max could see well enough to know it was holding a gun. Max slowly moved his hand towards his holster. "Keep your hands where I can see them or you're dead right now," the voice said. Max complied.

"If you're looking for the stolen ledgers, I put them in the kitchen pantry. No one would look there. They'd look in the obvious places; just as you have. It's too bad you had to keep snooping. I really have nothing against you personally, but you've insisted on forcing the issue."

"Then I must have been getting close," said Max.

"They say even a blind squirrel finds an acorn once in a while," said the voice, "and you were beginning to get a little too close for my comfort. Now I'll have to do something about it."

"Like what?" Max asked, stalling for time.

"A terrible tragedy, officer. I came home and heard noise upstairs and went up to investigate. Of course I went armed for my own protection. You can't be too careful these days, what with the rising crime rate. When I entered the room, I saw a man at my desk. He turned on me with a gun in his hand and I thought he was a burglar about to shoot me, maybe the same one that shot poor Danny Greene. In the dark, I didn't know who it was, and well, naturally I had to defend myself."

"I hope the money was worth it," Max said sourly.

"I'm not sure about the money, but keeping myself out of jail certainly is."

As he was talking, Max had been slowly backing away until he felt the desk beside him. He cautiously placed his hand on the surface and felt around for something he could use. His hand fell upon the cool roundness of a glass paperweight. It was just about the size of a baseball.

"Well, at least answer me one question first," Max said. "How did you..."

Still in mid-sentence, Max threw the paperweight hard at the figure in the doorway. The figure, preoccupied with Max's unfinished question, reacted a split second too late, firing just as the paperweight hit his chest with a thump. The sound of the shot echoed throughout the house as the bullet passed harmlessly where Max would have been if he hadn't taken the precaution of diving behind the desk.

More shots exploded in the darkness, deafening in the enclosed space and followed by the tinkling of ejected shell casings hitting the floor. Max fumbled for his pistol and cocked it as splinters of wood from the desk rained down on his head. Not wanting to expose himself, Max fired once in the air, hoping to force the figure to back off.

"You bastard," the figure hissed, "What the hell did you throw at me? That hurt."

"You're breaking my heart," Max answered. "The next thing that hits your chest will be a slug," Max peeked out from behind the desk to get a better shot.

The figure was gone.

Max looked around the dark room trying to see if any of the shadows had a human form. Where had he gone? Max listened carefully, but his ears still rang from the noise of the shots. The figure could be anywhere.

Still there was no sound.

Max's mind raced to analyze his situation. He was on the second floor in a room with only one way out; the doorway where the figure had stood. What if the man had simply ducked behind the doorway and was waiting in the hall? What if there was some sort of passage into the room he had missed and the man was about to appear behind him?

Max fought back a rising sense of panic and tried to reason out the best thing to do. He figured the man was probably lurking somewhere so he could get a shot without exposing himself, and the man would not make a sound until Max came to him. The only way Max could go was out the door of the room and down the steps.

He listened some more. The ringing in his ears was fading now, but he heard no other sounds.

Max quietly shifted to the other side of the desk. What would the killer be expecting him to do? What would he be counting on? If he were lurking in the hallway, he'd be hoping to get a shot when Max tried to get out of the room. But maybe he was waiting downstairs near the front door. That way he could pick off Max as he went down the stairs and had no cover.

"I counted five shots, but I heard the shell casings hit the floor, so that means he's using a semi-automatic with a clip," Max muttered to himself. "The clip probably holds at least ten rounds, so I can't slip away while he reloads."

The engineer side of Max's brain kicked in. If the killer lived here, he would know the best place to lurk unseen, so he was probably right outside the door in the upstairs hallway. Max thought it was unlikely the killer could have gotten all the way down the stairs in the few seconds between his last shots and when Max looked out from behind the desk. Besides, he thought, the stairs were bare wood and creaked; anyone descending rapidly would have made a racket that even the ringing in his ears couldn't cover up. No, the man with the gun had to be waiting right outside the door.

His best chance seemed to be to make a quick dash out the door so the killer wouldn't have time to react. The stairway was straight and Max knew he could get down to the bottom in a few seconds. From there, he would have the drop on anyone coming down the stairs after him. In fact, if he kept shooting from the bottom of the stairs, he could probably keep the killer pinned down long enough to get out the front door.

Holding his gun at the ready, he took a deep breath and whispered "Well, here goes."

Max burst through the doorway and reached the top of the stairs in a fraction of a second. Behind him the killer fired. Max felt a sharp pain in his ankle and found himself tumbling down the stairs. At first he thought he had been shot, then realized the truth was almost as bad. In the darkness he had stepped on the glass paperweight still lying on the floor after striking the killer in the chest. His twisted ankle stabbed with pain as he rolled and tumbled down the stairs.

Another shot came from the top of the stairs, this time plowing into the railing beside him.

To his horror, Max came to rest on his back about halfway down the stairs, completely exposed. He aimed his pistol in the darkness and rapidly fired back at the killer to try to hold him off. Firing constantly, Max dragged himself the rest of the way down the stairs.

Then he pulled the trigger and nothing happened. He knew was out of ammunition. The killer knew it too, and started walking down the stairs to finish off his crippled prey.

Chapter 24

An eagle falls

The killer was about halfway down the stairs when the front door suddenly crashed open, swinging violently on its hinges and slamming into the wall. Someone clicked a switch and the house was flooded with light.

Up on the staircase, the killer, gun in hand, squinted in the glare, trying to make out who the new intruder could be.

"Police! Drop the gun. Now!"

The killer's gun dropped on the wood staircase with a loud thump. Three men stood in the doorway. Otto Pfeiffer bent over Max.

"Are you all right, Hurlock?"

"I am now. I guess you got my message."

Pfeiffer nodded. "That we did, but it took some pressure from your Mrs. to get us to take it seriously. We agreed to come by here and see what was going on. Then when we heard the shots, well here we are."

Max smiled. "Well, as you said, she is a mighty persistent and persuasive woman."

"Max!" Allison burst through the doorway and knelt down to hug her husband.

"I'm fine, Allison. Really."

"So this is our killer?" Otto had turned his attentions to the figure on the stairway, now being handcuffed by Detective Edwards.

"Oh, yes," said Max, struggling to his feet with some difficulty on his swelling ankle. "Allow me to introduce the killer of Miriam Taylor, Robert Bradwell, Danny Greene, and almost Max Hurlock. This is the man we've been calling Mr. Eagle, but you may know him as Fred Madison.

"Fred Madison?" said Pfeiffer. "Isn't he Charlie Bradwell's business partner?"

"...and his accountant," said Max. "He's been embezzling from Bradwell properties since the war. He set up Eagle as a phony front company to receive bogus payments for work never done. He also skimmed rent money and raised rents without notice and pocketed the difference. Later, he used the money he embezzled to get into bootlegging, using Eagle as a money drop. That's how he knew Tim Walsh and how he knew Danny Greene was close to finding out the truth about the Taylor-Bradwell murders when Walsh thoughtlessly told him about what Danny Greene had said at the Volstead Tavern. Madison thought Danny Greene was in Florida, so he broke into his house to look for Danny's documents. Only Danny wasn't in Florida. He showed up unexpectedly and Fred shot him."

Pfeiffer interrupted. "Wait a minute. Why would Madison kill Miriam Taylor and Robert Bradwell?"

"Robert Bradwell was working at Bradwell Properties and started getting suspicious of Madison. Charlie Bradwell was preoccupied with getting clients, and left his partner to handle the day to day running of the place. He didn't watch over Madison closely enough, but Robert had a degree in accounting and he soon knew something fishy was going on. I'm not sure how Madison figured out Robert was on to him; maybe he inferred it from questions Robert asked or records he asked to see, but somehow he found out Robert was on his trail. Once he knew Robert was suspicious, Madison had to do something about it."

"You mean Charlie Bradwell didn't know?" asked Pfeiffer.

"Not a thing. Robert wanted proof before he accused someone so important to his father, so he worked in secret. He didn't even tell his brother Peter for fear he would slip and tell Charlie."

"If Peter didn't know, how come his fingerprints were on the papers Danny Greene had?" said Edwards.

"It was because of the secrecy. Robert prepared a summary of his concerns in ledger form and wanted Danny Greene to analyze it, but he didn't want anyone to know he was doing it. He was concerned he might be noticed with Danny Greene, and word would get back to his father or Fred Madison, but Peter was just entering Rutgers in the accounting courses. No one would think it was strange for him to be talking to a local accountant, so Robert asked Peter to deliver the papers for him. Unfortunately, the secrecy worked against him, because Peter thought that Robert's great interest in the fine points of embezzlement meant that he was stealing, and Peter didn't want any part of it. In fact, Robert's secrecy backfired so badly, we all thought Robert was the one embezzling."

"Very imaginative, Mr. Hurlock, but you can't prove any of this," Fred Madison, now in handcuffs, grumbled.

"Oh, but we can," said Max. "Mr. Madison has the books he stole from Bradwell Properties stashed in the kitchen pantry. I think an audit of his shenanigans will prove enlightening. I think you will also be able to match the bullet that killed Danny Greene with the pistol you see lying on the stairs. A look at Madison's bank accounts might prove enlightening as well. I think we have some good evidence in the Taylor-Bradwell killings too, as I'll come to in a minute. It might even be in Mr. Madison's interest to confess and possibly avoid the electric chair, but that's up to the prosecutor."

Madison was silent.

Max continued, "Madison planned to kill Robert Bradwell to cover up his embezzlement. I think he had some idea of making it look like suicide by shooting him at or near Miriam Taylor's house, but was hesitant because shooting him outside might have roused the neighbors and made it harder to get away. He had a stroke of luck, however. When he arrived at the Taylor house, he noticed that Robert had parked where his car wouldn't be seen and that the only light was in Miriam's room. He broke into the place and waited downstairs for Robert to emerge. Then two things happened; first, he realized if he shot Robert after the couple had obviously reconciled, the suicide theory would not be believed. Second, he saw Robert's gun, probably on the hall table where Miriam had left it for Robert to take home, and knew he now had a chance to make the suicide look even more convincing. He may not have known it was Robert's gun. He may have thought it belonged to Mr. Taylor, but the important thing is that the gun could not be connected with him and its presence was perfectly consistent with the suicide story."

Madison still didn't speak.

"So everything was going well, but he still had a problem. Even if he shot Robert and got away clean, he still had to deal with the likelihood of Miriam telling everyone that Robert no longer had a reason for killing himself. So now he had to kill her as well."

Even Otto Pfeiffer was shocked. "Good God!" he sputtered.

Max nodded. "I'm afraid so. He went up the stairs with Peter's gun and somehow managed to kill them both. Then he locked the bedroom door from the outside, slid the key back under the door so it would look like it had been locked from the inside, and walked away, secure in the knowledge he had covered up his crimes. Secure, that is, until he heard about Danny Greene."

"You suspected something like that all along," said Allison. "That's why you asked Charlie Bradwell if the room had wooden floors or carpeting. With a hard wooden floor, he could slide the key well into the room like he was playing shuffleboard."

"I was just weighing possibilities at the time, but you're right."

"But if Danny Greene had papers that incriminated Fred Madison, why didn't he go to the police? What was he waiting for?"

"I think he was waiting until it was time for the audit to see what they found and to find out if the audit firm was in on it as well."

"One more question; what made you suspect him?" said Pfeiffer. "You hardly mentioned him before."

"Yes," chimed in Allison. "You never gave me a hint either."

Max smiled. "It was Detective Edwards who put me on to Fred Madison."

Everyone looked amazed, including Edwards.

"When he told me about investigating the crime scene at Danny Greene's house, he said he had noticed a faint odor of cigar smoke. It was gone by the time everyone else got there, but Edwards noticed it. I didn't think much of it at the time, but on my way back from Rutgers tonight I suddenly remembered it, and remembered that Mrs. Greene told me Danny never smoked. I already knew that Fred Madison was a cigar smoker. It all fell into place after that."

"Well, I'll be damned," said Pfeiffer. "You mean Detective Edwards helped crack the case?" Pfeiffer looked as if someone had just told him that Santa Claus was real.

Max nodded. "Absolutely. He's observant, and that counts for a lot."

"What about the proof you mentioned?" asked Pfeiffer.

"As I said," said Max. "I believe the Danny Greene murder weapon will be found to belong to Mr. Madison, and we certainly have a strong motive once the ledgers are examined. In the Taylor-Bradwell case, we have proof as well. Remember the lady who saw the man standing on the lawn that night? I think she saw Fred Madison when he stood looking at the window and figuring what to do next. What's more, I'll bet she could identify him."

To everyone's surprise, Fred Madison began to laugh.

"So you're the great detective they had to import all the way from the sleepy south, eh? Well, you've assumed a few things, my friend."

Max smiled. "I'm sure I have some of the details wrong, but you committed three murders and there's enough evidence to convict you of at least one of them."

"Oh, I realize that now," Madison said evenly, "It's just that I resent the way you're making me out to be Professor Moriarity, when I'm just a simple accountant who got into trouble."

"A simple accountant who happens to kill people," growled Pfeiffer. "You're a real Boy Scout."

"If you want to set me straight," said Max, "I'm listening."

"A room full of detectives and no one can figure out the real story. Oh, I admit our southern friend here is close, certainly a lot closer than anyone else managed to get, but he's missed a lot. First of all, I was not the mysterious man on the lawn looking up at the window that night. I really resent it that you think I'd be that stupid. I stayed in the bushes well out of sight. You should have figured out who the man on the lawn really was."

"So who was it?" Pfeiffer asked.

"Robert Bradwell, of course."

Madison withdrew a cigar from his coat pocket and regarded it.

"I always knew these things would kill me one day," he observed. "I just never expected them to do it in quite this way."

"Quit stalling, Madison," Pfeiffer warned.

"Patience, officer. First of all, I never set out to kill anyone. Yes, I was embezzling, but the company was still solvent, and we were getting along fine. It all started when Charlie Bradwell went away to war. I had some financial problems, and I needed money badly. One day I borrowed a few hundred from the company and adjusted the books to cover it. I felt it was only fair since I had the whole burden of running things now that Charlie was gone. Charlie had always had money.

His family was well off, but I had to scramble my whole life."

"I scrambled too," said Pfeiffer, "but I never killed anyone."

Madison ignored the remark. "Well, it soon got to be a habit, and by the time the war was over, I had skimmed over a hundred thousand. I had even set up Eagle as a dummy company and made payments for imaginary work. I raised rents on our properties and kept the rates the same in the books and kept the difference. Later, I got into financing bootlegging. That's where I met Tim Walsh. I did a lot of other things, but you get the idea. It worked out pretty well at first. Charlie was always busy beating the bushes for new properties and tenants, so I was left alone."

"Then Robert came along," said Max.

"Right. Robert changed everything. He was nosy and he had a degree in accounting. Pretty soon he was asking questions about the books and about Eagle. I used the legitimate Eagle Property Maintenance for some real jobs, so I had my activities covered pretty well, but I could tell Robert was getting suspicious. Pretty soon he had convinced Charlie to have our next audit done by another company. Up till then, I'd had fake audits done by another dummy company. Charlie never knew the difference, but now he said he'd let Robert pick the auditor. The next audit wasn't due for several months, so I knew I had to do something before then."

"So you decided to kill him?" Pfeiffer asked.

"No. I told you I never set out to kill anyone. I tried to avoid hurting him. I tried to steer him in other directions, and maybe get him to lose interest, but nothing worked. He stuck with it. Then Miriam Taylor broke her engagement with him and I hoped he would be so distracted he would lay off, but it made him worse. He dug even more, apparently trying to do something to impress her. I realized it was him or me, and that I'd wind up in jail if I didn't take drastic measures. I knew I had to eliminate Robert, but how? Then one day I heard him tell Doris that he was going to make a final try that night to get Miriam to reconsider, and I saw my chance. It would be the perfect time for a suicide when she rejected him. I waited for him to leave the Taylor house that night. I had a gun I had bought in Philadelphia that couldn't be traced. I would shoot him as he left and leave the gun at his side; a clear case of suicide for unrequited love."

"Weren't you afraid they'd reconcile?" Allison asked.

Madison shook his head. "I asked around about her and found she had broken engagements before, but had always broken them permanently. I didn't think there was a chance she would ever take him back. I waited in the bushes near the street and finally Robert left the house, but he stopped right on the front lawn near the driveway. He kept looking up at her window and pacing back and forth. I was all ready to shoot him, but he never walked close enough and I wanted to stay concealed. This went on for maybe 15 minutes until he finally decided to go back for one last try. I told you he was persistent. He finally went back in and all I could see was the one light in her window and I thought maybe he had talked her into it after all; maybe they were even up there doing, well, you know."

"We know," said Max. "Go on."

"In his haste to go back, Robert had left the front door open, so I followed him, listening all the way to try to find out if they had reconciled. In the front hallway, I could hear voices from upstairs. Robert was doing his best to convince her to take him back, and she sounded as if she was starting to consider it. As I listened, I looked on a hall table and saw a pistol. I had no idea whose it was, but it was a perfect way of making Robert's death look like a spur of the moment suicide. So I picked it up and waited for Robert to come down, but the more I waited, the more it sounded like she was going to take him back. That would have destroyed the idea of Robert committing suicide, so I went up for a closer look."

Allison shifted her feet, visibly uncomfortable at where this narrative was leading.

"The door to her room was open about halfway. They couldn't see me because the light in the room was much brighter than the dim light in the hallway. Robert was standing in the doorway with his back to me, leaning against the doorjamb. Miriam Taylor was sitting on the bed with a robe wrapped around her. It was obvious what had happened. Thinking Robert had gone home, she must have started undressing for bed while Robert was outside pacing. Then she threw on a robe when she heard him back in the house calling her. The more I listened, the more clear it became that she was going to take him back temporarily, or at least consider it. I knew that suicide because of rejection was out as long as Miriam was around to refute it, so I had to kill her too. I crept up in the darkness and shot him in the head. Then I burst into the room to shoot her almost before his body hit the floor. She was immobilized with shock from seeing Robert shot. It was over in maybe two seconds. It was only then that I noticed the gun I had picked up was only a .22, so I shot them each several more times to make sure they were dead."

"Then Robert was standing in the doorway when you shot him," said Max, "but he was found lying beside her. How did that happen?"

"I arranged them that way to protect myself," said Madison calmly. "I set it up in a way that would guarantee the bodies would be moved before the police or the coroner could properly analyze the crime scene. I dragged Robert and laid him over her. I knew that the bodies would be quickly removed for reasons of decency. That's exactly what happened."

Everyone looked at each other for a moment, stunned by what they had just heard.

"You're quite the model citizen, ain't ya, Madison?" said Pfeiffer. "What about Danny Greene?"

"I never meant to kill him either," Madison insisted. "Tim Walsh told me about what he said and I thought I could find out what he had and remove it while he was away in Florida. Then he could talk all he wanted and it couldn't hurt me. I had hardly gotten there and started going through his papers when he walked in. Fortunately, I had a gun and he didn't."

Pfeiffer pulled Madison towards the door.

"Now you can come down to the town hall and sign a statement- as soon as we find those ledgers."

Max was on his feet now, still nursing his sore ankle. Detective Edwards was back from the kitchen pantry in a minute, holding up the missing ledger books in triumph.

"The only thing I can't quite figure out," said Max, talking to Madison, "is how you found time to follow me without being missed at the office."

Madison frowned. "What are you talking about? I never followed you; I had more important things to do than to dog the footsteps of an amateur gumshoe."

"But then who was.."

Detective Edwards smiled sheepishly. "That was me, Mr. Hurlock."

"You?"

"That's right," said Pfeiffer, looking embarrassed. "I wasn't sure just what you were up to, so I told Detective Edwards to tail you for a while. He stopped a few days ago."

Max shook his head. "That's the trouble with this modern world; nobody trusts anyone anymore."

When Madison and the police had all filed out of the house, Allison turned to Max.

"My hero," she said, with genuine affection.

"Aw, shucks," Max replied.

"But don't you ever do anything like that again!"

Chapter 25

Down the shore

The next day, Max and Allison prepared Gypsy for the flight back.

Charlie Bradwell drove them out and thanked them profusely as Max carefully poured cans of gasoline into the fuel tank and oiled up the rockers on the engine. Allison, meanwhile got the luggage stowed and put on her flying jacket and leather flying hat. The farmer watched them with interest, asking detailed questions about the intricacies and costs of flying.

"That looks mighty nice, Miss," he said, noticing the white silk scarf Allison was tying around her neck. "It's too bad nobody'll see it up there."

Allison smiled. "It's not a fashion item. Max has one too. With a silk scarf you can turn your head freely as you fly without rubbing your neck raw on your jacket collar. It's a trick pilots used during the war so they could constantly look around for the enemy."

"You know," the farmer said finally, "I just might get me one of these flying machines. Maybe do a little crop dusting."

With a final goodbye they climbed into the cockpits. The farmer volunteered to start the engine by turning the curved propeller. The engine sprang to life with a burst of noise and smoke and Gypsy bounced down the field and lifted into the air. As they rose over Moorestown, Allison motioned Max to look down. They were passing over the Taylor house.

The afternoon sun turned the Chesapeake Bay into a sheet of blazing light stretching to the southern horizon as they crossed back into Maryland. A little over an hour later, they were passing over St Michaels and beginning their approach to home.

A few weeks later, the autumn sun shone down warmly on the Miles River on Maryland's Eastern Shore. Out on the water the crab and oyster boats, their white hulls reflecting on the ripples, worked their crab pots or tonged for oysters. On shore, the trees were still green, but there was a little coolness in the air at night, warning of the approaching winter. The wind rustled the leaves and carried the occasional squawks and honking of v-shaped flights of ducks and Canadian geese, appearing black against the clouds as they passed overhead on their long flight south.

Behind the white clapboard house, Allison stood up from kneeling in her garden and wiped the loose dirt from her hands.

"Whew! If I could grow tomatoes the way I grow weeds, we could start our own cannery. These weeds really took over the place while we were away."

Max emerged from behind the garage carrying a dripping bushel basket filled with crabs. Several of their blue-tipped claws protruded from gaps between the basket staves.

"Hey, farmer Allison; I just emptied our traps on the pier. There must be two dozen crabs here all ready for dinner tonight. What do you say we go into town and pick up the mail, then come back and put on the crab pot?"

"Sure," she replied, wiping her forehead. "Why don't you crank up the flivver while I wash up a little?"

A few minutes later they were motoring in their Model T down the St Michaels road, its oyster shell roadbed crunching under their tires.

"This car is getting a little cranky, Max," Allison observed. "I just saw a new Chevrolet utility coupe advertised in the paper for $720. With that check you got from Charlie Bradwell, we could buy several of them."

"Maybe next year. Meanwhile, there's plenty of life left in the old Model T," he observed.

"Fine. Walking is good exercise," Allison replied.

"Well, it's great to be back," Max remarked. "But soon it might be too cold to paint the house this year. It's my last chance."

"No," she corrected him, "you had your last chance when that Fred Madison oaf was trying to shoot you."

"That was a little scary. I guess I should have waited for Pfeiffer," Max admitted.

"I guess you should have," Allison agreed. "I'm too young to be the widow Hurlock. Besides, I'd look lousy in black."

"Nonsense. You'd look great in anything."

They were in the town now, a scattered collection of weathered wooden buildings bordering several boatyards and seafood processing buildings along the Miles River. As they passed the cannery at Navy Point, Allison spotted the Adams Floating Theater.

"Oh, good. It's still here," she said with delight. "Max, let's pick up tickets to tonight's show. We'll have the steamed crabs then go out for a night at the theater."

"Great idea," agreed Max. "We'll stop by as soon as we get the mail."

The St Michaels Post Office was a small clapboard building right on the main street. The postmaster handed them several letters. One was for Allison from Modern Girls Magazine. She grabbed it eagerly.

"They love my article!" Allison announced when she opened the envelope. "They want me to do a series on any topic I'd like. Isn't that the ant's pants?"

"Well you certainly worked hard enough on it," Max noted, "and through some pretty unfavorable conditions, too. Not only that, but your research uncovered some important clues in the Taylor-Bradwell case. Speaking of which, here's a letter from Charlie Bradwell."

"I hope no one else has been murdered," said Allison. "Moorestown's a small enough place as it is."

Max read the letter. "No, no; he's just thanking us again and bringing us up to date. It seems Tim Walsh just got a big contract with a legitimate importer and he has all the trucking business he can handle now. Peter is doing great at Rutgers, and Charlie says he is making a lot more money now that Fred Madison is no longer stealing it from him. The local prosecutor has announced he will be seeking the death penalty against Madison. And look. Charlie sent a copy of the Chronicle with one of Pedigree Pettigrew's articles about the case."

Max scanned the front-page article. "It looks like out reporter friend got to make a big page one splash."

"I'm happy for him," said Allison, "but he's still an abrasive little man."

Max read the article. "Well, it seems our pal Otto Pfeiffer is getting a lot of mileage from this case. The papers are calling him the 'Wizard of the Pine Barrens' and he's being hailed as a sort of detective genius. To his credit, though, he did say that he had a lot of help from an out of town investigator named Max Hurlock."

"Good for him," said Allison. "At least he didn't try to grab all the glory."

"Yes, he's gruff, but he's a professional. Hey, what's this?"

A paper fell out of the envelope and fluttered to the floor.

Allison picked it up. "It's a check with a note attached. It says 'Here's a little share of the extra money I'm making now. Consider it a bonus. You earned it; you cleared Robert's name and I'll always be grateful.'"

Allison looked at the check.

"My, my," she said quietly. "Who says crime doesn't pay?"

Max looked at it and whistled. "Wow. Nothing like having a satisfied client," he remarked.

Allison was looking at another letter. "Max, look at this fancy envelope. It's engraved. And look where it's from. Do you know anybody at this place?"

Max peered at it carefully. " I don't even know anybody who knows anybody there. Let's see what they want." He opened the envelope and unfolded the letter. "Let's see...Dear Mr. Hurlock We note with interest your success in the Taylor Bradwell matter and wonder if you would be available......hmmmmm."

"Well, don't keep me in suspense, Max, what do they want?"

Max handed her the letter. "Are you up for another little trip?"

Allison's eyes widened as she read. Finally she put the letter down and sighed.

"Well, Max; we'd better get Gypsy gassed up. It looks like painting the house is going to have to wait a little longer."

The End

Notes

The Wilson-Roberts case

(Death of a Flapper is fiction, but it was inspired by a real life crime; the Wilson- Roberts case of 1929.)

Just after midnight on the night of June 1, 1929 wealthy Moorestown attorney and financier John Wilson and his wife were returning home after playing cards with friends. As they approached their spacious Tudor-style house, they noticed a light on in their daughter Ruth's room. The Wilsons went inside and knocked on Ruth's locked bedroom door, but there was no answer. Ruth Wilson and Horace Roberts had been engaged some months earlier, but she had broken it off two months ago. Roberts had become despondent and depressed, but kept visiting Wilson, hoping to change her mind.

John Wilson ran to his bedroom and climbed out the window to a communicating roof to make his way to Ruth's window.

Ruth lay face down on her bed, nude except for her shoes and stockings and a light coat. Horace Roberts, completely nude, lay partly on her and partly on the floor where he had apparently slumped. There was blood on his head as well, and beneath his hand was a .22 pistol. Incredibly, both were still alive, though a closer look revealed both had suffered multiple gunshot wounds to the head.

Along with local police, Burlington County Chief of Detectives Ellis Parker was called in to investigate. The crusty, homespun Parker was a legend in New Jersey; his deductive skills and ability to solve the toughest cases earning him a reputation as "the American Sherlock Holmes". (See Master Detective, by the author.)

The locked room seemed to indicate suicide, while the multiple gunshot wounds pointed towards murder. Ellis Parker, after a one-day investigation, concluded that Roberts had shot Wilson, then killed himself. The gun was found to belong to Horace Roberts' brother, Walter

The sequence of events seemed to be that Roberts had made a last effort to get Ruth Wilson to take him back and was refused. He left, worked up his courage, then stormed back, and surprised Ruth as she was getting ready for bed. (The bed was still made up when the bodies were discovered on top of it.) The partially undressed Ruth threw on a light coat to confront Roberts at the doorway to her room. Roberts shot her twice and she fell across the bed diagonally with her head towards the foot of the bed and her feet towards the adjacent doorway. Roberts came in the room, locked the door behind him, undressed, (His clothes were found neatly stacked on the floor.) then stood over the dying Ruth and shot himself. He fell over her and partially slumped to the floor.

The victims were buried, but townspeople, particularly relatives of Horace Roberts, began to express doubts. Public pressure mounted until the case was reopened before a coroner's jury.

On the day of the exhumation and the inquest, 30,000 visitors crammed the streets of Moorestown, rubbing elbows with the local population of 6,000. A coroner's jury affirmed Ellis Parker's conclusion that the case was a murder-suicide. The crowds melted away, and the case was once again closed.... for the moment. If the authorities were through with the case, however, the public wasn't. People still talked about the mysterious circumstances and were skeptical about the inquiry's conclusions. Bradway Brown, who lived across the street from the Wilsons, was a friend and former suitor of Ruth Wilson, and a classmate of Horace Roberts. Brown hinted to friends that that there was more to the story, but the inquest was complete and it would take something startling to open it up again.

Almost four years later, Bradway Brown was found shot to death in his home with a pistol in his hand. Once again, Ellis Parker was called in, but this time, Parker declared that Brown had been murdered by someone who tried to make the crime appear to be suicide. Several people reported that for the past few weeks, Brown had been telling friends that he had discovered the real story of the Wilson-Roberts case, and that he knew the identity of the real murderer.

Now the floodgates of public attention were opened once again. A few weeks later, Horace Roberts, Sr. publicly called for a new probe of the Wilson-Robert case. Roberts freely admitted he stood to gain $30,000 from an insurance policy if the death of his son were to be declared murder rather than suicide. Former coroner Benjamin Farner claimed the case had been hushed up back in 1929, by a powerful politician

The rumors, sniping, and public speculation continued to build. Ellis Parker stood by his original conclusion and turned a disapproving eye on the hysteria.

The Grand Jury convened once again on March 4. The powerful state politician who told Farner to "lay off the inquest" turned out to be state treasury secretary A.C. Middleton, who denied applying any pressure. He merely made the request, he said, to avoid further heartache to the families involved.

On March 10, the Grand Jury reached its verdict. Roberts had murdered Wilson, then taken his own life, the same finding Ellis Parker had reached after his one-day investigation four years earlier

A few months later, Ellis Parker found and arrested the killers of Bradway Brown. The murder had been the result of a burglary gone wrong. Brown had come home and surprised the intruders. There was no connection with the Wilson-Roberts case after all. The Wilson-Roberts case was closed for good, even though the whole sequence of events seemed so unlikely and so many loose ends and unanswered questions appeared to hang over it.

Today the Wilson house still stands on a tree lined street in Moorestown looking much as it did in 1929, and the room where Ruth Wilson and Horace Roberts lost their lives still keeps its secrets. Few people seem aware of the case today. The present owners of the house were not even aware of its history until several years after they moved in.

The Curtiss Jenny (Chapter 2)

The Curtiss Jenny, so named because of its official designation as JN, was the first aircraft to be mass-produced. Turned out by the thousands during the First World War, the Jenny was a two-seat biplane trainer that was also used for aerial reconnaissance. The Jenny also saw action in Mexico in the U. S. Army's pursuit of Pancho Villa. After the war, the army (There would be no separate air force branch until after the Second World War.) sold many of the Jennys back to the

Curtiss Company, who refurbished them and sold them to the civilian market. The flood of cheap Jennys kick started American civil aviation as hundreds learned to fly and made money by staging airplane shows that featured aerobatics, stunt flying, and airplane rides for a fee.

Chesapeake Bay Log Canoes (Chapter 2)

So called because they were originally built from sections of hollowed out logs, Chesapeake bay log canoes were once the work boats that harvested bay oysters and crabs for restaurant tables and homes all over the east coast. Log canoe races originated in the practice of racing the boats to Baltimore or some other port to sell the catch, since the earliest arrivals normally got the best prices. By the 1920s, however, these graceful and well-designed craft had been largely supplanted by motor driven boats, or by the simpler and easier to manage Skipjacks, and many lay rotting on muddy stream banks or marshlands. A few were preserved and used in races such as the one described in the story. The awarding of a ham to the last place finisher so that he can use it to grease the hull for future races is an old tradition. Several dozen of these boats, some dating from the 1800s, survive, and can still be seen in races in the summer months around St. Michaels, Oxford, and Claiborne, Maryland. The boats named in the story are all still racing today.

The Adams Floating Theater (Chapter 2)

The James Adams floating theater was one of a number of such vessels (barges, really) that plied the rivers of the south from 1919 to about 1930. Before television and movies took their place, floating theaters brought excitement and live entertainment to otherwise isolated river towns. The actors lived on the boat and put on shows at different towns throughout the warm months. In 1924, New York writer and Algonquin roundtable member Edna Ferber visited the Adams floating theater to gather material for her next book. The result was *Showboat*, a best seller that was later made into the phenomenally successful musical. A foundation is presently trying to raise money to build a replica of the Adams floating theater.

Mary Miles Minter (Chapter 3)

One of the most successful movie stars of the early 1920s, Mary Miles Minter was considered a rival to Mary Pickford. She was born Juliet Reilly, and under the thumb of an overbearing stage mother, became an actress at age 6. But by age 11, she caught the unwelcome attention of the anti child labor Gerry Society, so her mother changed her name (and birth certificate) to that of an older deceased cousin, Marie Miles Minter. Minter was in numerous movies and was admired by men and women alike. She starred in several films by director William Desmond Taylor, and was infatuated with him.

Taylor was found murdered in 1922 in his home in Hollywood, and both Minter and her mother were suspected. The crime was never officially solved, but Minter was found to have lied about both her relationship with Taylor and her movements on the night of the murder. Although at the height of her fame, Minter's reputation with the public was permanently damaged and her career ended, although she made enough from investments to live comfortably until her death in 1984. On her deathbed in 1964, silent screen actress Ella Margaret Gibson confessed to the murder of William Desmond Taylor, although she had never been a suspect.

The Florida land boom (Chapter 7)

When Max and Allison think Danny Greene has gone to Florida, Allison remarks that she hopes he doesn't buy land and settle there. This is a reference to the great boom in Florida real estate in the early 1920s. With the advent of the automobile and better roads, Florida real estate and planned developments in that state became the basis of many fortunes. People in the north bought lots sight unseen from magazine and newspaper ads. The increasing values seemed to have no end. Land prices increased so rapidly, speculators were buying lots one day and reselling at a profit the next. In 1925, however, the land boom started to run out of people willing and able to pay the ever increasing costs. The bubble broke and thousands of buyers and developers were left with land and loans they could not afford.

Suzanne Lenglen (Chapter 16)

Arguably the first woman sports star in history, Suzanne Lenglen was born in France and was driven by both her own ambition and parents who pushed her mercilessly. In 1919, she beat seven-time champion Lambert Chambers to win at Wimbledon in a match many have called "the greatest and most exciting women's final ever played."

As her fame grew, she became a genuine sports hero beloved by both the public and the press. In 1920 she appeared in makeup and a dress that consisted of a scandalously short skirt and a tight fitting, sleeveless top. One player said the outfit was a "cross between that of a prima donna and a streetwalker."

Lenglen dominated women's tennis until 1927 when American Helen Wills took over as the greatest player.

Ozzie Nelson (Chapter 18)

If ever there was a big man on campus, it was Oswald George "Ozzie" Nelson, best known as the creator and star of The Adventures of Ozzie and Harriet, one of the earliest and most successful sitcoms in television history.

Just as depicted in this book, Ozzie Nelson was the quarterback of the Rutgers football team, member of the boxing team, band leader, star of the debate club, and generally one of the great overachievers of Rutgers history. (He graduated with a law degree.)

Born of well to do parents in Jersey City, New Jersey, Nelson combined a first class business mind with a strong drive and ambition. He was totally unlike the somewhat passive and bland character he later developed for television. After graduating from Rutgers, he formed the Ozzie Nelson band, married his vocalist Harriet Hilliard, and began to perform on the Red Skelton radio show. He developed and produced the Adventures of Ozzie and Harriet radio show, and later successfully sold the TV version of the show for which he is still remembered.

Rumrunning Raids (Chapter 19)

The description of Tim Walsh's arrest for rumrunning is based on an actual New Jersey incident in 1925 that came to be known as the Rancocas Creek Rumrunning Scandal. Acting on a tip, State Police found a large group of heavily armed men unloading $300,000 worth of bootleg liquor from a sand barge tied up at a pier on Rancocas Creek near Bridgeboro, New Jersey. They arrested 55 men and took them to Burlington to be arraigned. The men were all released on bails ranging from $200 to $500 each, totaling less than the bribes the men had offered the arresting officers. When it was later discovered that the men had all given fake names and had therefore escaped prosecution, charges of collusion and corruption filed the air. A grand jury was convened to investigate Prohibition enforcement in Burlington County and handed down 95 indictments. Several officials were put on trial for malfeasance, but the evidence was insufficient to convict.

The Exclusionary Rule (Chapter 24)

In the final chapters, Max Hurlock breaks into a house to secure evidence. He is not a member of the police and has no search warrant, so it would seem that any evidence he found would not be admissible in a court of law.

In the early 1920s, when the story takes place, however, the so-called exclusionary rule, which states that evidence obtained by an unreasonable search can not be admitted in court was not in force in state courts for violations of state law. The rule was first instituted by the US Supreme Court in the case of Weeks v. United States in 1914, but only applied to federal courts. State courts remained free to treat evidence as they saw fit and many were not too particular. The limitation of the rule to federal courts was confirmed as late as 1949 in the case of Wolf v. Colorado. It was not until the case of Mapp v. Ohio in 1961 that the Supreme Court ruled that the 4th amendment mandated the exclusionary rule to state courts as well.

About the author

John Reisinger is a former coast guard officer and engineer. He lives with his wife and research partner Barbara on Maryland's Eastern Shore. John writes and speaks on a wide range of historical, crime, writing and technical topics, and is the author of several books, including Master Detective, Death on a Golden Isle, Nassau, and Evasive Action.

And don't miss other adventures of Max and Allison Hurlock as they investigate murder and mayhem among the well-to-do in the Roaring 20s.

Death on a Golden Isle

On an isolated island off the Georgia coast stands America's most exclusive club for the most wealthy and powerful men in the country. Outsiders are not welcomed and nothing is permitted to interrupt the rhythm of daily life.

But when one of the members is poisoned at the club dance in 1923, all eyes turn to his new wife. Is she a gold digger or innocent victim? She calls on Max Hurlock to find the truth, but can an outsider break the wall of silence and suspicion?

The victim's wife swears she is innocent, but why is she spending so much time with Bwana Pete, the big-game hunter, and if the victim died from poisoned coffee, why was his dying word "cocoa"?

For more information, visit www.johnreisinger.com

Other books by John Reisinger....

Master Detective: The Life and Crimes of Ellis Parker, America's Real-life Sherlock Holmes

The story of America's greatest detective and his tragic role in the Lindbergh kidnapping investigation. He obtained a signed confession but went to prison for his trouble.

"Fascinating reading for true crime fans and mystery buffs alike."....Max Allan Collins, author of The Road to Perdition.

"...a masterpiece of a biography." ... Troy Soos, author of The Gilded Cage.

"...a story powerfully told."...Roger Johnson, in the newsletter of the Sherlock Holmes Society of London.

Evasive Action: The Hunt for Gregor Meinhoff

A tense manhunt through WWII Canada for an escaped German POW with an explosive secret that could change the outcome of the war.

"Fast paced, well-constructed...a first-rate adventure yarn." ... John Goodspeed, Easton Star-Democrat book review.

Nassau

Civil War blockade runners turn a sleepy tropical port into a boomtown as they await their next runs through the fire and steel of the deadly Union blockade.

"the final chase scene was among the most exciting things I've ever read." ... Dr. Ken Startup, history professor and VP for Academic Affairs, Williams Baptist College.

Reading group guide

Death of a Flapper:

How was Prohibition circumvented and what role did speakeasies play?

As the story progressed, what character did you suspect was the killer and why?

How does the story make Robert Bradwell's possible guilt seem uncertain?

What sort of red herrings appear in the story and which are most convincing?

How does the local police force help Max? How do they hinder him?

How would the investigation of the murder have been handled differently with today's technology?

How does the publicity and the small-town setting affect how the case is investigated?

In what ways are Max and Allison a reflection of the 1920s and of their backgrounds?

How do Allison and Max work as a team and how do they sometimes come in conflict?